A PLACE CALLED THE TREE

GINA MOROSEY

Nerd Squad Revolution

Nerd Squad Revolution

To my husband and our extraordinary children for teaching me true love.

And to those who haven't quite found their place. You are more than you can even imagine.

"Every kid, no matter where they come from, no matter their socioeconomic status, they have a home here. They have a place here where they can be involved."

Kyle Karum, SHS Choir Director

Chapter 1

I'd decided a long time ago that there were more benefits to being a choir kid than a drama club kid. In most schools, the two were interchangeable. In my school, choir's funding was better because the Parent-Teacher Association donated to it. Those kids won awards with their names engraved into plaques. The auditorium sold out with all their loved ones. There was the promise of popularity and, best of all, they had their special spot under The Tree.

I, however, was not a choir kid.

I took a bite of my mashed potatoes that I'd bought for a reduced price, staring out of the cafeteria window that separated the world of free lunches and echoing chatter from the world of designer bags and brand-new cars. Outside, Braden Gregory and the choir kids were sitting under The Tree with plates of fresh pizza slices served from the north wing. The grass around them glowed in the late-winter sun while, in my world, cafeteria lights magnified everything I refused to accept: Grade D food, hand-me-down jeans, and a life I would change in a heartbeat.

Choir kids claimed the north wing territory at Tipton High—home of the Cardinals and the biggest gymnasium in the state of Indiana. The north wing stood alone, separate from the main school building. It looked like a huge brick box and housed the gymnasium, health classes, and a small kitchen which served pizza during lunch hours.

From the cafeteria window, I watched the choir kids grab their food and scatter around the tables in the hall next to the north wing kitchen, all except for one small group who favored the outdoors.

What was it about that tree they always chose to sit under? There were a bunch more just like it planted in a line which stretched all the way to the tennis courts. Granted, they weren't as big and hadn't quite bloomed. The leaves of that favored tree drooped from the branches like a dying green firework, and to hug the trunk would be like hugging the big belly of Buddha.

Maybe if you squinted—if you squinted really hard—it looked kind of magnificent.

I pulled the letter from my jacket pocket, scanning my table of theatre friends who still conversed about upcoming auditions.

"It's *The Miracle Worker*, dumbass," shouted my friend Justin from across the table before he flicked a spoonful of corn at Becca. "And to your dismay, you're going to be Kate Keller, the star, the sexiest mom of the 1800s."

We were senior drama club kids. The ones who might have had a few coins in our pockets, but nothing more. The ones who found peace with our piece in the puzzle.

"Kate is most definitely *not* the star," Becca said, turning to me. "The wild and fabulous Helen Keller is."

There were over a thousand kids in Tipton High, most of whom would be remembered for something. Even for a public school, everyone had their "thing". They knew what they wanted and they were good at it.

My yearbook superlative—if I was ever important enough to have one—would be:

Leah Roy - Drama Club Queen

I folded the letter so Becca couldn't see it and quickly tucked it into my Calculus book.

I glanced out the window, zooming in again on that place called The Tree, hoping one day my good grades might give me a smooth life like those choir kids had.

Tipton High's popular clique consisted mostly of choir kids. It was more expensive to be a choir kid. Their uniforms cost a pretty penny and they got to order their musical costumes straight from Broadway. Drama club had a thrift store packed closet that housed our dusty costumes. Even the musical tickets cost more. Drama club was just glad if anyone paid three bucks to see our shows.

Unlike choir, drama club was funded strictly by ticket sales . . . or a lack thereof. I should have been thankful to the choir kids who auditioned since their friends and family always beefed up our audience.

Choir kids.

I wondered if any of them were going to audition for the drama club play. *The Miracle Worker.* The show I had been waiting for since the beginning of the semester. A few choir kids would pop in each semester, lollygag right through auditions, and steal a big role from us. Maybe it looked good on their college applications or maybe they just liked being coolest in the room.

To put it frankly, they *were* the more talented bunch, but I'd never tell a drama club kid that. Either way, I promised myself that I wouldn't let them overshadow me. I would get the part of Helen Keller even if I had to claw my eyes, pierce my ears, and never speak again.

Braden chuckled with a few others, probably about Laurie Hamilton—someone just as short and pale as me, only a hundred pounds bigger. She took the heat from them as she trailed the sidewalk to the cafeteria, giving up on sitting anywhere near *that* tree.

It was pretty much known that The Tree was reserved for that group only. It was bigger, shadier than the rest, and it belonged to them. We didn't cross lines at Tipton High. Doing so left a person exposed and vulnerable like that scene in *Friends* when they walked in on a stranger sitting on their sacred orange couch.

Yeah.

We don't do that.

Sure, there were other popular kids like the cheerleaders and the "too good for the arts" football players, but at our school, the arts were actually a cool thing until cliques had to divide that, too. Popular kids took over choir while drama club had been dominated by the kids who didn't want to go home after school.

My thumb ran across the tips of my fingers at the thought of being viewed like Laurie Hamilton.

Puberty had brought on a terrible case of the body blues. I was only five feet tall on a good day. Even though people said I had a body to kill for, I didn't believe it. When I looked in the mirror, I saw a fragile girl with stringy brown hair stretching down to her tailbone, a girl who only looked pretty when she was sweating because it put some color in her cheeks. I didn't see an ass when I turned to the side, but I heard otherwise when freshmen passed me in the hallway.

My upper arms were strong, maybe because I had big boobs. Most girls envied my boobs, so I suppose that was one thing going for me.

Having turned eighteen earlier that month, I felt like I should have had more self-esteem.

I liked my smile a little. It lit up my eyes—my entire face, actually.

Braden's eyes followed Laurie until they landed on me.

The words "unicorn girl" echoed in my memory.

I jerked my head away, closing my eyes to the sheer embarrassment of having been caught staring. I hated being caught staring. It was like being caught with your hand in the cookie jar, only Braden was no cookie.

His boyish laughter bounced inside my brain like a boomerang —no matter how hard I tried, I couldn't get rid of it. I'd never been able to forget it since the first time I'd heard him in middle school. It was the kind of laugh that sent a trickle of electricity down my spine, what I imagined love at first sight felt like. Only in my case, Braden Gregory was an asshole and I hated him.

Scotty Hunter joined The Tree and plopped his gym bag next

to Braden. I knew Scotty from our pathetic mom-forced appointments with Mr. Hillman.

Hillman was a freak of nature—a teaching beast. His main classes were English Literature, but he also taught Theatre 101 and directed drama club for free and, as if that weren't enough, he minored in Psychology and majored in living a lonely life which qualified him to counsel students before school.

My sessions weren't until 7:30 a.m. on Tuesdays, but my mom had to be at work earlier so I had to wake up at ridiculous o'clock on those days. Since being promoted to manager of the Home Inn, my mom never risked being late. She was my only ride if I didn't want to walk to school.

I wondered if Hillman was swarmed with students during the other mornings or if Scotty and I were the only losers to see him. We shared joint appointments with Hillman to talk about basic things: our moms, school, pressure, etc. There was comfort knowing we weren't allowed to talk about our sessions with other students. Sometimes Scotty wouldn't show up and I'd have Hillman all to myself.

I only went to him because I thought it would make my mom happy. God, did I just want her to be happy. Hillman would sit there with his leg propped over his knee, assuring me that my mom only wanted what was best for me. I would sit with my hands folded together, assuring him with a slow nod before glancing away.

Apparently, having teenage mood swings and looking like my dad worked against me with my mom. I could only guess that every time she looked at me during one of my "attitudes", I reminded her of the crazy person she'd left behind, and if crazy was hereditary, then she was going to fix me before I ended up like him.

Hillman's sessions worked for now, but my mom was on some desperate hunt for a "real" psychologist. Someone who could prevent me from being just like my "crazy schizo" dad, and since

Hillman didn't give out pills like candy, she would find someone who did.

Before my very first session, Hillman had got stuck scheduling auditorium time with Mr. Steele, so Scotty and I waited in the small walkway near his classroom. It would have been socially unacceptable not to communicate, so we were sort of forced to look at each other.

Looking at each other forced a half-smile. Smiling forced a quick, "Hey," which forced a, "What's up?" After the third late appointment, it stopped feeling like something forced and more like a comfort. We started to actually talk.

Scotty reminded me of one of those ancient naked statues with a square face and curly hair. He wore clothes though—mostly his wrestling jacket with a pair of jeans that brought out his dark-blue eyes.

I wasn't exactly attracted to him. Not to say he wasn't cute or anything, I just wasn't into blonds. He didn't exactly support blonds in the smartness area either. Talking to him made me want to cross my eyes and smack my forehead. Between his southern accent and middle-school vocabulary, I figured the teachers prob-ably pimped his grades to keep him on the school's basketball team. Most of the time, our opponents creamed us, but Scotty's fast dribbling and clean shots through the hoop were the only reasons we had ever come close to winning.

Even though I had met the soft side of Scotty, there was no gray area in Tipton High, so he still fell under the jock clique. He did have gentle eyes though. They were eyes that said, *"It's okay, I'm not a total asshole."*

Scotty came from the north side of town, which was where most of the popular kids lived—right behind the high school. His parents had divorced when he was two, so he lived primarily with his mom.

"My old man's some sort of franchise boss or something," he

told me one day while we were waiting for Hillman. "I couldn't care less. It's been forever since I've seen him."

I rested my back against the wall, watching him from the other side of the walkway.

"I haven't seen my dad in years," I told him.

"Yeah, well, my mom thinks the imbalance of testosterone in my life is why I bust chairs against my bedroom wall."

I glared at him. "You did *what*?"

"She thinks I'm so angry 'cause my dad's barely around. I told her I'm angry 'cause she's on my ass about everything. The arguing drives me nuts." He thrusted his hands into the air. "What am I supposed to do? Throw *her* against the wall instead of my chairs?"

My face tensed. *How many chairs does this guy have?*

"How about taking it out on practice?" I asked.

"Doesn't work. Now she's makin' me see Hillman."

Some mornings, we contemplated skipping out and grabbing coffee at the Quick Stop gas station down the road, but guilt stopped us. Hillman wasn't the kind of teacher worth ditching. Talking to Hillman made us feel like we were hanging out with the loner uncle we'd never had. He had these strange quirks like randomly showing up with a goatee or setting drama club meetings at odd times.

During our conversations, Hillman stayed pretty silent. Sometimes he would stare a little too long, casting an awkward cloud over us which forced more information from us, just to fill the silence. Being the only black teacher at Tipton High, I was sure he sometimes felt a little like Scotty and I: judged, misunderstood, secretly lonely.

He didn't make us feel like we were a problem though. Most of the time, he would just toss us a pop and listen to us ramble on about our annoying moms who blamed everyone in the world for their struggles.

Most of the time I'd spent with Hillman felt like a weight

being lifted off my shoulders, even if we weren't talking about problems.

It must have been helping Scotty, too. As the sessions progressed, he complained less about his mom.

"I got rid of my desk chair, stool, and couch chair," he said one day. "Now I just punch my pillows instead."

I liked that Scotty and I had a lot in common.

Except that he was a choir kid.

Chapter 2

The last bell rang. My locker opened with a pop.

Auditions, I reminded myself with a deep breath. *Auditions are today. Today very soon. Like twenty minutes soon.*

My knees shook like baby rattles until two hands blinded me. "Guess who?"

I giggled, knowing exactly who it was by her deep voice. Despite our age, she still had middle-school tendencies.

"Becca?"

Her black hair bounced off her shoulders as she popped in front of me, wearing the widest grin I'd ever seen.

Becca Hoang was the rebel in her clan. Being the only English-speaking person in her Vietnamese family, she refused to invite us to her family get-togethers so she wouldn't have to translate everything from her overly excited relatives to us.

I wish I had known more about where I came from. All my mom ever said was that we were "American mutts" mixed with pretty much every European nationality—"an extra sprinkle of Italian."

When Becca's grandparents bought her new jeans for school every year, she ripped holes in them and drew on intricate dragons and animals. She rocked black nail polish and eyeliner, yet still radiated that exotic beauty most girls our age would've killed for.

"Damn, Leah. Your shoulders are tense. Auditions got you all wound up?"

"I'm a cat near water." I scanned through my textbooks before jamming all of them into my book bag.

"What do you have to be nervous about? Hillman could literally ask you to stand up and say nothing, and you'd still be the star."

"I'll stand up, say nothing, and drop to the floor with my teeth chattering. Cold readings are cruel and unusual punishment. Speaking of punishment . . ." I swung the strap over my shoulder and pushed my locker door closed until it clicked. "You still grounded?"

"Nope." Becca began a backward walk down the hallway. "Mom said that since I keep skipping out on visits to my dad's, my punishment would be—get this—an actual visit from my dad. He showed up for a couple hours last night, asked the basic questions—*How is school? How are your grades? When are you coming to visit your family in Vietnam?*—then he left. I told him to give me a warning before he barges in like that."

"So that you can skip out again?"

"Yup."

"He's your dad. Let him see you."

"Would you let your dad see you?"

I looked to the ground and rubbed my arm.

"Okay. Cats aren't *that* scared of water, Leah." She nudged me. "You get like this every time. And every time, you do fine."

"It's just that I starred in the last play already, so if I screw up, Hillman will cast Rachelle. I wouldn't blame him anyway. She's going to massacre everyone in the club if she doesn't get her turn at the lead."

"You're either good or you suck. Rachelle sucks and everyone knows it. She brings enough masculine energy to make up for our lack of dudes. Hillman would be off his rocker to cast her anyway. She doesn't even look like Helen Keller. You're the one that passes for a six-year-old."

I flashed her a fake smile. "What's up with Hillman's schedule? Did you hear the announcement this morning?"

"I about died."

We repeated Principal McCoy's southern accent: "Auditions for *The Miracle Worker* will begin in Mr. Hillman's classroom at exactly 3:47 p.m."

We laughed. Becca spun around and walked beside me.

"Seriously, Leah. Worrying creates wrinkles, and wrinkles will prevent you from getting the part."

"What's another challenge?"

"Challenge? You are the ultimate line learner. And Helen Keller doesn't even have lines so just imagine how Oscar worthy your performance will be."

"But she has a script full of blocking. I've never had a part where I had to memorize only actions. Can you imagine having to create memory in your body, not just in your brain?"

"If Hillman doesn't cast you, I swear I'll choke him out."

"Please don't. I kind of need him alive."

"I'll consider sparing him if you promise me that when auditions are over, we're gonna kidnap Justin and crash the basketball game."

"Yeah, sure." I grew quiet, unable to shake the nerves of auditions.

"You know I love you,"—Becca burned me with that x-ray stare—"but you can't worry forever."

As soon as my mouth opened to respond, my eyes widened as I spotted the words THE MIRACLE WORKER on a blue book being carried down the hallway, the lettering seeming to glow, as if to lure me into its world.

"Hey!" I shouted to the girl hurrying down the hallway. "Where'd you get that script?"

She turned around. It was Tamara Jackson, the student director for the third year in a row.

"What? This?" She held up the script, catching her breath.

"Yes. Where'd you get it?"

"Mr. Hillman." She spun around and continued her sprint.

"Please let me see yours. I promise I'll give it right back."

Turning her head just enough for me to hear her, she said, "Can't. Cold reading."

When she disappeared, I was pretty sure all the blood had drained from my body.

Kids bumped into me as I stood there, gazing down the south wing hallway.

"I despise the earth and all who inhabit it," I said.

Becca rested her elbow on my shoulder. "You won't be saying that when you get the lead. You'll be bouncing on your little Helen toes."

As soon as we reached Hillman's classroom, I stopped before the door. Thoughts about The Tree rushed through my mind as they often did during my bouts of anxiety.

Sometimes I would go there after school when no one was around. The brick of the north wing looked even redder under the sun. Wooden benches lined the sidewalk which stretched all the way to the student parking lot. I'd settle into the soft grass that cushioned my body and stare at the sky through the leaves, wondering why those choir kids had it so much easier.

The sound of them practicing in the auditorium would reach my ears and I'd dream about what it would feel like to wear one of their purple uniforms—the white rhinestones lining my neck, the ruffles flowing lightly at my ankles, the snugness of the perfectly-fitting dress, showing off the woman I was becoming.

My chest filled with a wholeness when I imagined my parents watching me from the crowd as I sang the songs of spring.

I glanced over at Becca, wondering if she could hear my heart thumping, but her eyes were glued to her cell phone.

I wanted to leave.

Run.

Hide and never come out.

"It's gonna be okay," Becca said, still clicking her keypad.

I cleared my throat and nodded. "It's no big deal. I'm just feeling a little bleh, that's all."

"Let it out, Leah."

"It's just that . . . I wouldn't have to worry about this if I was one of those jerks at The Tree. Those kids have it all together, don't they? They can just raise their hands and get a part, while we have to suffer all this nerve damage. They never even meet deadlines. I always end up whispering their cues."

"Feel better?" she asked.

"How are you not nervous?"

"I only audition for these plays because you dragged me into this."

I glared at her.

"Okay, and to ditch my dad, but still."

"Give me some of your chill," I said. "You make everything look so easy."

"You can have a little bit." She squeezed her thumb and index finger together. "But I need the rest."

She slipped her phone into her pocket.

"Life's easier when you don't think too much about it," she said.

"Sorry, but that's a challenge I *can't* accept. Where will I go after school if Hillman doesn't cast me? I can't get a job. Mom would guilt-trip me into paying bills."

"Did you tell her about college yet?"

"Seriously? I'm not ready for one of those conversations about how she also wanted to go to college, but it isn't in our blood, and how we can't afford it, and how I'll be paying off loans for the rest of my life."

I turned the knob and pushed open the door.

Since the new semester had started, I'd been in Hillman's classroom at least thirty times aside from our sessions. As soon as the last bell rang, drama club kids would hurry over just to hang out or talk about theatre.

It was the "cool" thing we did.

Hillman was writing something on the chalkboard as I walked in—all twenty feet of him, his facial skin smooth without that goatee. He was as tall as the giant beanstalk and just as difficult to reach, though he hid it behind a friendly face.

"You've got this," Becca said, squeezing my arm before darting off.

I lost her to our cafeteria table friends which included Riley, Abigail, Hannah, Alexa, and Mikayla sitting in the first couple rows. Justin and Cameron, the only two consistent drama club guys, sat with them as well. Drama club was always short on guys.

I plopped my bag next to the first desk in the last row. The yellow classroom walls taunted me with their joy, but before I sat down, my eyes caught something all too familiar.

THE MIRACLE WORKER

The title seemed to glow again, teasing me with the knowledge that the words I needed were right behind the cover.

"Nervous?" Hillman stood in front of the chalkboard.

He wouldn't have asked if the others weren't carried away in their own conversations. He wasn't one of those jerky teachers who used humiliation as a teaching tool.

"No," I lied. "Are you?"

"Why would I be?"

"Spending the next two months with a group of truly disturbed and hopelessly dramatic people? I'd be running for the hills." I leaned forward. "Do we at least get to look at the script for a few minutes?"

Hillman walked back to his desk and sat down, watching me with those deep-brown eyes as if he could read every thought racing through my mind.

I squeezed the cuffs of my gray sweater jacket before I got up and stepped to his desk.

"I don't need long." I pointed to the script. "I just want to do my best at Helen."

He lifted it. My eyes followed the book before meeting his stare.

"Helen doesn't have lines," he said.

"But the blocking is even harder. Shouldn't anyone auditioning for Helen get a sneak peek?"

"No."

"What if you guys audition me for Anne Sullivan or Kate Keller, or anyone with lines?"

"You do understand what a cold reading is, correct?"

"I've had enough of the cold."

There was a pause when he glanced out the window. It was the end of February and rays of sunlight beamed through.

He looked back to me and sighed. "I have copies of specific scenes that I want auditioned and I won't give out those copies until it's your turn."

He smiled and placed the script back down.

I huffed and walked back to my seat, glancing at my friends before sitting down. Becca was telling them something that had happened to her that morning—something about a vacuum and her mom—but the others burst into laughter before I could get the joke.

A wad of paper suddenly bounced off my shoulder.

My friend Justin hollered, "Leah, what's up with you today? Too good to sit with us?"

I turned. Justin Doyle . . . the ginger Josh Groban. He had been both a choir kid and a drama club kid in his freshman year, but since choir was also an actual class, he'd quit to make room for more academic credits.

Now he was entirely invested in drama club.

"The wild and fabulous Helen Keller needs to concentrate," I said back.

Since I'd known him, he had always been a performing arts

enthusiast. During my first day of sixth grade, he was the one assigned to show me around. Plays and musicals were all he could talk about—stuff that I didn't know much about at the time. That same day after school, he'd brought me to his mom's hair salon to get my hair trimmed. Afterward, I had to promise him that I would never, *ever* let my hair grow split ends like that again.

We'd been friends ever since.

"Shut up, Justin." Becca leaned over and flicked him on the forehead. "Only fools have time to fart around. She actually has a shot at this."

I lost their attention when Justin flicked her back, starting a flicking war within the group.

I playfully rolled my eyes and refocused on my thoughts.

Helen Keller—a champion of life who overcame the odds against her—had lived in Alabama. She was blind, deaf, and mute, only a child when her teacher Anne moved in to help her. Helen got really pissed off when she didn't get her way, slapping her teacher in the face. Many times.

I glanced up at Hillman; that didn't seem like a bad idea. He was being so stubborn about the script.

What Helen knew was that the world was dark and quiet.

Very quiet.

Loud voices poured through the classroom door and I looked up. Thank all the gods and all the heavens that I was still sitting, because my legs liquefied as soon as he entered the room.

There he was—Braden Gregory—class clown and one of the most popular guys in school. Time ceased to exist. The voices and people around disappeared and all I saw was him showing off his lopsided grin right out of one of those cheesy romance films.

I wouldn't say he was particularly hot though. Maybe I saw him for the jerk he had been in middle school, laughing at my mismatched clothes or mocking my shyness as I quietly answered a question when the teacher called on me.

He was different now, even different looking. I mean—if I cared—he was overdue for a haircut. That thick brown hair really accented those green eyes that turned into crescent moons when he smiled.

Braden stood with forced confidence—his nervousness was written in the awkward way he glanced around.

When he looked my way, my insides turned so warm that I was sure I'd faint. I pressed my fingers over my temples, hiding my face from his view.

Oh how I wished he weren't cute . . . and kind of nice these days. It would've made hating him much easier.

When I bit my lip, the slow motion ended. His fellow choir friends—Sara, Rachelle, and Scotty—followed him as he made a beeline to my group of friends.

I'd had only one crush before—Matt Hendrix—an upperclassman drama club royal. I was only a freshman when I'd met him. He was the star in *Pirates of Maribel Island*. Holding hands was as far as we ever went and, I had to admit, I became a really good hand holder, so good that I was ready for our next step to be a kiss had I not caught him backstage kissing Jordan Green.

Jordan Green was not a girl.

Maybe it was my own paranoia getting the best of me, but I'd never heard of Braden having a girlfriend. Ever. Not only that, but he had an odd sense of fashion. The guy wore clothes that were a little too tight and he donned a yellow and red polka-dot tie over all his shirts. He always wore a black bowler hat like Charlie Chaplin and fancy brown grandfather shoes. Even though he used to be a pretty good wrestler, his involvement in musicals didn't exactly help ease my gaydar suspicions.

I'd never heard about him dating any of the pretty girls he hung around with. If he really was gay, it must have been hard to keep such a secret in the world he lived in. I sometimes wondered if that was why he picked on other people.

Scotty lifted his fist and shouted a jocky greeting to Hillman before slipping smoothly into a desk seat.

For years, I'd overheard that group talking about The Tree as if it bled magic sap.

"Hey man, you going to The Tree for lunch?"

"Meet me at The Tree during passing period."

"Let's talk about it at The Tree."

They blended in like chameleons while I laid low to avoid being targeted. Who would have thought public school would be so hard? If I could be a choir kid for a day, I wouldn't have to avoid anything or anyone.

It wasn't that I wanted to be friends with any of them, but I was curious.

Me with the popular group? Socially unacceptable. It was fun to think about anyway—a different perspective with me on the other side, looking toward the cafeteria from the north wing.

I'd once read that we become who we surround ourselves with, and maybe I wanted something different for my future instead of divorces and penny pinching. I wanted college. I wanted to break through those limitations that society had tied around me just because of who my parents were and what they'd chosen for their lives.

I came from poverty and a family of divorce. Maybe that was how I became so good at theatre. Most of the choir kids came from wealthy families, or at least families that didn't sit at the kitchen table deciding whether to go without water or electricity for the month. Working low-paying jobs around the clock was how my parents survived, but I always wondered if getting by would have been easier if one of them had a good college degree.

Despite my curiosity, my loyalty was with my drama club friends—friends I wouldn't leave for anything.

Braden and Scotty struck up a conversation with Justin and a couple others while the girls sat a couple seats away. I kept glancing over, worried they might be picking on Justin, but then Justin's laugh went off like a horn in church.

Scotty kept glancing at Sara, too scared to get her attention. I knew it from the way he rubbed his hands together under the desk and looked away when she turned around.

"We found two male actors, Mr. Hillman." Sara pointed to Braden and Scotty. "If you need more extras or help backstage, we might be able to draft a couple more."

Becca mouthed the words KISS ASS.

Sara was a Californian, practically another species to Hoosiers like us. Nobody else had her cream skin and perfect blond hair that glistened under the light.

In history class last year, I'd caught a glimpse of her report card —an obnoxious mixture of A minuses, A's, and A pluses.

Braden treated her like she was a princess; opening doors, buying her coffee from Quick Stop, listening to her go on and on about whatever photos she had to take for the Yearbook Committee. Sometimes I wondered if he was deaf. Her voice carried this sharp tone that could really get on your nerves after a while, but he seemed unfazed. It killed me how people like Sara flew up the social ladder, much like how the loudest singers in choir took up all the solos . . . just because they were loud. Even Rachelle—former drama club enthusiast turned choir kid suck-up—knew her way up the ladder.

Hillman lifted his head from the papers he was grading.

"We need as many males as we can get." He looked at Braden and Scotty. "Nice to have you both interested. We have rehearsals three evenings a week. I hope this won't interfere with Mr. Steele's rehearsals?"

When Braden spoke, his voice was a little deeper than I remembered.

"He knows we'll be doing drama club, too. He's totally fine with it as long as we memorize our lines."

Great.

"Will it be too much for you?" Hillman asked.

"No," Braden said. "I'm helping my dad less around the shop. Freed up some time."

Hillman smiled. One of those smiles that conceal what a person was really thinking.

He probably knew those kids would give him a run for his money.

Chapter 3

Last semester was one of those times I would miss my bus on purpose after school and walk to The Tree. I wouldn't be caught dead sitting there during school, so I waited until school was out and the coast was clear.

Resting my back against the trunk, I'd think about all the things I wanted for my future, like a college degree, a nice car . . . to live like the choir kids.

Fitting the image of who I wanted to be would finally give me everything I had ever wanted and, for once in my life, I would know what it felt like to not be pointed at by some jocky jerk or high-society adult just because I couldn't afford new clothes or a decent haircut.

It was during one of these moments, sitting against The Tree, when I shifted down the trunk and something crunched under my palm. I looked down.

A small piece of plastic stuck slightly out of a patch of unearthed grass. If you didn't look hard enough, you couldn't tell anything had been dug up since not much grass grew around the trunk anyway. I tugged at it, and out came a small plastic sandwich bag containing a folded piece of paper.

That was the day I unofficially met Robert.

I could never forget that first letter as I opened it in my hands. It read:

wednesday, november 12, 2008

> *"Don't cry when the sun is gone, because the tears*
> *won't let you see the stars." Violeta Parra*
>
> *all i can do is surrender to this void in my heart*
> *and wait for something good to replace the pain. i hope*
> *anything or anyone can save me from myself. it's dark*
> *in a world without meaning, without knowing myself. i*
> *will wait for the answers. i will wait to feel whole again.*
> *Robert*

I felt like I was breaking an unspoken confidentiality agreement, eavesdropping on someone else's thoughts. I hadn't intended to respond. After all, he was probably waiting for someone else, not some Tipton High senior who stumbled upon his letter.

The letter stayed inside its plastic bag on my bedroom desk for weeks until I found another one during my after-school daydreaming session:

> *thursday, december 4, 2008*
> *"Argue for your limitations and, sure enough,*
> *they're yours." Richard Bach*
>
> *this is one of my favorite quotes. it helps me*
> *through the toughest days.*
>
> *i used to love this school. i used to love this tree.*
> *this tree was the only place that made me feel alive.*
> *that was until you left and took a piece of me with you.*
> *the people in our lives should be the ones who build us*
> *up, empower us, give us strength.*
>
> *how is it that once they are gone, everything can*
> *change?*
> *Robert*

I wanted to answer his question. He had a right to know that he wasn't the only one feeling that way, and who better to understand change than the girl reading his letters?

In Tipton County, clouds could quickly turn into rain, so I was glad Robert had enough sense to bury his letters in a plastic bag. He must have wanted somebody to find them if he cared enough to protect them. I figured nobody was writing back since I hadn't found response letters. Maybe I could help him find who he was looking for or maybe I just couldn't shake my curiosity. He seemed desperate.

I understood desperate.

So, I wrote back.

Monday, December 8, 2008

Dear Robert,

I don't have any special quote to put at the top, but I do have something to say. I found your letters here after school. I'm probably not the one you want to hear from. I'm just a student at Tipton High. I like to sit here sometimes, thinking about how my life changes, too. Even though I've been in this town a while, I still worry.

People leave. I leave. New town. New school. New faces.

It's like being on a merry-go-round that keeps spinning faster and faster, shreds of my spirit disappearing in the wind. Sometimes, sitting here makes me feel as if I've jumped off for a moment. I can slow down, see straight again, and figure out where on earth my life is headed.

I guess I just wanted to say that you're not alone.

Pen Pal Tina

In his response letter a couple days later, I learned he used to attend Tipton High with his high school sweetheart in the fifties, and that they left each other notes under The Tree.

We would each leave a letter weekly, sometimes more, sometimes less. From then on, I started considering Robert a friend.

I never looked at The Tree the same again. Its meaning seemed older, wiser, and more complicated than I could ever understand—too good for me or the choir kids to claim.

In his writing, Robert expressed his deep desire to come back and find a letter from his sweetheart, even after all those years. I sort of felt bad for finding the letter at all, but I quickly learned how much we had in common.

He wrote about how she'd ended up moving away with her family before they graduated, never getting a chance to say goodbye.

I told him about the choir kids who took over his tree, all my teenage angst about the future and where I fit in, how I wanted to go to college with the scholarship I had.

It wasn't a "cool" scholarship by definition. It was one for low-income households that would pay for half of my tuition if I made good grades and stayed away from detention and the principal's office. It would help a lot, but I would still have to take out loans. I told all this to Robert, all my struggles and doubts.

Writing to Robert was an outlet that drama club couldn't give me. When I was on stage, I was somebody else. When writing, I was the real me, even if I used a fake name.

I sometimes wondered when he came to bury the letters, and if he lived nearby.

I felt bad for the guy . . . his being abandoned . . . his loneliness.

My mom had moved my sister and me to many states—seven to be exact. All big towns. New school every year until moving to this Small Town Nowhere when I was eleven, just in time to start sixth grade.

In one of my letters to Robert, I wrote how I understood his sweetheart. She probably had to go because her family made her. My mom had her reasons for moving, but unlike most people in Tipton County, I actually wanted to stay.

Friday, February 20, 2009

Dear Robert,

What is it about The Tree? You once told me it was the only place that kept you alive, but I want to know more.

I just can't stand it. As if those choir kids have nowhere else to eat their overly priced lunches.

You're right though. I have to stop focusing on what doesn't matter. It won't even matter after this year when we all graduate and realize that there is more to life than stupid cliques. What matters now are auditions for the play.

I like The Miracle Worker. It proves that we can overcome our biggest challenges. I just can't believe it will be my last play here. What am I going to do without drama club?

I guess we all have things that keep us alive. I wonder what mine will be when high school is over.

Pen Pal Tina

Chapter 4

I chewed on my lip and ran my hands through my hair just so I could sneak a peek at the royalty among us. Becca looked at me, pointing to Braden as I shook my head with every neck muscle.

Before I could say anything, Braden spoke over the group. "Earth to Helen Keller over there. You know you might actually have to talk, right?"

The room quieted. Tamara wrote ferociously into her notebook while Hillman clicked away on his computer.

It didn't hit until a few seconds later that Braden was referring to me. My body froze. The embarrassment of being singled out crept into all my nerves.

So what if I was being quiet? Why did the popular kids get to define that as a flaw?

"Anna Sullivan doesn't have forever," he said. "Or maybe she does. Who knows."

My chest tightened and heat rushed to my face.

I blurted the first thing that came to mind. "It's Anne Sullivan, smart one. *Anne.* You wouldn't know that though since all the teachers pass you out of pity."

I was hoping for a comeback or anything to show that he was the jerk, not me.

Everyone stayed quiet.

I looked down, tapping my fingers on the desk.

Maybe I shouldn't have said that.

Hillman rose from his desk and scanned the room. Glancing at the clock which read 3:47 p.m., he grinned.

"Welcome back, everyone. As you all know, our final production of the year will be *The Miracle Worker*. There will be two show nights. First, I must inform you that scripts for this show will cost fifteen dollars due to low funding. On the bright side, we're pleased to have new faces with us. Sara and Rachelle have already dipped their toes in the last production. Scotty, Braden, would you like to tell us a little about yourselves and what brings you both to drama club?"

Scotty stayed seated and tapped a pencil on his desk. "Hey y'all, I'm Scotty Hunter. I'm a pretty good singer. I wouldn't say I'm like Bocelli or anything. Mr. Steele's always casting me in the musicals, so I must be all right. I get to be Aladdin this year. I'm a basketball player, too. I'm hoping Mr. Hillman gives me a small part because my acting blows."

He got a laugh for that one.

Braden stood and looked around the room. Before I had the chance to shield my face, his magnetic eyes caught mine and I became his focal point.

I guessed I deserved that.

"Hey, I'm Braden." He raised his hand for a quick wave. "This is my first time in drama club. Sara said there weren't enough guys, so I figured I'd take a jab at it. I usually do musicals. This year I'm the Genie in *Aladdin*. My dad owns the Gregory Auto Shops. I help him out sometimes at a couple of the stores. Since it's senior year, he's letting me out of the auto cage for a while so I can focus on school. Yeah. So. I like plain cheeseburgers, long walks on the beach, and dancing in the rain. Thank you."

He gave a semi-bow, people clapped, and I wiped a bead of sweat off my forehead when he finally dropped his magnetic eyes.

Auditions proceeded as they usually did. Hillman and Tamara huddled together before calling out who would go up. Different combinations were tried out. Sara was auditioned with nearly everyone. Not only did she have perfect hair, but she was also talented, as if the role of Anne Sullivan were made for her.

Becca auditioned as Helen's mother, Kate Keller, with her oh-so-sarcastic eagerness. She glanced at me during her audition with eyes saying, *"This is all your fault."* I was proud of her for toughing through it though. If not for Justin and me nagging her to join, she'd have to spend play rehearsal evenings with her dad.

When it was Rachelle's turn at the monologue audition, I tensed.

If Cruella de Vil and Penelope Cruz were to collide and become one person, that would be Rachelle Rodriguez. I first met her when she joined drama club our freshman year. She'd transferred schools when her family moved from Texas to Small Town Nowhere.

From what I'd heard, her family spoke only Spanish at home. She had this cool flow in her accent, too. When I asked her one time about her nationality, she lifted her head without answering and started talking to someone else. Justin nudged me and said, "She speaks the I'm-better-than-you language." Since then, she joined choir and upgraded to the group at The Tree, abandoning her fellow drama club members as if we were chopped liver.

Who could blame her? Maybe she wanted a better life, too.

Tamara gave her a nod and Rachelle began reading. Other than her deep, husky voice, she had a chance at Helen Keller. I thought so, anyway. She was curvier than me and would make a better Anne, but I liked the way she put her anger into her performance. It reminded me how healing theatre could be for bottled emotions.

When she was finished, she took her seat.

"Leah," Hillman called.

The hairs on my arms tingled.

This was it. This was as prepared as I was going to be and I just had to deal.

I stood, making no eye contact with anyone as I walked to Tamara and Hillman.

Hillman handed me the paper but didn't release it from his grip until I looked at him. He gave me one slow nod. I thought I smiled, but my face was numb.

As soon as he released the paper, I made my way toward the front of the room.

"Braden," Hillman said.

My feet stopped.

I heard Braden get up and I quickly turned.

"Mr. Hillman," I said. The room quieted. "Are you sure . . . I mean . . .?"

Braden took the paper from Hillman and turned around. His magnetic force almost took hold again, but I imagined my eyes were invisible to his power.

Hillman said, "We just need to test the chemistry."

"You can test me with Scotty," I said, almost regretting speaking at all.

"Don't worry," Braden said. I avoided his magnet with all my might. "I'm not a mean Captain Keller. I won't spank you if you misbehave."

The room giggled, and he slid up to the front as if the path were paved for him.

I exhaled through my nose and glanced at Becca. She gave me the thumbs up.

Braden stood beside me, his energy swallowing my bit of confidence. I lifted my paper without looking at him.

"Whenever you're ready," Tamara said.

I focused on the paper.

"Uh, Tamara," I said, scanning the lines. "This is a scene between Captain Keller and Anne Sullivan. I want to audition for Helen Keller."

"Everyone will be considered for every part."

I looked at the floor, realizing most of the others had already tried out, and all that was left was me and Braden.

Concentrate.

What did I know about Anne Sullivan? She was Helen's teacher. Growing up in a group home wasn't an easy challenge for her to overcome. The Kellers hired her to move into their household for the purpose of helping with Helen's behavior.

The first line was mine.

Stage fright. I gulped air. *Totally normal.*

I quickly memorized my first chunk of lines.

"Captain Keller, pleased to—"

His magnet caught me as soon as I looked up, those same eyes that had caught me staring from the cafeteria window.

I forgot my lines.

I forgot my own name.

A small smile grew on Braden's face, almost as if he were enjoying this torture. Those wide-set eyebrows made him look even happier.

Gosh, it was just the popular boy effect, I reminded myself. Just some cute, stupid boy who thought he could have another girl on his arm.

"Leah?" Hillman called out.

Braden's thick brown hair stood up in all kinds of directions, making me wonder if he owned a mirror.

His eyes were a darker shade of green than I remembered. A few faint freckles popped from his sun-kissed skin. "Freckle face," I could have called him.

Oh. God. Focus.

The actions read that I was to reach out my hand, so I did. He grabbed it as the fully embodied Captain Keller would and shook it with strength.

With his voice deep and mighty, he read, "Ah yes, Miss Sullivan. We have been expecting you. I hope your trip here was as smooth as your hands."

His eyebrows rose and paused for effect. The room rumbled in quiet laughter, surely winning him comedic points.

"Read the lines as they are written," Tamara said.

Braden delivered his next line, taking another step toward me. My mouth tightened into an upward curve.

He was trying to break me, but I wouldn't surrender to his humor.

"I understand you come from a group home of girls. You must have a lot of experience dealing with challenges. I hope you are prepared for the job."

I forced myself not to look at him, but he emphasized the words "girls" and "experience" and "job".

His gaze devoured me.

I bit my tongue, my lip, the inside of my cheek. I was pretty sure my cheek started bleeding.

"Braden," Tamara grunted. "Lines. As. Written."

Braden cleared his throat, but not the smirk on his face.

"*And* the suitcase—" he read, reaching out for an invisible suitcase.

"I'll take the suitcase, thanks."

"Not at all, I have it, Miss Sullivan."

"I'd like it."

"I couldn't think of it, Miss Sullivan. You'll find in the south we—"

"Let me."

I pulled the invisible suitcase back, but he nearly jerked it out of my grasp.

"—view women as the flowers of civiliza—"

"I've got something in it for Helen!"

Braden brought his hand to his face and glared at me with exaggerated shock.

A laughing sensation began to rise from my belly to my chest.

No.

I forced it down.

"Well then." Braden stepped forward, removing his hand from his face. "I hope Mrs. Keller informed you about Helen's condition."

I glanced at my paper. There were no such lines. The scene was over.

Improvisation was okay, I told myself. If Braden could do it, then I could do it better.

"Depending on how you see it, this could be a small *job* or a very *big* one indeed," he said.

Becca hollered a catcall noise.

I'm going to kill her.

"Well, Captain, I have quite the resume." My voice broke. "I understand this will not be an easy task to undertake since I am not used to handling . . ."

I sucked in some air and controlled my lips.

". . . *small* jobs like yours."

He raised his eyebrows so high I thought they would fly off his face.

Where did his confidence come from? Was it just a gift from being born into a family that had everything? Or did it come from that sly grin that wanted to shatter me into a million pieces?

Don't laugh, I reminded myself. Breaking character is the death of an actor. Catching stupid, lusty feelings is the death of a human being.

I waited for him to continue, but he let the silence linger.

Just when I thought I had it under control, the sensation rose to my neck and projected out of my mouth.

I laughed.

The room exploded into applause and cheers, all the while I couldn't stop laughing.

Braden's chest rose and fell a few quick times, but his eyes didn't fall from mine. I detected some sort of victory in his smile.

It was then when my lips snapped shut. I covered my mouth, realizing I had just committed theatre suicide.

For the first time ever, I broke character. My theatre career was officially over.

Damn you, Braden Gregory.

The cheering continued and soon my shoulders dropped. I looked at Hillman who was nodding while writing something down. Becca rose from her seat, clapping. Then others rose from their seats, joining the applause. Shaking my head, I turned back to Braden. There he was—calm and unaffected.

Was laughing a part of the character? The script?

I glanced over the lines, but nowhere did it say to laugh.

"Good *job*, you guys," Hillman said. "You can have a seat."

I looked up, but Braden was already making his way back to his desk. I watched him sit down, noticing something deep, almost secretive in the way he looked at me before I took my seat.

To make matters worse, I didn't even get to audition for Helen Keller. Devastation began crawling over me, but every time I had lifted my hand to ask for my chance, Hillman and Tamara called another pair to audition before me and Braden.

I blew it and I knew it.

When they finally answered my raised hand, Hillman announced that he and Tamara had seen everything they needed to see to make their decisions.

"The cast list will be posted next Monday morning on my classroom door," he said.

That was it.

I bombed my audition all because I couldn't stay in character. As much as I wanted to blame Braden, I should have been strong enough to not laugh.

Before I left the room, I spotted Hillman smiling at me. I smiled back, hoping for some kind of reassurance, but he just nodded as I walked out the door.

I made my way down the hallway with Becca and Justin. Without a chance to scold Becca for her catcall, I heard my name.

"Leah," a voice called. "Hey, Leah."

I turned around as Braden jogged toward me. He stood almost a foot taller than me, but then again, everyone was taller than me.

Becca and Justin went ahead after Becca had quickly turned

around, winked, and pointed to Braden. I began planning how I was going to get her back for that until Braden's voice interrupted my thoughts.

"That was pretty funny, huh?" he asked, as if we'd always known each other. "You think Hillman will cast us together?"

I just looked at him, pretty sure my face was tense and twisted. His clean scent and polka-dot tie pulled my attention.

"What's with the terminator face?" he asked.

I let out a quick breath, correcting my slumped posture.

"What do you want?" I asked.

"What?"

"Why are you even talking to me?"

He wore a contented smile and shrugged one shoulder.

"It's just some joke to you, isn't it?" I said. "Your little shenanigans in there could have cost me the part I wanted."

Before I turned around, he said, "Leah Roy. You only have yourself to blame."

I glared at him, pretending not to notice his smooth face—no sign that facial hair had ever existed.

"This isn't a joke," I said.

"Lighten up, Paul Simon. I'm just messing with you."

I only knew Paul Simon because my mom loved the music video with him sitting in a room with Chevy Chase. She'd always say that nobody could listen to that song and be angry at the same time.

"Really funny," I said. "I'm not an idiot."

"Didn't say you were."

"I get it. Paul Simon's a short guy. I'm a short girl. Did you get your fill so you can go home and feel better about yourself?"

He shifted his weight to one side. "You don't know Paul Simon, do you?"

"I know Paul Simon."

"No, you don't."

"Yes. I do."

"No. You don't."

"Paul Simon. He sings that one song. You know, the one where he's sitting in that room with—"

"You have no idea," Braden interrupted. "So you know one song. Big whoop. I bet you don't even know any of his songs from Simon and Garfunkel."

"Simon and who?"

"Wow. And you said you weren't an idiot."

"I'm not an—"

Scotty darted past us, nearly tripping over his own feet. "Hey, dude, can you drop my books off at the locker room?" His sneakers screeched louder than his voice echoing down the hallway. "Coach Garcia's gonna make me run five freakin' miles if I'm late again." He pressed his hands over his head. "And my gym shorts. Shit. You know my combination."

Apart from the few drama club members who walked past us, the south wing hallway was empty.

"You're late already," Braden said.

"Yeah, in like two seconds. I promised him I'd be there before five o'clock."

"Scott, get it yourself. A little more running won't kill you."

"But my crazy mom will. Come on, dude, I need that shit before Garcia catches me without it again."

"What's he going to do? Beat you with his whip?"

"Fuck off, Braden!"

He was nearly out the door. His face drooped in helpless defeat as he looked at me.

I cast a compassionate nod.

"Don't bail him out of this one," Braden said. "Coach Garcia needs to teach him a lesson."

"Give Leah my combination," Scotty said, swinging the door open. "She's not a sarcastic dick like you."

Braden watched Scotty disappear. "His mom really is a hard-ass."

"I know." I caught myself, but he didn't push it any further.

"I was over at his house a lot during winter break," he said. "All they did was argue. Drove me crazy. It was like she didn't have his dad to push around anymore, so she took it all out on him."

I didn't really know what to say. I was still processing that Braden Gregory was talking to me. I was still trying to convince myself that I didn't like it.

His eyes swept up and down my body—their warmth heated every part he looked at.

My shoulders melted, my lips moistened, and my hair felt like it was going to burn into my scalp. I recoiled as if looking at him would have made me forget my own name again.

Ugh. Maybe I was going "crazy schizo".

"Basketball game. Tonight. Your life will change once you *really* know Paul Simon." He wrote down Scotty's combination on a piece of notebook paper and handed it to me.

"What's this?" I noticed a phone number underneath.

"Text me your address," he said. "I'll pick you up during half-time."

"Half-time?"

"I work concessions until then."

Maybe he wasn't serious. Maybe it was one of those famous movie jokes where the popular guy tricks the girl into believing he actually likes her.

"Come on," he said. "Don't give me that 'girl is too good for the guy who pours his heart and soul into asking her out' attitude."

"Asking me out?"

"You know, out of that cave you hide yourself in. A little fresh air will breathe life into that pretty face."

My face burned. I wasn't sure if I was still annoyed with his confidence or attracted to the challenge.

"Just so you know," I said, "I like being by myself. It beats being like you and having to try so hard to get people to like me."

"You don't have to try so hard."

I searched his expression, but he wore that same contented smile. A wave of confusion and curiosity filled my gut. The need to run snuck up on me, but my shoes burned into the floor.

This guy was good. *Really* good.

"I have plans," I finally said.

Braden pulled out his phone and gestured for me to take mine out, too.

"Seriously. I have plans," I repeated.

"I know. You're going to the basketball game and I'm going to school you on Paul Simon."

"I prefer to stay in my cave, away from entitled hotshots like you."

I folded the paper and began walking toward Scotty's locker as Braden followed. It was the dented one right across the hallway from Hillman's classroom. I'd seen Scotty kick it one morning when it jammed before he realized I was standing outside of Hillman's door.

It popped open after I clicked in the combination.

I grabbed a bag that I assumed contained his gym shorts and pulled down the only two books I saw.

"Just so you know, I wasn't comparing you to Paul Simon's height." Braden's tone softened as he leaned closer to my ear. "He has the voice of an angel."

My lips parted.

I gently closed the locker, feeling my heart thump all the way up to my ears.

My hand lowered to my pocket where I pulled out my cell phone and sent Braden Gregory my damn address.

Chapter 5

I hopped into Braden's purple minivan while he sang the high notes from "Hey Jude" by The Beatles. He turned up the volume knob before backing out of my driveway, the steering wheel taking a brutal beating to his drumming hands as he sang higher.

He wasn't a good singer.

His voice was nice and everything, but he couldn't hold a note to save his life. Why in the world would Mr. Steele cast him in musicals?

Braden tipped his Chaplin hat forward and I guessed I was supposed to do the same with my baseball cap.

"You like Nike?"

His question caught me off guard.

"Your hat." He pointed. "It says Nike."

"Oh." I blushed. "Yeah. I didn't even realize it. It's my mom's."

"This is my grandpa's." He adjusted his hat.

"Reminds me of Charlie Chaplin."

"My grandpa loved Charlie Chaplin. He loved The Beatles, too. God, I love The Beatles, don't you?" he asked, turning the volume down.

I knew of The Beatles from my mom blasting their music at her ex's pool parties.

"I like one of their songs," I said. "The one where it gets kind of scary."

"'Revolution 9'?"

"It starts out kind of happy, then gets really loud."

"Ahh, you mean 'A Day in the Life.'" He took his eyes off the road for a second to glance at me. "Leah Roy, the girl who doesn't even know Paul Simon knows one of The Beatles' songs. A good song, too. I'm impressed."

My skepticism of him still overpowered any fuzzy feelings that filled my gut.

"Don't be. I really don't know much about The Beatles. That song, though, I like it a lot." I gave him a side glance. "And I know Paul Simon."

It was a three-minute drive from my house to the high school. Sometimes Justin would drive Becca and me home if he didn't have to work. It took about twenty minutes to walk when I missed my bus, which was always a risk when I buried a letter after school.

I'd have to wait until most kids were gone, run to The Tree, bury the letter, and run to my bus, hoping it would still be there. Sometimes I'd catch the bus right before the doors slammed, but sometimes I'd miss it and spend a little more time at The Tree before walking home. The only problem with walking home was crossing the highway because it curved before the road leading to my house. If you weren't fast enough crossing the road, you'd be splattered.

I snuck a glance at Braden's back seat and swore there could have been a family of rats living somewhere under all the balled-up papers and fast-food wrappers. I noticed some papers were old homework assignments. One was graded an A. Another was a B plus.

"Someone does their homework," I said as we neared the high school.

"What?"

I motioned to the back of the van.

"Oh, right." He exhaled. "My van is pretty much the only place where I can be myself. At home, everything has to be clean . . . organized . . . perfect. My parents drive me up the wall."

"You bona fide rebel," I said. "It's pretty cluttered under my bed, if that makes you feel better."

"Leah Roy. A rebel herself," he said. "That's the only place you can have your clutter, huh?"

"I guess."

"Mr. Green gave me some extra time on my paper. I've been working on a paper about Jeff Buckley. What'd you write about?"

"I chose to write about that Joyce Carol Oates story 'Where Are you Going, Where Have You Been?'" I paused. "But that was due last week. How much time do you need?"

"You can't rush art. I told Mr. Green I wanted to get it just right. No one should be allowed to half-ass any story about Jeff Buckley."

Braden suddenly turned up the volume when a Tracy Chapman song came on. While singing her part, he pulled into the parking lot and found a spot far away from the gymnasium.

"Seriously?" I laughed under the music.

Like all the great singers, Braden raised his hand to his face when higher notes came. His upper arm flexed as he got into it, and as he sang to me, I became fully aware that this was Braden Gregory, but at the same time, it wasn't. Not the Braden I thought I knew anyway.

Sitting in his van while he sang to me was like a sweet dream that I didn't want to wake up from. That wasn't reality. Reality was me zipping up my jacket and going home to a tuna casserole dinner while Braden hung out with his friends and made fun of people who ate tuna casserole.

After his voice cracked for the tenth time, he turned down the volume.

"My falsetto is good, but my chest voice needs work. Mr. Steele said most of my power has to come from my stomach muscles."

"No kidding," I said.

"Slow and steady. Too much will hurt the vocal cords."

"Adding extra high notes isn't exactly starting out easy."

"But my vibrato is really good. It's in my blood. My mom sings in the church choir. She could be an opera singer." He started singing again, emphasis on the shaky vibrato.

I was grimacing on the inside, but I just nodded as he finished.

"Honestly, Mr. Steele probably thinks I suck. Sometimes I think he only casts me in big roles because I entertain the audience so much."

"You seem to make a lot of people laugh," I said.

"I made you laugh today, didn't I?"

My gaydar on Braden was officially destroyed when he looked at me with that tame, sexy grin. I rubbed my arm when the heat set in. Yeah. He wasn't gay. His stare could send orgasmic waves rippling through my body.

"Hey, don't flatter yourself," I said, swinging the door open. "That script has a ton of lines that could be twisted by a bunch of hormonal teenagers."

As we walked in, we brushed into each other a couple times. I tried to ignore it, but my stomach jumped each time Braden's skin touched mine. He smelled like a freshly showered jock mixed with what I assumed to be the natural scent of his home—clean with a hint of old.

He led me to the concession stand where he'd worked the first half of the game. On our way, Scotty jogged to the team bench and waved at me. After auditions, I'd snuck his gym bag and books into the boys' locker room while Coach Garcia was drilling everyone on how "we owe this top-notch school an unforgettable season."

Top-notch. Sure.

"My little brother's here with his buddies," Braden said, lifting his chin to someone.

"How old is your brother?"

"Fourteen. My parents take off to their vacation house on the weekends. Trevor stayed behind this time. They're having some kind of track team lock-in at the bowling alley tonight. The kid's a track star. Ran all the way here from our house."

"Wait, you have a vacation house?"

"More like a vacation cabin. And it's not mine. It's my parents'. They sort of share it with their friends. Their friends are weird."

"If I had a vacation cabin, I'd be there all the time."

"It's cool and everything, but after so many weekends there, I sort of grew out of it. I like having the house to myself."

I nodded, pretending to understand the rich life. I used to love going places with my mom and her friends, like when we'd go camping at this cheap place about thirty minutes away. I'd savor the smell of the charcoal as it burned in the grill, the sound of their laughter, the light music in the background. Her friends were cool —especially when they were sober.

"Come on in," Braden said.

He opened the side door to the concession stand. My belly churned when I noticed California Sara serving customers. She flashed us her beauty pageant smile, her hair falling in her face as she poured hot cheese over nachos.

I walked past Braden.

It was boiling in that small room, maybe from the hot dog cooker or the stove which heated the cans of nacho cheese.

Braden offered me a hot dog, which I declined, but I accepted the Dr Pepper he snapped open for me.

I pulled my jacket sleeves over my hands. "So tell me . . . out of all the things you could be doing with your Friday night, why serve drinks at a basketball game?"

"We get paid minimum wage for it actually. Looks pretty good on college applications."

"Are you going?"

He rubbed his neck. "Eh."

"Oh please," I said. "Have mercy on the enthusiasm, will you?"

"It's just that—I don't know—my parents went to college, so it's kind of expected that I go, but I'm just burnt out."

"I'm guessing business school or something?"

"My dad owns the Gregory Auto Shops in Tipton County. Not exactly something I'm thrilled about taking over. Maybe I want to travel for a while. Been stuck in this small town my whole life. We've only ever traveled to the same places. Gatlinburg and . . . Gatlinburg. I'm feeling a little restless, you know what I mean?"

I thought about all the times I'd moved.

"Restless. You'd like my mom then."

When I heard the next order for Sara, I pulled out two Cokes and a Sprite and handed them to her.

We helped Sara through the next half hour. Braden was a natural at taking orders and delivering them. Since math wasn't exactly his strong point, I counted out the change.

Sara grabbed me by the shoulders.

"You. Are. A lifesaver. Most of these people aren't even ours, they're the opponents, and I swear they're just out to get me."

We served the last few customers. Once the line was gone, the game was easier to see.

Sara waved at Rachelle who came over pulling a small wagon full of drink cases. She shot me a dark look, staring a bit too long before handing Sara the drinks.

"So, Leah Roy." Braden's voice distracted me. "What's your typical Friday night deal? You ever come to these games?"

I turned to him. "I come with my friends."

"They seem cool. I talked to Justin a little at auditions. Haven't seen much of him since he quit choir. That kid's hilarious."

"And has no filter. He's always telling me when I'm not matching or when I look like a streetwalker."

"Streetwalker. Nice."

"I don't know if you've seen that glittery-looking salon on Second Street? His mom owns it. I let him trim my hair every month. And Becca was kind of a package deal after I met Justin. They're best friends."

"Becca's the bouncy girl with the short hair, right? We've had a few classes together. I don't think she likes me much."

"I didn't think she liked me either. I met her soon after I moved here."

"Sixth grade." He smiled.

I was surprised he even remembered.

"We've been friends ever since our science teacher paired us up for a project. She was the only one who refused to dissect the frog. She ripped the gloves off my hands and lectured me about why we shouldn't harm animals."

"I remember that," he said. "Thought it was just a rumor though. They were already dead, so what was the big deal?"

"She loves animals." I smiled at the thought. "Becca is tough. I kind of wish I had her spunk."

"Okay. Two things. *Streetwalker*? You wish you were *tough*?"

"Justin's right. I have no style. I either look like a bookworm or like someone looking for tricks. And yeah, Becca doesn't take crap from anyone."

"Well, first of all, you're really pretty. I wouldn't use the word 'streetwalker' to describe you."

I wished there was a button to drain the color in my cheeks. I just glanced at Sara who was chatting with another customer.

"And second of all, I've seen how tough you are. You fought for the lead in this play. I wouldn't mess with you." He winked. "Even though it might be a little fun."

"Clearly."

"And you like unicorns," he said.

Unicorns.

I pretended that I didn't hear him because the last thing I wanted was a reminder of why I had always hated him. Sort of liking him now felt nicer than wanting to dump a bucket of red paint over him during his musical.

As the game reached the fourth quarter, the crowd cheered, sometimes letting out their disappointment if the other team came close. Which they did. A lot. Scotty's nerves must have been getting the best of him.

When the concession line slowed down, Braden turned to me. "Wanna get out of here?"

I wanted to ask where. I wanted to ask a million questions, but his fingers on my wrist had my tongue all tied and twisted. A casual grip over my hand. Gentle, yet strong enough to promise safety in his presence. With no time to overthink, I nodded, temporarily surrendering to his gaze.

Grabbing our Dr Peppers, he opened the side door and followed me out of the stand. He let go of my hand and waved at Sara and Rachelle.

I gave them both a half-smile. Sara gave me a Miss America wave with a smile that nearly blinded me, while Rachelle just leaned over the counter and watched me walk away, her glare beating bruises into my face.

I followed Braden's lead.

"She's not so bad once she knows you," he said.

"I'm pretty sure Rachelle hates me."

He laughed. "She's like that with everyone at first. She was like that with me a little. Her mom met my mom through church. My mom kind of helped them adjust to town and learn English. I don't think Rachelle likes this town much. Or anything really."

We neared the front walkway of the bleachers and began making our way through.

Braden turned away from the cheering crowd and spoke so close to my ear that I could smell his cool, mint breath. "Take one long look at all these people. They don't even know for themselves what they want, so how are *we* supposed to know what we want to do with the rest of our lives? They're only cheering because they think it's what everyone else wants them to do, but they know the other team is better." He shook his head. "Nobody wants to be alone."

"Don't you think they're cheering out of loyalty even if they know their team sucks? Like if your brother was the worst runner on his track team, wouldn't you still cheer for him because it's the right thing to do?"

"But he's not the worst," he said. "He wins every race. Just like you're the best actress in drama club, but you know Hillman wouldn't cast you as lead again."

That burnt.

"He'll be fair to the others and give a suckier actor the chance to lead. Even though he knows picking you would be the right choice."

"I always figured Hillman would be fair," I said.

"Fair isn't the same as honest, Leah. Look at all these people."

I glanced around, studying their faces, seeing the doubt behind most of their forced smiles as the buzzer horned another point for the opponent.

"They're just being fair," he said, "but they know the truth. The truth is that our team is playing like shit. My parents act the same way at my brother's track races, except they do that for the other kids because they know Trevor will win. He always wins."

"Doesn't he love running?"

"About as much as Scotty loves his mom right now. My parents raised winners, not losers. They'd cast the guilt cloud over us for months if he didn't win those races . . . if I didn't star in the musicals or win my wrestling matches."

Hearing this made me wonder if he even liked theatre. I began to wonder who Braden really was and what he would have chosen for himself.

"How do you deal with the pressure?"

"Music," he said, staring ahead. "And my grandpa. I used to talk to him a lot. Visited him every summer until he moved to Alabama a few years ago. He has this way of making people feel free."

"I haven't seen my grandparents in years. We used to visit them every summer, too, but we haven't had the money."

"Money. Always money. My grandpa didn't care to make

money that important. He's simple. Tough like Chuck Norris. He's seventy-two years old, but he's ripped like a forty-year-old. Smartest man I know."

"Seventy-two? Wow."

"He was always at home chopping wood and working in the garden when I was there. He was my idol." We turned the corner. "I could talk to him about anything and he would always have something wise to say. My dad didn't get along with him though. He called him a know-it-all lumberjack living by the seat of his pants and always told him to settle down somewhere."

"And Grandpa Norris is . . . where?"

"No idea. When I was about fourteen, my dad stopped talking to him. Now I'm not allowed to see him, but I talk to him behind my parents' backs."

"Everyone should get to see their grandparents. It's our right. If they didn't get along, why would your dad ever let you visit him in the first place?"

"The same reason all those people are cheering."

I glanced at the crowd as we passed another set of bleachers.

Fair.

I thought about my mom and how long she had to put up with my dad and all that fighting. Maybe she tolerated the situation for us . . . to give us as normal a life as possible. But what about her? What was fair for her in all that?

Braden was right. Eventually the truth comes out and that truth can be a tricky situation.

He was quiet for a second, seemingly lost in thought.

"My grandpa always talked about all the places he'd been," he finally continued. "I've always wanted to go on a road trip because of him, but not the kind you see in all the movies where everyone goes to all the big cities. Just someplace simple, places not a lot of people see. Going to Alabama, for instance. I mean, who takes a road trip to Alabama?"

"Helen Keller's house is in Alabama," I said. "I'd love to see that."

"To visit the house of someone who overcame the impossible. Yeah. I get how that'd be cool."

"I like true stories. The good ones anyway. They make me believe in people . . . in myself."

"Don't you?"

A hint of vulnerability attacked my mind, but as I remembered the touch of his hand over mine, I felt safe.

"We could all use a little more faith," I said. "Couldn't you?"

"Something like that."

When we left the building, the wind blew past us. Braden readjusted his hat.

"Come with me," he said, taking off almost too fast.

He led me through the parking lot. His clean scent traveled behind him, filling my nostrils with its goodness. I wanted that feeling of his fingers on my wrist, of his skin brushing against mine, but wanting that feeling could have become an addiction if I wasn't careful.

"What about you, Leah?" he asked, slowing down and straightening his posture as we neared his van. "Do your parents put you in the pressure cooker?"

I thought of my mom and Beau, and how they had already started drinking before I left. Rock music blasted from the computer speakers, all while Beau hollered at the Indiana Pacers playing from the television screen.

"Light a fire under your balls you dumb, lazy-ass dipshit!"

Alcohol gave people a colorful vocabulary.

"The total opposite," I told Braden. "It would be a dream to go to college."

"So go."

"Right, because it's just that easy? There's no such thing as long-term planning in my ever-changing life. Who knows when we'll move again."

"Move?"

"Moving is my life. That's how I ended up here. It was the fourth and, hopefully, final time she left my dad."

"Damn. You moved around four times?"

"More, actually. I'm just counting the times that lasted longer than a couple months."

"Why so many times?"

I thought about all the moves and how my mom managed to slip in her second marriage during one of them. It only lasted a few months before she filed for divorce and went back to my dad.

"Who knows?" I said. "Love. Kids. Trying to make it work. I have to give her props for trying."

"He must've been a real winner." Braden looked at me for a long time. "Sucks for him."

He opened the side door of his van. A few empty pop bottles spilled out.

Braden lifted our Dr Peppers in his hands.

"These are probably all shaken up now," he said, tossing them into the garbage that was on his back seat.

They landed on some papers, exposing a bottle of what I assumed was aspirin. He quickly pushed it under the seat while shuffling some papers around. The noise distracted me from the moment.

During our counseling session that week, I noticed that Hillman had organized some papers on his desk. I suspected he was a bit of organized chaos himself since a rough night of sleep always showed under his eyes.

That goatee he'd gotten rid of would have been useful. Something about a little scruff made tired eyes less prominent.

While we talked, he asked me about my dad. I gulped my pop, then took another long pull.

"Statistically speaking," Hillman began, "there are at least a handful of students in each class who struggle with some sort of mental illness. It's more common than you think and nothing to be ashamed about. The definition is often misunderstood. Things like depression, anxiety, obsessive compulsive disorder . . . these all fall under mental illness."

"Really? I always thought it was the more serious things like schizophrenia and bipolar and those people everyone calls 'crazy'."

"Unfortunately, that's a negative connotation associated with mental health."

"Is loneliness a mental illness?"

"That depends."

"On what?"

"Well, I suppose on how deep it goes. Everyone gets lonely, but it doesn't always lead to depression or anxiety. Most of the time, there are other issues at play."

"Oh." I bit my cheek.

"What are your thoughts, Leah? Why would your mom think you fall under this category?"

"I don't know. She probably thinks if I'm sad then I will become depressed which will lead to bipolar and eventually find its way out through schizophrenia. Apparently, all roads lead to schizophrenia. I was only eleven years old when we moved here and she started saying I would end up just like my dad if I didn't stop my mood swings and find a way to deal with the changes."

I just wanted to get away from the topic as fast as possible, but my deflection never worked on Hillman. Sooner or later, I knew he would pull it out of me.

"I only ever saw some powder on the coffee table once," I said. "I was eight, old enough to know it was something bad. I remember coming home from school. My mom and her friend were talking about something in the kitchen. Their voices were really low, so I couldn't understand. I thought my dad was at work or maybe at the store, but when I tried to go to the bathroom, the bathroom door was locked."

I closed my eyes.

"My mom came into the hallway with this worried look on her face. She looked kind of scared and told me to let him be. I didn't know what she was talking about until I tried to open the door again, but it wouldn't open. When I put my ear against it, I heard some mumbling. My mom grabbed me hard and told me to come into the kitchen with her, but I didn't want to. I peeked through the keyhole and that's when I saw him."

Hillman nodded. "What did you see?"

Cars honked and zoomed by.

Braden lived right by the interstate, down the road from the string of hotels including the Home Inn where my mom worked.

In the dark, it still looked like an amazing house, but not like the one I had pictured. Instead of a mansion with a pool in the backyard, it was a one-story, light brown stone house with a half-blooming flower garden surrounding it.

At least three new vehicles were parked in the driveway that stretched toward the back door. They had two large garages behind the house. One was closed. There was a shiny orange Mustang in the open garage. I didn't know much about cars, but I knew Mustangs because my mom's ex had a green one.

Braden parked toward the side and led me to the back door. Noise from the interstate died down once we were inside, but it was still slightly noticeable.

"How do you sleep?" I asked.

He threw his keys on the counter. "Usually on my back."

I giggled and glanced around. I expected brand-new furniture, large rooms, and high ceilings, but instead, the kitchen was much smaller than mine though they had marble counters and a smooth stone floor. Old dolls and collectible stuffed animals filled their living room, and family photos took up a lot of the wall space without looking too cluttered. Their furniture looked heavily used, probably since Braden had been a small child. That must have been where the old smell came from.

Braden walked me through. His parents' bedroom door was open. The light was off, but I noticed they had made their bed. Braden's room was smaller. He had a simple twin bed, his walls were painted a dark shade of red, and a dusty guitar rested in the corner.

"Do you play?" I asked.

"Used to until my grandpa moved away. My parents pushed me into learning the piano."

"Will you play something for me?"

He hesitated, gliding his fingers over the strings.

"I haven't played much since he left. It'll probably sound like shit."

I had never been in a guy's bedroom before—at least not one that was straight. I hid my nervousness by scanning his stack of books that rested on a small shelf.

"Not much of a reader?"

"A few a year. I just finished this one." He pointed. "*A Million Little Pieces* by James Frey. It's really inspiring. You want to borrow it?"

"No, thanks. The play will keep me pretty busy." I stood, watching Braden adjust the long sleeves on his red shirt. "Didn't you like . . . have plans with friends or something?"

"I don't hang out much anymore. They just sit around Starbucks or linger around the high school parking lot."

I raised my eyebrows, surprised that this boy I used to hate was more like me than I ever thought.

"What do you want to drink?" Braden headed to the kitchen.

I followed behind.

"We have Dr Pepper, apple juice, and iced tea."

"What are you having?"

He pulled out the Dr Pepper.

"Something tells me that entire two-liter is yours." I smirked.

He poured our drinks and led me into the front room where the lighting was dim, making everything appear even older.

"Do you guys collect antiques or what?"

"My mom does. Stuff costs a fortune."

"You seem to live pretty . . . simple."

"My dad didn't grow up with money. He saves most of it. He even makes me earn my own money at the shop. Been saving for a couple years now. My van used to be my mom's. He always says that if I want a new one, I have to pay for it myself. Other than offering to pay for my college, he's never really just given me anything."

He sat on the piano bench and I sat on the rocky cushion of a very old chair. I placed my drink on the side table . . . coaster underneath.

"You really saved Scotty's ass today," he said. "Coach Garcia's been threatening to bench him."

"Why would he do that? Scotty's one of the best players."

"Garcia's getting fed up with blond boy always being late. I bet Scotty's getting tired of waking up so early for those therapy sessions with Hillman."

For a second my stomach burned. Braden went on.

"Scotty has basketball practice, choir rehearsals, and he's class Vice President. He had to quit his job at Sonic just to find time for all of this. Then he has to go home and do hours of homework like the rest of us. I can't believe he remembers to put on pants in the morning."

I pictured Scotty sitting there during our morning conversations. He was such a big guy. Talented, too. Maybe not the brightest, but a nice one anyway, and I wondered if he ever thought about giving up a little more just to have his sanity back.

I looked around the room, noticing the pictures of Braden's family.

"That's your little brother?" I asked, pointing to a framed photo of a sweaty boy holding up a medal.

"Yeah, that's Trevor."

"He looks a lot like you," I said.

"Lucky guy."

I searched for a picture of the grandfather he had mentioned, but the other two photos were of his parents.

"Grandpa Norris . . . he's your dad's dad, right?"

Braden nodded. "But he's a lot cooler than my dad. He never did what anyone expected of him."

"Such as?"

"They expected him to come around more, be on time, dress appropriately, talk a certain way. Stupid things. Showing up at my grandma's funeral wearing a red tux really got my dad's blood boiling. He said he wanted to honor his wife's life, not mourn the minute she died. She loved red."

"I think that's sweet."

"So is grabbing his guitar and jamming to 'Stranglehold' by Ted Nugent during the viewing."

My eyes popped and I couldn't help but giggle trying to imagine someone playing that song at his own wife's funeral.

"Hey, he promised my grandma that her funeral wouldn't be a mourn fest."

"I'd call The Guinness Book on that one."

"I understand him. It's uncomfortable shaking hands or acting interested when someone from my family or our social circle talks about stuff that I'm not interested in. They want me to dress in suits with bow ties. Bow ties are the bane of my existence. Neckties are my thing. Cool, do-it-yourself neckties. Not bow ties."

"Bow ties . . . the end of the world."

"No. Diabetes is."

I frowned.

"Trevor's diabetic. Guess that's why my mom and dad thrive on predictability. Makes them feel safe. They finally let me stay here by myself this year instead of going to the cabin with them. I'm almost eighteen. Eighteen, Leah. They wanna show that they trust me and everything."

"They'll have to once you're in college."

"That's the thing . . . I don't even know if I'm going. Maybe if they weren't always on my case about it, I'd be more motivated. Study music history or something. Right now, I think it'd be cool to live really cheap somewhere and just write songs . . . play guitar again . . . chill."

"That would be cool if you can do it. I mean, if you're able to earn a small living off it, then why not?"

"Wouldn't you?"

"College would mean everything to me," I said. "I'd be able to give my kids everything that my parents couldn't give us. The only problem is that I'd be the first person in my family to actually go to college."

"How's that a problem?"

"No money to pay for it."

"There's scholarships, grants. There's all kinds of things that can help."

I explained to Braden about my scholarship for low-income households and how that scholarship money will only cover part of my tuition.

"I just want to provide a life that's as easy on my kids as possible so they don't have to worry about things that kids shouldn't have to worry about."

"Life is full of worries, Leah Roy. They won't stop just because you have a degree."

"I know this small town isn't the most exciting place in the world, but it's the first place I've actually been able to call home. I still worry, but I worry less here."

"It makes sense, you know."

"What does?"

"You wanting to go to college. You being so good in theatre. You really want someone to hear you. Think about it. Theatre is the place where people have no choice but to sit there and listen to you for two hours."

I'd never thought about it that way. I didn't want to go home after school because I felt out of control at home. I wanted to be anywhere else and theatre always seemed like a good choice. Being in someone else's shoes brought some relief.

We talked for a while more about college. I was glad Braden knew how to listen and didn't always have to respond with an answer. Sometimes he would just agree and that was enough for me.

After playing me a couple songs on the piano, he went over to his computer and burnt me a CD of all these songs he swore would change my life. Then he played piano and sang some more. The front room window could have shattered under his voice.

He could play better than he could sing.

I didn't tell him that though.

"Hey Jude" was his favorite to play on the piano. While he sang, he kept looking at me. He spoke loudly over the piano that he admired the power of Paul McCartney's voice in that song compared to other songs.

My eyes shot open and I felt goosebumps crawl over my skin when he shouted for me to sing with him. Stage fright in front of Braden? He was the one who could barely hold a note, but I was still too nervous. What if he thought I sucked?

I refused and would have rather broken my own arms before singing in front of him, but then he gestured for me to sit next to him. We were close enough that our sides were touching. He put my fingers on certain keys and told me to repeat them while he played the rest. All the while, I didn't want his hand to fall from mine.

As he began to sing again, I pressed the keys and sang with

him. My nerves slowly softened once I started singing, but that was short lived. When I felt his eyes on me, I forgot the words, so I just listened to his voice. How could his eyes alone have that effect on me? Maybe it was the potential thoughts behind them that mattered so much.

I wanted the song to last longer, but when it was over, I let my hand fall from the keys and finally looked at him.

He leaned closer to look at me. I thought he was going to kiss me, but instead, he carefully lifted the hat off my head. He smiled and took my hand, holding it for a moment, whisking me away on a current of stomach flutters and fuzzy tingling throughout my chest. His soft skin and gentle grip made me want to hold on forever, but after our hands slowly parted, I pressed my fingers back on the keys where he joined me in playing the song again.

We watched a movie. *Rebel Without a Cause*. The only light came from the television screen. I was so nervous sitting next to him that I barely paid attention to what was going on. My hands remained on my lap where they sweated into my jeans.

Braden must have sensed my nervousness when I caught him looking at me, and just as I hoped, he took my hand in his, clammy and all. My nerves were shaky at first, until I realized he just wanted my hand and nothing more. I relaxed into his side, letting my head rest against his shoulder.

After the movie, he drove me home. It was a quiet ride as I searched for words to understand the warmth I was feeling, but I couldn't really find them. The only way I could describe it was when I looked at Braden, familiarity channeled through me, and there was comfort, maybe in his faint scent or in the way he tilted his head when he turned the wheel, that made me feel as if we were more alike than anything else.

He pulled into my driveway.

"Hey," I said.

He looked at me. The engine still rumbled as he came to a slow stop.

"Didn't you say you were going to school me on Paul Simon?"

He took off his Chaplin hat and placed it on my head. After giving an approving nod, he said, "Patience is a virtue, Leah Roy."

I blushed and slid out of the passenger seat. As I turned to leave, Braden rolled down the window and called out.

"Hey, Leah."

I looked at him over my shoulder. His face reminded me of someone who had been searching for a book in a bookstore and, after hours, finally found it.

"I like unicorns, too," he said.

I couldn't recall a moment where I felt as whole as I did right then.

Chapter 6

On Monday, Principal McCoy delivered the morning announcements over the intercom. In all his southern twang glory he mentioned that, "Scripts for *The Miracle Worker* are ready for pick up in Mr. Hillman's classroom no later than 3:47 p.m."

No cast list yet, but at least the scripts were ready.

By the time the bell rang, I dashed out of the science lab.

Every drama club member needed a script. Even crew members needed to mark the points in the script where props were to be set up on stage.

I was only a crew member once and vowed never to do it again. It was during my first drama club experience my freshman year when I was cast as an extra in *Pirates of Maribel Island*. Not only was I an extra, but I also had to run a few apples next to a village house so that the main character could pretend to eat one during his monologue. I was pretty proud of my apple-setting abilities, and my ability to stand there and make ghastly facial expressions as a concerned townswoman.

It wasn't that being an extra or a crew member was bad or anything, I just had this eagerness to do something different.

Being new to drama club, I didn't know any of the members except for Justin. He had been trying to get Becca to join for a while, but she refused until I dragged her along to help with props. I got to know Hillman a little and wanted to sneak a peek at his mysterious life after he shut off the auditorium lights and locked the back doors.

The others would ask him all kinds of questions like, "Hey, Hillman, got a main squeeze?" or "Hey, Hillman, who're you shacking up with?"

I wondered, too. I didn't know why I always imagined him living in a tiny house in the woods with plain wooden furniture and not much to do other than read and grade homework. The only peek I got was the inside of his perfectly clean green car when he hopped in the driver's seat and drove away.

I pushed through the swarm of students filling the school hallway until I burst through Hillman's door. Some students from his last class were still collecting their things, including Braden who was scooping up his books.

Nerves got the best of me, so I pretended I didn't see him. I hadn't talked to him since Friday night after he dropped me off at home.

"Hey, Leah," I heard him say.

My heart jackhammered my chest.

He was all I could think about that weekend. I'd sat on my bed for hours with my cheap flip phone—yes, flip phone—in my hand, wondering if it would be loserish of me to text him. I'd plowed through my chores and homework, going through the motions as if he weren't the only thing on my mind. Part of me wanted to hate him all over again. It'd be easier that way.

I swallowed a ball of air before turning around toward Braden in fake surprise.

"Braden, hey," I said, my voice a little too high.

He wore his polka-dot tie and big brown shoes, his grin too big to ignore.

I wiped a long strand of hair out of my face and motioned to his books. "I didn't know you took Theatre 101."

"Yeah, it's pretty cool. We're learning how to position our bodies on stage. Never turn your back on the audience."

I nodded, remembering my sweaty palms at his house.

"Well, anyway, can't be late for second period. Catch you

later." He grabbed his books and walked to the back cabinets to return something.

I swallowed another ball of air while a tune played in my mind. It was one of those happy Paul Simon songs on the CD Braden had burnt for me. I couldn't remember the name of it, but it had been stuck in my head all day.

Something about diamonds and shoes.

As I reached Hillman's desk, his brow arched.

"What?" I hoped my face wasn't as red as I imagined.

He was doing that mind-reading thing again, so I stared back, telepathically telling him to knock it off.

"When will the cast list be ready?" I asked.

"We're still making the best fits, but we will let everyone know soon."

He then pulled out a gorgeous stack of shiny blue scripts and plopped them on his desk. I exhaled, holding my finger up.

"One, please."

He wrote my name down on a sheet of paper, then handed me the Holy Grail script.

It called to me. It whispered my name in a soft, come-hither voice.

I brought it to my ear to make sure I wasn't losing my mind.

I was.

When I opened it, I flipped through the freshly printed pages, inhaling that comforting scent of a brand-new book.

"That'll be fifteen dollars," Hillman said.

I did a double take. "What?"

"The script costs fifteen dollars," he said.

"Ugh, I completely forgot. Why, though? You never charged us before."

"Funding is too low, I'm afraid. Didn't make enough with the last show. We have to start charging for scripts."

I checked my pockets, my bag. Nothing.

I passed Justin in the hallway. Justin was the kind of friend that always had an extra piece of gum or a quarter, but not this time.

A school newspaper article once explained that rich kids grow up to become rich, and poor kids grow up to become poor. It went on to say that kids born into rich families have more access to the best opportunities. They would grow up to be happier, healthier people, one of the many benefits of having a stay-at-home parent giving them love and attention.

Rich people had the luxury of spending time and money on opportunities that would advance their futures, while poor people focused more on getting by, day by day. A child born into a rich family would most often have their college paid for, giving them a better chance at accumulating wealth throughout their life.

I grew up hearing my mom complain about living paycheck to paycheck while her boss was already planning her next two vacations.

I didn't want a future filled with resentment and struggle and just trying to keep my head above water. Planning a vacation without a worry, living like the kids at The Tree . . . that was what I wanted.

I just had to figure out how.

monday, february 23, 2009
"Life is a dream for the wise, a game for the fool, a comedy for the rich, a tragedy for the poor." Sholem Aleichem

everybody wants what they dont have tina. when you fixate on those kids you will lose sight of what matters. those kids, that tree, they wont be there forever. then what?

The Tree was something different for me. it was a

place that kept me close to sweet angela. it was during a time we didnt have cell phones and internet. guess what we did? we wrote letters and buried them at The Tree. letters. i know. writing. paper. how ever did we survive?

i used to think it was my love for angela that kept me alive. without love, what sets our hearts on fire? but now, now i think it was the hope. hope kept us alive.

if you open your eyes tina, you will find yours.
robert

Becca, Justin, and I hung out at his mom's salon after school. Those were the only moments I actually felt cool by Tipton High's definition.

The small salon was in an old downtown building, the only part of Tipton County that still held that small-town feel, having been established in the 1800s and all. The buildings were connected, each shop painted a different earth-toned color on the outside. Tall, rectangular windows lined the second and third floors while the entrances to each shop were nearly all glass.

The door jingled as we walked in. I plopped into a salon chair to skim through college brochures while Justin gave Becca's hair a wash in one of those cool salon sinks.

"A blue-black ombré," Becca repeated to Justin. "And don't skimp out on the blue."

Another lady walked in with her daughter and checked in for their appointment. The salon was less busy on weekdays after school, but the other two workers were busy with an older customer who demanded that her hair be cut exactly how it was last time.

"I'm so late," I grunted.

"Aunt Flow not coming this month?" Becca asked, staring at the ceiling.

"Applying," I said. "It's probably too late now. I've got that scholarship but haven't applied anywhere. I don't know what's wrong with me. I feel like I'm wasting a good opportunity. Everyone keeps talking about where they've been accepted already."

"You needn't worry, my dear," Justin said. "There are schools that'll accept late applications. Don't wait much longer though."

"All that money," I said. "Financial aid helps, but who wants to spend the rest of their life paying off student loans?"

"Struggle of the century." Becca closed her eyes as Justin massaged her hair. "You've got the grades though. That scholarship is a saving grace."

The night before, I'd been leaning over the kitchen counter, shuffling through some college brochures my homeroom teacher had handed out, when my mom got home from work. After she threw her jacket over a chair, she eyed the papers in my hand while speed texting. She didn't say anything other than "Oh, those again" and "You know that's going to be expensive as hell."

College had always been something she wanted to do, but two kids and a deadbeat husband kind of killed her dreams of becoming a nurse.

Justin started humming a show tune as he tilted Becca's head up after the rinse.

"The thought is exciting anyway," I said, flipping through the pages. "Can you imagine us in college? How awesome would that be?"

"Yay, school forever," Becca moaned as Justin wrung out her hair with a towel.

I smacked her with the brochure, feeling sort of guilty that I hadn't told either of them about my little rendezvous at Braden's house that weekend. I could imagine Justin's blazing eyes and Becca teasing me on the importance of safe sex.

"I have to do something with my life, you guys. I couldn't even buy a script today. What's that going to look like a few years from now? Debt, unpaid bills, endless frustration."

"With your SAT score, you won't have to worry about money," Becca said.

"Yeah, what'd you get, a 1500?" Justin asked.

I turned my head to look at him. "1500? Is that even possible?"

"Rumor has it that Joseph McIntire got a 1500."

"Hence why he's valedictorian."

Justin said, "Doing what you love doesn't always mean a fat paycheck. Like cosmetology. Now where's the money in this? You guys don't even pay me."

"I think I would be happy being a teacher," I said. "Hillman seems happy enough, doesn't he?"

Becca laughed as she made her way to the hair dryer. "The guy needs a lover."

Chapter 7

When Wednesday came, it was the first time I saw Braden since our awkward meeting in Hillman's classroom. He volunteered as the main office assistant during second period with duties that consisted of organizing files, helping visitors, and dropping off mail to teachers' classrooms. I knew that because Justin had done it and said it was way better than study hall because he got to eavesdrop on the office gossip.

Braden walked into my health class showing off his all-too-lovable dorky grin as if he knew all eyes were on him. He was wearing a short-sleeved yellow shirt with that polka-dot tie, and walked as if the stack of paper he was holding would fly right out of his hand like loose dollar bills.

It reminded me of when I'd asked my mom for the script money earlier that morning. She'd squeezed her wallet, telling me, "Money doesn't grow on trees."

Afterwards, I'd checked my coin jar, but there was only enough for a couple bags of chips from the vending machine. When my mom reluctantly came into my room with the money, I was told to inform Hillman how crappy it was for us to have to pay for the script.

I wasn't going to deliver the message.

Braden handed my teacher part of the stack, then caught me watching as he turned to leave.

He stopped for a brief moment, my face flushing under his gaze.

His smile warmed my cheeks, and he waved as if he wasn't sure I'd wave back.

I did.

Now all eyes were on me.

I cupped my hand over my forehead and looked down. How was I going to get through the next two months?

Shortly after Braden left, my teacher walked by and plopped something on my desk.

I peeled off the sticky note that read: *for leah roy.*

Printed on the bright blue book was:

THE MIRACLE WORKER

That Friday, I saw Braden at his locker before he took off in a hurry to first period. I had the fifteen dollars in my pocket, ready to shove in his face, but I didn't see him the rest of the day.

After school, I spent my time in the school parking lot with Becca and Justin waiting for the basketball game to start.

I took out a pen and notebook.

Friday, February 27, 2009

Dear Robert,

My eyes are wide open, too pissed off to see what you're talking about.

What am I, his charity case now? Braden Gregory bought me the script. He's this entitled rich boy, one of those kids at The Tree, who needs to do things like that to feel better than people. Ugh. I could have paid for it myself. I don't need him feeling sorry for me.

It seems that things have changed since your time here, Robert. The Tree has been tainted by people like Braden and hope has turned into a fight for survival.

Pen Pal Tina

Before the game started, I snuck away to bury the letter.

Becca led us toward the bleachers, her blue-black hair perfectly straight and shiny. She didn't even need to brush her hair for it to look that pretty. Justin, on the other hand, with his hot Irish hair, had seen more combs and oil treatments than Sara Washington had seen the beach.

The game had barely started. Patriotic teachers and cheering parents in all their team spirit attire surrounded us.

In my head, I heard Principal McCoy's intercom voice from earlier: *"Now remember, Tipton High students, purple and white aren't just our school colors, they represent our persistence, ambition, and pride. I hope everyone shows up to support our team. Break a leg tonight, boys."*

I looked to my right and grimaced as one of our own slipped to the ground. Our cardinal mascot was damn near knocked over as another player collided with him.

Justin's pale round face and orange hair lit up as we walked under some gymnasium lights.

"He paid for my script," I said.

They both looked at me.

"What are you talking about?" Becca asked.

"He seriously paid for my script."

"Who?"

"Braden. He was still in the room when I went in there to get one. He must have overheard me talking to Hillman."

"Sounds like someone's got a crush," Justin teased.

A crush.

Was I crushing on Braden?

"Are you kidding me? I don't have a crush on Braden Gregory. He's not even my type. His hair is too messy and his book bag is always empty. The only reason I even talk to him is to be cordial for this play."

"I was talking about Braden having a crush on you, but now that you got all defensive . . ."

Truth be told, I couldn't get Braden out of my head no matter how hard I fought away his image. I'd seen him walking from his van that morning, battling my sincere feelings for him and the fact that I had become his good deed of the week.

I was the poor girl and he was the hotshot.

I asked myself what a hotshot was doing driving something only a soccer mom would be proud of. Worse than that, Sara Washington got out of the passenger seat, carrying her designer bag. I didn't know which was worse, the fact that he drove a purple minivan or the fact that he was bringing royalty like Sara to school in it.

And to think I could have liked him.

Justin snapped his fingers in my face to get my attention.

"We can forget about it," Justin said. "But just so you know, you were amazing during auditions, Leah. I had a feeling Braden would try to mess with you, but you lasted a lot longer than I would've under his irresistible smoldering spell."

Becca led us up the bleachers, but the spot we had our eye on was now taken, so we weaved through the rows in search of another. There was a loud whistle from the floor, shoe screeches, and some disappointed "awes" around us.

A brush of air blew my hair back. Too many people. I straightened my hat and zipped up my gray jacket, both of which had belonged to my mom. I remembered finding them in one of our storage boxes after we'd moved to Small Town Nowhere, among other clothes of hers that I hijacked for the twenty-first century.

"No," I said. "It's not over yet. Especially not now."

"Who do those choir kids think they are anyway?" Becca asked.

"Let's direct that question to Justin, their new BFF."

"You know what they say." Justin looked up as if he were imitating Dracula. "Keep your friends close but your enemies closer."

I shook my head; a small smile cracked from the corners of my mouth.

"Come on, girls." He nudged me. "Don't be jealous. They're

not that bad. They're as excited about this play as we are and, if you think about it, they're just trying to help."

My voice tightened. "I know, but it's like an invasion. Don't you feel a little pissed off that more and more of them are coming? They think they can rule everything just because it's senior year. Haven't they already been accepted to college? What do they need this for?"

They both shrugged their shoulders.

"I think it might be cool to be a part of that group," Justin said. "Who doesn't want to feel like they're a part of something different for a change?"

Becca frowned at him. The type of frown a veterinarian might give before euthanizing a cute little hamster.

"Oh, Justin, you wish," she said.

"Yeah, maybe I do. What's so wrong about wanting more, and extending my circle of friends?"

"Loyalty," I blurted. "Integrity. Your dignity, for God's sake."

I could barely stifle my emotions. Not just because I had become some sort of "help the homeless" case for Braden, but because he spent so much time with Sara. Anytime I passed him in the hallway, Sara was beside him yapping away about the Yearbook Committee or whatever school newspaper article she was working on. I wasn't going to be just another girl on his arm to boost his ego, and I certainly wasn't going to be another joke.

We walked into the last half of the bleachers before finding an empty area at the top near a group of Tipton High stoners.

I plopped down on the seat and drained my lungs of air. I kicked off my shoes and dropped my shoulders and, for a short moment, I actually didn't care who was looking at me.

Justin sat down with a euphoric expression on his face, as if he'd just gotten laid, while Becca slouched against the empty row behind us. We were so high up that the basketball players looked like colorful M&Ms dribbling across the floor.

I pretended to understand basketball. Every time the crowd

cheered, booed, or stomped their feet on the bleachers, I knew something had happened. The band would blast their horns, cheerleaders would then do their robotic dances, and it would continue like that for hours.

"Should we invite them to sit with us?" Justin said, pointing to Sara and Rachelle as they walked up the bleachers.

My throat went dry. "Uh, absolutely not."

"Leah, give them a chance," Justin said. "They're nice girls. Don't you think it'll be agonizingly awkward if they sit right by us and nobody talks?"

The area around us was pretty much the only available spot unless they chose to sit right next to people, and we all knew it was socially unacceptable to do that.

"He's right, Leah," Becca said.

I folded my arms and looked at the M&Ms. Scotty was dribbling the ball across the floor, going for a shot that bounced off the rim.

When I glanced over to Sara and Rachelle, I noticed they had spotted us. I felt Justin's and Becca's eyes on me.

"Fine." I did feel sort of guilty since Sara and Rachelle looked like lost puppies and all.

Justin flailed his arms about in the air as if he were disappearing.

"Up here," he shouted. "There's room up here. Come join us."

When they approached, Sara beamed and spoke as if she'd just ran a marathon.

"Hi, you all. This spot free?"

"Of course," Justin said. "Sit. This place is packed tonight."

Sara waved at me.

I raised my hand.

Rachelle didn't acknowledge anyone. She was overdressed for someone going to a basketball game with her dark-red lipstick, tight clothes, and animal print hooker boots.

They sat down on the row in front of us. I watched in shock as

Sara pulled items out of her bag like Mary Poppins—seat pads, blankets, and coffee mugs probably full of tea or hot chocolate. It wasn't even cold.

"You came prepared," Becca said.

Sara looked over her shoulder and handed a mug to Rachelle.

"I brought an extra blanket if you want one. Nothing like being comfortable."

"I'll take it." Justin snatched the purple blanket from Sara before Becca could refuse. "Oh my God, this is so soft. Merchandise?"

All I could think was how nice it must have been to own cute little things like that.

"Actually, I borrowed it from Braden," Sara said.

I looked up when she said his name, hoping my interest wasn't too obvious.

"No concessions tonight?" I asked.

"Nope. Tonight's free. Can you believe this is my first actual game since I moved here? I've been so busy."

"Spill it, Sara. How amazing is California compared to Indiana?" Justin leaned forward as if missing this information would have been the end of the world.

Sara went on to describe what I could have described myself: Tipton County had a tighter community, safety, cornfields, Big Red pop.

The next ten minutes passed while I pretended to care about what they were talking about by nodding here and there. Becca was slouched over, coloring on her jeans with a black pen.

The game hadn't progressed. Not that I knew of.

I looked down to the walkway in front of the bleachers. Thinking I had spotted Braden, my neck turned to fire, but it wasn't him.

I noticed Sara pull something else from her bag when my focus drifted to the paper she was holding.

"Where'd you get that?" I asked.

She turned to me a bit too quickly.

"I got it from Mr. Hillman." Her voice was so high I thought all the animals in Tipton County would come flocking to her feet. "Tamara and Mr. Hillman were in such a scheduling mess today, I decided to sign up to be his assistant."

I cracked my knuckles with my thumb, feeling a sudden rush . . . a need to protect what was mine.

"I didn't know there was a form to fill out," I said, wishing I could have just snatched the paper from her hands and run it all the way back to Hillman's classroom where I had been his unofficial assistant until California Barbie showed up.

"He was super relieved to know that someone would be around to help."

I watched her finish filling out the paper. What would I have said anyway?

No, Sara, you can't be Hillman's assistant because that's kind of my thing.

I felt Becca press her shoe over my tapping foot while Justin went on about Rachelle's boots.

Rachelle wasn't much of a talker, but when she did talk, you'd think a husky prostitute with a slight Spanish accent was propositioning him for a roll in the sack.

"Besides," Sara continued, "Tamara is the student director. She has enough on her plate. I'd handle the tasks of planning the rehearsal schedules, set-building plans, props, brochures . . . little things like that."

Little things. I almost vomited.

I cleared my throat. "I know all the responsibilities. I've been his assistant before. Have you ever done something like this?"

"I have support in case it gets difficult. Rachelle will help. Scotty and Braden will, too. You know, the new members are sacrificing a lot for this play. I hope the others will participate a little more so that we don't have to carry the entire load."

Becca made an expression as if to say, *"Hello, we're right here!"*

"Drama club members sacrifice a lot." I straightened my back and spoke so that each word came out strong. "Most of us have jobs or activities after school and we all have kept up our grades so that we can do this."

Sara shrugged her shoulders, signed the sheet at the bottom, and placed it into her bag.

The hairs on my neck rose. Though Sara wasn't looking, Becca was and she grabbed my fist until I unclenched.

Oh, Sara. A week's worth of sunshine bottled into one tiny Californian body. She wasn't fooling me.

"Why can't you just leave it to the people who actually know what they're doing?" I asked.

She turned just enough to blink at me. "It's nothing to get upset about. It's no secret that the club needs a tad more organization, and I'm willing to help with that. Save you the time and energy with the promise of a job well done. I'm doing you a huge favor if you think about it."

I wished someone would have sneezed right into her mouth. Why did the high and mighty kids always think they were doing people like me a favor?

"You're just helping Mr. Hillman with some things and he's done fine without you and your friends. You can't just come here, wave your fairy godmother wand and make everything perfect. We need good actors. A good show."

Sara shrugged her shoulders again. "Nothing wrong with a few fresh faces. Say that three times fast." She snickered and placed her hand on Justin's knee.

I shivered.

There was nothing wrong with the choir kids helping out, yet it shook my world.

Theatre was my escape from evenings of searching for coins between couch cushions and struggling to get my chores done. Theatre was my excuse not to be home. It was my sanctuary. My place. I had something I could call my own, something to retreat to after a long day when I didn't want to go home—that was drama club for the majority of us, and now the choir kids were going to waltz right in and take our opportunities?

Rachelle turned to me like a cat about to pounce on prey.

"You know," she said, "I don't think this would bother you if you hadn't bombed your audition."

My heart raced faster than Scotty speeding across the floor.

I rose from my seat and pursed my lips.

"We'll see," I said.

Sara looked at me. Becca and Justin glanced at each other.

I told them I was going for a drink.

As soon as I began stomping down the bleachers, the announcer yelled, "Score Tipton High!"

The bleachers vibrated under my feet like an earthquake. Clapping and cheering from all around filled my ears.

As I reached the walkway between the bleachers and court, I heard Becca calling my name. She sprinted over and grabbed my shoulder.

"Dumb bitches, right?"

"That's an understatement."

I stormed toward the concession stand, lucky to have found seventy-five cents that morning. Sometimes, Beau emptied his pockets before bed and left it all scattered on the kitchen counter.

Becca pointed to my feet. I'd forgotten my shoes, but I didn't care.

"You're not going home, are you?" Becca asked. "Because I'll walk with you. Beats hanging around here for two hours."

"I'd never give them that power. I'd rather stew in the awkward tension until one of *them* breaks and goes home. And seriously, what's going on with Justin? It's like he sees an opportunity and shoves us aside."

"I don't think it's like that. You know Justin. He can't resist fashion talk, all the glitz and glam."

We were quiet while standing in a line that was taking forever.

If that's what the group at The Tree was like, then I wanted no part in it. Being molded into a Barbie girl from the West coast wasn't what I had in mind.

The mystery of The Tree was what drew me in. The ideas they might have thrown around about life, the conversations, the reason they carved their initials into the trunk, all the secrets of that life—that's what I wanted to be a part of. Something genuine, something that mattered . . . not Sara's stuck-up ways.

When the man in front of me grabbed his popcorn and turned away, I froze.

Braden was working the concession stand, looking a little different until I remembered that I still had his Chaplin hat.

He watched me, looking relieved to see me. Another guy was working beside him, but before I could switch lines, someone else ordered.

I had choices here, I reminded myself. I didn't have to stay and face off with him. I could run. I could turn and run all the way down Cottage Road, cross the highway to hell, and barge through my front door.

Our eyes locked.

"Dr . . ." I said. "One Dr Pepper."

Braden turned to the fridge behind him and pulled out a Dr Pepper. At the same time, I took out three quarters from my pocket, but he denied my money with a wave of his hand.

"It's on me," he said.

Really?

More charity?

I slapped the seventy-five cents on the counter and took the bottle from him.

Our fingers brushed. My spine did that electricity thing again.

His smile faded to confusion. Before I stepped out of the line, I stopped.

My thoughts shot back in time to being in seventh grade, waiting in the lunch line. I needed some extra help with my science work, so I had gotten out of class late. By the time I got in line, my friends were already sitting down with their lunch trays.

These two boys were messing around in front of me—the kind of boys who had to find something to fill the awkward silence after they ran out of things to talk about.

That *something* was usually their next joke.

It was Scotty and Braden, though I barely knew them then. They both wore new polo shirts and blue jeans with no holes. Scotty looked like Napoleon Dynamite. I didn't know Braden's name at the time, but I remembered thinking he looked like a mixture of James Dean and Edward Norton.

Napoleon Dynamite tapped James Norton on the shoulder and pointed to me. I looked away.

I sensed what was about to happen when that hint of doom invaded my gut. I wished I could have just left the line and gone to my friends, but I had skipped breakfast that morning and was feeling the rumble in my empty stomach.

"Nice shirt," James Norton said to me, touching the sequins.

I was wearing a light-blue shirt with a shiny picture of a unicorn on it—something my mom had bought for me from a thrift store. Definitely not something you wanted to wear if you wanted to be considered a "chick" or a "babe".

I didn't say anything. I just shrugged one shoulder and looked away.

"You like unicorns, huh?" James Norton asked. "Do they have those where you come from?"

He poked his friend while they both erupted into uproarious laughter.

Kids around me joined in.

As the laughter grew, some kids started saying, "Unicorn girl! Unicorn girl!"

My face turned to stone, but the worst part was that James Norton . . . Braden didn't care.

I closed my burning eyes wishing I could have disappeared.

Becca pulled my arm again, bringing me back to the present. I heard the cheerleaders in the distance as tears blurred my vision. I could have gone with her and finished watching the game. I could have cheered and joined the others stomping on the bleachers to encourage our team, but I jerked my arm back and whipped forward where my hands landed flat on the concession stand counter.

"People like you think you can just come here and take what doesn't belong to you. You think you have a right to laugh at anybody who might be a little different than you because if they're not just like *you*, then there must be something wrong with *them*, right?"

I took a quick breath.

"I know you bought that script. I don't need your charity, Braden, so you can scratch that off your college application." I shook my head. "I was so stupid to think you were different."

I expected surprise from him, maybe even a little defense or a tongue-tied response, but he grabbed something and leaned over the counter. His eyes fell over me, probably reading the vulnerability in my slumping posture.

Then he handed me a hotdog.

On his face returned the same relieved smile he'd greeted me with.

He raised his eyebrows, tilted his head, and said, "You must be hangry."

Chapter 8

"Yes!"

Burning before my eyes was the cast list—the portal to the world I had been seeking since the beginning of the year.

I jumped up and down like a giddy girl, not caring that other kids were crowded around Hillman's door where the cast list was posted. I needed to see it at a million different angles to believe that I would be playing the part of Helen Keller.

"Oh my gosh, Becca, do you know what this means?"

I grabbed her and forced her into a tight hug.

When she pulled away, I clapped.

"Drama, drama, drama," she said.

My eyes roamed back to the cast list, then to the others who had shown up to see their fate. I hugged my castmate, Riley, who had been cast as Kate Keller, Helen's mother.

When Justin saw me coming for him, he backed into a corner. I slowly approached him, my overflowing love seeping from my outstretched arms.

"Come here, tiger," I said.

"Spare me, darling. You hurt."

He backed away until Becca and I had him cornered. He surrendered with his arms wide open to embrace me and said sweetly, "You deserve it."

"Damn, Leah," Becca said. "I haven't seen you this excited since Evel Dick won Big Brother."

When Hillman auditioned me as Anne Sullivan, I thought my chances were over. Part of me went home afterwards wishing I had truly sucked at Anne, just so he would consider me for Helen. To my lack of surprise, the role of Anne went to Sara who had also been cast in a smaller role in *Aladdin*. Who better to play a know-it-all teacher than her?

Relief washed through me when I thought about my role.

Helen Keller.

Someone who'd faced more obstacles than the average person would ever know. I got to *be* her; to put myself in her shoes. I liked Helen Keller. People thought she was sick or something . . . challenged even. Of course, she faced huge obstacles, but she was no different than the rest of us. She just couldn't communicate her thoughts and feelings, and that had to have been a frustrating life, knowing others were speaking for her and making all her decisions.

I hoped I could make her light shine even if it was just a high school play.

Rachelle also came to check out the list, and snickered a cold "Congrats" to me. Becca hissed as she walked away.

To Rachelle's utter dismay, she had been cast in a small role as one of the blind girls. Luckily for us, Mr. Steele had already cast her as Princess Jasmine, so nobody would suffer the wrath of Rachelle.

Becca had happily discovered that she'd been cast as one of the blind girls, too, while Justin bragged about being cast as the doctor in the opening scene. It was a smaller part, but he'd never let that dim his limelight.

Kids came to the list full of hope. Some left with bright faces while others walked away with slouched shoulders. I remembered those awful times when I thought I sucked, thinking there was no way I'd ever be good enough for a bigger part.

Then I looked at the cast list again—the beautiful paper of names.

Scotty popped in for a quick peek.

"James Keller," he said, turning to me. "I'll be your brother for the next couple months. Always wanted a little sister."

"Don't let that go to your head," I teased.

Hillman finally showed up to open his classroom door for first period. He stood beside me, glancing at the list.

"You did good, Leah." His keys jingled from his hand. "I'm sure you and Braden will work great together."

I didn't know how it happened, but it happened fast. My body froze in place as Hillman strolled away. I felt Becca and Justin watching me.

I looked below my name and there it was, written in black, bold letters:

CAPTAIN KELLER - BRADEN GREGORY

"Oh. Shit."

Becca came up to me. "Ya missed that little detail, didn't cha?"

It's okay. It's going to be okay.

I swallowed hard. How did Braden get cast as Helen's dad? He could have played James or even one of the servants who wouldn't have much to do with Helen, but Captain Keller?

"I mean, what's the worst that could happen?" I asked.

Justin stepped to my other side. "Helen could rip his head off like a praying mantis."

monday, march 2, 2009
"And when we speak we are afraid
our words will not be heard
nor welcomed
but when we are silent
we are still afraid.
So it is better to speak." Audre Lorde
i needed angela even more after she moved away.

*she ignited that flame in my heart. her love showed me
that i was more than i could ever imagine.*

*things certainly have changed since my time. people
used to need each other. people used to depend on each
other. now people have gotten used to suffering alone.*

you don't have to suffer alone tina.

*have your eyes softened enough to see that maybe
this boy was trying to be kind?*

robert

I knew things about Braden, things he tried to hide from the people who mattered.

I remembered evenings when drama club and choir had to share the stage for practice. Drama club would be on stage while choir rehearsed their musical in the classroom until it was time to switch.

During our breaks—when I didn't feel like socializing—I'd grab a snack from the north wing vending machine. I'd take my Payday candy bar and sit around the corner near the locker rooms where I knew nobody else would be. On one of those days, when I heard someone coming, I hid from view. It was last semester after we had finished our final dress rehearsal for a play called *The Fairy*. I thought I was alone until I heard his voice.

Braden often had the same idea, to get away for some privacy. I always got lucky he never caught me sitting there in case he was feeling a little humorous, except for that one time—the time I swore the jerk Braden I thought I knew was somebody else entirely.

I usually heard him on the phone with someone who I assumed was his mom, but I guessed it could have been anybody.

He'd always be explaining himself—why he was out so late, why he was doing choir at all, why it meant so much to him.

"I told you we had practice tonight," he said in a controlled tone.

Normally, I would have mocked his conversation in my mind —feeling happy that the poor rich boy had a problem—but that day was different.

"You've had my schedule since the beginning of the school year. I'm seventeen. I shouldn't always have to tell you where I am."

I rose from the ground, careful not to make any noise.

"Are you serious?" His voice deepened. "I can't just do that. You're always drilling me on commitments. I made a commitment to be here, not there. It was *your* choice to sign me up for that crap, not mine. I told you, I don't need it."

I heard the weight in his long sigh followed by a break in his voice as if he were holding back tears.

"Fine. Bye."

I waited until I thought he was gone, but as I walked into the hallway, he turned his head to me.

He was leaning against the wall wearing a defeated expression. A shadow of dread passed through his reddened eyes when he saw me standing there.

I squeezed my empty wrapper and stepped to the exit door.

"Hey," he said.

I cleared my throat and grabbed the door handle.

"Moms are difficult," he added.

I turned to look over my shoulder, barely making eye contact.

"I know."

My palms began to sweat as I clutched harder on the door handle. I wanted to leave, but a pang of guilt pounded my gut.

I turned around.

"You okay?" I asked.

His eyes rested over me.

I knew he wasn't okay by the look on his face. It stared at me in the mirror every morning as I would get ready for school, listening to my mom's demands for what I was to clean when I got home.

"Yeah," he said. "My mom can be kind of a tight-ass."

I wanted to say the same thing. The truth was that my mom was hard on me, unfair at times, but I could leave the house anytime I wanted and do anything I wanted.

"My mom's usually too busy to notice me," I said.

His light-brown hair was a mess and dark circles rested underneath his eyes, though I'd never noticed them before.

As he pushed himself off the wall, he forced a small smile. "See ya, Leah."

He said my name.

He knew my name.

I watched him slip his phone into his pocket and walk down the hallway.

Before the first play reading of *The Miracle Worker* that week, we were all sitting in a circle by the time Braden burst through the auditorium door, overdoing his apologies for being late. Luckily for him, people were still talking because Hillman was busy fixing glitches in the sound system.

A finger tapped Becca on the shoulder. I looked up and it was Braden asking to squeeze in between the two of us. He wore those grandfather shoes and his ridiculous tie, smelling of clean clothes and a little bit of sweat.

She gave me a "wtf" look as she slid over.

Braden took his spot and exhaled as if he'd taken a long sip of pop. I caught a whiff of his fresh breath, wondering if he'd chewed gum or brushed his teeth after school.

He turned to me and seemed to consider the contours of my face. When he offered his hand, I guessed I was supposed to take it, but all I could do was look at him as if he'd just crawled out of a dumpster.

A pink tint grew on the apples of his cheeks while his innocent gaze lured me into whatever trap he was trying to set up.

"Hi, Leah." He reached out his hand to me. "I'm Braden."

I regained my composure. The way his eyes rested into mine made me want to take his hand, but I was still a little flustered by my reaction at the basketball game.

Even when he wasn't trying to be all cute and charming, his eyes still hypnotized me like right then, with the way they curved against his hopeful, boyish grin.

His hand hung in the air, waiting for me to take it.

I thought about Robert and his last letter—how he might have been right about Braden trying to be kind.

I took his hand in mine.

"Hi, Braden. I'm Leah."

7:24 a.m.

New Msg:

Jeff Buckley is great.

Sorry for not texting back.

Got busy.

7:26 a.m.

Msg From: Braden

hey leah

that excuse has been overdone

by me

mom piss you off?

7:30 a.m.

New Msg:

Yeah

Laundry room was a mess and I didn't take the dogs out

7:31 a.m.

Msg From: Braden

tough luck

doesnt his voice give you the chills?

7:34 a.m.

New Msg:

Jeff buckley? I'm still trying to get over it.

7:35 a.m.

Msg From: Braden

hah so you really listened

7:37 a.m.

New Msg:

Yeah so hey, I wanted to say thanks for getting my script.

I might have overreacted.

… might have.

7:39 a.m.

Msg From: Braden

independent woman.

overreact is my moms middle name

trust me its fine

i really didnt mean anything bad by it

7:40 a.m.

New Msg:

Why does she do that?

7:42 a.m.

Msg From: Braden

my mom?

she cant help it

her kid has diabetes remember?

where r u

7:43 a.m.

New Msg:

Just got off the bus.

7:45 a.m.

Msg From: Braden

geez thats torture. i always show up at 8:25

im still in bed

7:47 a.m.

New Msg:

Get out of bed. Ew. Youre making me uncomfortable.

7:50 a.m.

Msg From: Braden

okay im in the shower now

better?

7:52 a.m.

New Msg:

Stop it.

8:11 a.m.

Msg From: Braden

what r u getting me for my birthday?

8:13 a.m.

New Msg:

When is your birthday?

And Im not getting you anything.

8:16 a.m.

Msg From: Braden

this thursday

if you dont get me anything then i have to assume we arent friends

it will make me sad though. if we arent friends

im kinda putting this in your hands

8:24 a.m.

Msg From: Braden

leah?

8:29 a.m.

New Msg:

See you at rehearsal.

"Today we're going to do line practice," Hillman began. "The exercise will be as follows: I will put you all in pairs and you will sit anywhere in the auditorium to run lines, but you will first memorize the line before saying it. Your partner will make a note next to the line if you miss a word or say it incorrectly. We need to get those lines locked down."

He looked around the room and lifted his finger. I clutched Becca's arm. We were usually paired together and I had already practiced with her, so this would be a breeze.

"Riley will partner with Cameron," he said, and searched for others. "Let's see, Justin will partner with Abigail. Alexa with Scotty. Mikayla with Hannah."

I noticed Scotty wasn't there yet while Hillman paired the others. Hillman's eyes stopped at Becca.

"Becca with Rachelle."

Becca and I immediately locked eyes. "God no," she mouthed. She slumped in her chair and threw her head back. Rachelle wasn't thrilled about it either, considering her hateful look when Becca rolled her head around.

Once it hit me that I wouldn't be paired with Becca, there was only one more possibility.

I walked toward the ramp hall where Braden was standing.

I wasn't ready for it. I must have *really* embarrassed myself, freaking out about a script and a stupid unicorn shirt.

"Hey," I said.

"Hey, Leah." He cleared his throat.

"You finally got out of bed."

"Only to see you."

Damn you, Braden.

"Hey, you still have my Chaplin hat."

I remembered it was on my closet shelf. "I'll bring it tomorrow. What's your deal with that thing anyway?"

"It belonged to Grandpa Norris, remember? Don't you ever wear your mom's hats and feel like you're in her head?"

I also wanted to ask about the tie but decided against it.

I pulled the cash from my pocket and counted out fifteen dollars.

Pride. Maybe he was right . . . my mom would have done the same thing.

"Here's the money I owe you for the script," I said.

He took the money, squinted at me, and then put it in his pocket.

"Wanna practice in the ramp hall?" he asked.

"Anyone else in there?"

"No." Braden switched on the dim light. "Unless you want to go somewhere else?"

"Here is fine."

I followed him into the ramp hall, watching as he kept glancing behind to see if I was still there.

Doors lined the poorly lit hallway. One led to the stage. The others were storage rooms. We stopped along the wall away from the flickering light that needed a bulb change and took a seat on the floor across from each other.

"How are your lines?" I asked.

"I probably signed up for too much between this play and *Aladdin*. Didn't realize how much helping my dad at work would be."

"That's a lot." I situated myself Indian style.

"Especially since he's been on my ass about training me in management."

"Didn't you tell Hillman something about being *out* of the auto cage?"

"I did."

I could tell he wanted to talk about this by the way he paused for me to respond, but I didn't know what to say.

"I guess we can start with your lines and I'll take notes," I said, flipping through my script.

Braden ignored his script. He had both hands in his huge green book bag that never looked like he had anything in it.

"I know I was a total asshole back then," he said, pulling out his semi-damaged script. "I'm not one of those idiots who can sit and pretend like I don't remember how I treated you."

"Ancient history," I said. "We started over, remember?"

"If we're going to have a good show together, don't you think you should like me a little?"

Telling him I liked him would have exposed way too much. Telling him I didn't like him would have been a lie, but it would have gotten me out of a very uncomfortable situation.

"Okay," I said.

"So, what's your favorite band?"

I studied his face, wondering why the sudden interest.

"What?" he said. "We've only ever talked about the music I like. What kind of music do you listen to, Leah?"

I liked when he said my name as if it was the first time he was meeting me. His voice vibrated the wall against my back, running through my bones and finding its way out through my tingling fingers.

"Aren't we supposed to be running lines?" I flipped to the first scene. I looked up, immediately distracted by the curiosity in his crescent-moon eyes. "I . . ." I looked away in order to think. "I like . . ." *Oh, come on, Leah.* "You're just going to laugh at me again."

"Why do you think that's a bad thing?"

His gaze radiated a warmth that sent a heat wave from my head down to my toes. He tilted his head, waiting for me to answer.

"I like '80s music. Boston. I like coming home from school with Boston blasting from the computer stereos. That's the kind of band you hear and instantly know it's them."

"Great band," he said. "Your favorite?"

For some reason, I felt like telling him the answer to this question would somehow peel an item of clothing off my body.

"I don't know yet. I always feel as if I should like what my mom likes. Things have usually been her way or no way. My head gets all jumbled."

"It's the hat." He leaned back.

I began to wonder if he even cared about the play. "We really should be learning our lines."

"I'm lucky my parents don't care much for music," he said. "They're movie people."

I opened my script again but couldn't manage to say his first cue line. I just sat there with my focus on the page, knowing Braden's focus was still on me.

"My favorite band is The Beatles," he said. "I've liked them since I can remember. Their first bits of music were pretty good, then they just got better and better. I mean, the LSD probably helped. Some people don't think drugs make you a good artist. I think it enhances a person's talent. What do you think?"

"Are you asking me what I think about drugs?"

"Do you think drugs count? Should a person get the same credit for their work as if they'd done it when they were sober?"

"Well, they did it, right? It's still their work regardless, so yeah."

His expression held an ounce of pride.

By the time we actually got to running lines, I realized he probably hadn't even opened his script since getting it, even though it looked like it'd had the ride of its life in that book bag.

"Come on, Braden," I complained as he stumbled over a little chunk of lines. "Hillman's going to regret casting you."

Braden gave it a good attempt before he stopped me halfway through the first scene.

"You're pretty good at this stuff," he said.

"At what?"

"Learning lines, acting, getting into character. Guess I was wrong about Hillman not casting you as lead again just to be fair to the others. He knows good talent when he sees it."

I blushed.

"I get it, you know," he continued. "I don't know how you do it, but I know why."

"You do, do you?"

"You think that if you have all those lines in your head, then there will be no more room for your own thoughts."

"What?"

"You're afraid of your own thoughts. You're afraid of how you might screw up or how someone might react. Whatever baggage you're carrying caused you enough pain that it's all you can think about when your brain isn't preoccupied with something else. You wouldn't bother with these lines if you had nice thoughts." He waited until I looked at him. "Music helps."

Had my self-consciousness been that obvious to him? I began to feel myself sinking into my shell, but fought against it.

"Do you ever wonder how your life would be if you were good enough for the people who are important to you?" he asked, staring into my eyes under the dim light. "If you were good enough . . . do you ever wonder if you would still need theatre?"

I stopped myself from sinking deeper into myself. My eyes never fell from his, though every part of me felt exposed. As long as

I didn't agree with him, he would never know how vulnerable I felt at that moment.

"I don't care about all this as much as you do," he said. "Maybe I would if I was half as good as you, but hey, I have my own little obsessions that keep me busy when my parents drive me nuts. The Beatles being one of them."

I watched him. He watched me back.

"You're too hard on yourself, Leah Roy. If you are your own worst critic, is anything ever really good enough?"

I tried recounting the years I'd lived in other places, wondering if I had always been so obvious, wondering if I had ever had a friend who knew me so well.

I set my script aside, lightly exhaling from the psychological relief of finally feeling understood. I wondered if those topics were discussed at The Tree, if they questioned themselves as hard as they questioned others.

I tried to muffle my curiosity. "Okay, since you seem to know so much, can I ask *you* something now?"

"Shoot."

I cleared my throat and searched for my voice.

"You have this place you go to . . . you know, that tree by the north wing," I said. "What's the big deal?"

Braden rested his back against the wall and held the script between his knees.

"Don't you have one?" he asked.

"Have what?"

"A place you go to get away from the world for a while?"

I thought about it, but before I could answer, the back door shot open. Rachelle called out for Braden.

Braden squinted under the fresh bright light. "Yeah?"

"I found Scotty." Her voice was higher than I had ever heard it, a little shaky even. "He's freaking out in the locker room. Something about how his life is ruined, shitty mom, Garcia can go to hell. You gotta get over there now."

Braden was on his feet before she could finish. I laid my script down and followed, not caring that I wasn't officially invited.

Braden ran across the parking lot to the gymnasium. He swung open the main door and called for Scotty.

My thoughts drifted as I followed, retreating further inside my head with every step. I remembered my dad backing up with a football in his grip, telling me to "go long, go long." I ran as far as I could before he threw the ball, but I didn't catch it. It fell out of my grasp and bounced off the concrete while I panted. Tears filled my eyes as I picked it up, but my dad would clap and give me the thumbs up anyway.

Every time.

My face glowed when he would say, "Great job, Leah. You almost got it."

Braden shouted for Scotty again.

My eyes shot open to a crashing noise and what sounded like a lion roaring from inside the locker room.

We made our way over. The crashing grew louder.

Braden hurried in. Becca was already there, standing against the opposite wall with huge eyes. Rachelle stayed near the door and, from the looks of it, she'd never seen anything so violent in her life.

Braden rushed over and tried to put Scotty in some kind of manly hold, but Scotty shoved past him. He kicked a locker—no, beat the locker—until the hinges fell to the floor. Then he ripped the metal off and threw it against the wall with a loud roar. I noticed a few other lockers had already seen the same fate.

I wanted to ask him what happened, but I didn't want to make our visits with Hillman obvious. I hoped Scotty would be okay. That was all I could think as I watched Braden grab him one more unsuccessful time.

"Scott," Braden said. "Chill, man. What happened?"

One thing I knew for sure was to never tell a pissed-off person to chill.

Scotty flipped a bench over, picked it up, and chucked it against the lockers, leaving dents in them.

I turned and hurried over to Braden.

"Any ideas?" he asked me.

A row of foldable chairs lined the wall. Scotty shouted obscenities to each one he picked up and slammed against the wall.

I sure as hell wasn't going to stand in front of one of those doomed chairs.

I pictured myself standing in front of Helen Keller's house. Maybe the inability to see certain things in life was a blessing in disguise . . . not hearing the horrible things people said or seeing the horrible things they did.

I imagined Scotty as a modern-day Helen Keller when she was mad or frustrated, only her family didn't try to shove a bunch of pills down her throat. She became violent, messy, furious. They gave her everything she wanted, at least until Anne came around and demanded that Helen face her challenges.

"Take it out on practice," Braden yelled over the crashing.

"What practice?" Scotty shouted. "There isn't gonna be any more practice."

I turned to Rachelle who shrugged her shoulders. Becca tossed another foldable chair to Scotty.

He caught it and beat down another locker. A wooden stool was next. Scotty whipped it through the air until it shattered against the wall—I shielded my face as broken pieces flew in our direction.

"Guess this is all a part of being bipolar, huh, Mom?" He smashed the locker with his knee, or maybe he smashed his knee. I couldn't tell. Blood covered his knuckles though.

"Huh, Coach?" he yelled, backing away from the locker. "Guess I'm just too friggin' crazy to do somethin' I love!" He smashed into the locker again before Braden jumped in and pulled him back.

"Knock it off, man. They'll expel you."

Scotty turned to us. Red blotches covered his face and his eyes brimmed with tears.

"What does it matter now?" he shouted. "What does it fuckin' matter now?"

He tried to pick up another chair, but Braden pulled him down to the ground. Scotty punched the side of the locker before pressing his hands over his face and letting out a throaty scream.

"I hope she's happy," he yelled. "I hope she's real happy now."

It was quiet for a long minute as Scotty sobbed into his palms.

Becca walked over to us. I glanced at Braden who glanced at Rachelle who glanced at me.

What did people do in moments like those? Sometimes a pat on the back wasn't the answer. Anger wasn't an honest emotion anyway. I knew that from my many pillow punching episodes and, as I watched Scotty, I recognized his soaked palms as the real truth.

I thought of my dad again, seeing him through the bathroom door keyhole before my mom jerked me away. He was sitting there in the corner of the bathroom with a newspaper in his lap. I heard his low voice but couldn't understand what he was saying. There were mumbles, nonsense, talking to something that wasn't there. Looking at him was like looking at a zombie version of him.

Fear crept into my little being and found its way out through my fists banging on the door, as I cried for my dad to come out. His face wasn't the face of my dad, but of some blurry, disoriented stranger who hadn't slept in weeks.

I looked up when Scotty finally pulled his hands from his face.

"Garcia called me to his office after school." His voice cracked. "Told me I'm booted from the team."

For a while, nobody knew what to say. During our sessions with Hillman, Scotty would talk so much about how basketball had been a saving grace and how he couldn't imagine himself without it. I always thought of Scotty as this big tough jock. Seeing him now all broken down . . . he was stronger in a different way, a way I had never considered.

"I'm so sorry," Rachelle said. "I know how much that meant to you."

Braden sighed. "Late again?"

"Naw, man, I wasn't late." Scotty got up and ran his hand through his hair, hitting a few knots. "It's my mom. She thinks I'm not 'well enough' to play."

"So she takes basketball away?" Braden said. "I don't get it. You're in choir and drama club, and—"

"Yeah, forget it."

We were all quiet as Scotty went on.

"She thinks I'll be too burnt out for college. She's lettin' me finish out choir and this play because she thinks those are easy for me, but she convinced McCoy and Garcia to take me out of student office and kick me off the team." He shook his head. "Hillman must've gotten to her. He must've gotten into her head."

I felt a sudden wave of self-consciousness when he mentioned Hillman. I looked at Braden and Rachelle, but their focus was still on Scotty.

"No," I said. "I mean . . . I don't think Hillman would do that. He's not like that."

"It doesn't matter anyway. Nothin' in the world can convince her I'm okay."

I thought about my mom and all the times she'd taken her frustration out on me—yelling at me about the bathroom being dirty or why I hadn't put leftovers in the fridge since I was the last one to eat dinner. I also wanted to yell. I also wanted to complain about things she hadn't done right. Her words hurt. A lot. She made me see Hillman, too, but even after all of that, she would never take away theatre.

Chapter 9

If I could thank my mom for one thing—besides giving birth to me—then it was for making my gift picking job much easier.

She offered to take me to the drug store on her way to the party store—I didn't bother to ask why she was going there. When she pulled up to the front doors, she told me I had exactly five minutes. That time crunch sent me through the store like lightning.

I walked directly to the card aisle.

A regular present might not have been good enough anyway, so I decided to get Braden a birthday card. Simple and not much room for error. It had to be something he would like . . . something with music, maybe?

Excitement morphed my face; that was until I realized all the good cards had been picked over. Was everybody in town born in March?

I scanned the selections over ten times, but all that was left was a funny card for a twenty-first birthday. I took a deep breath and grabbed it.

When we got home, I hurried to my room and shut the door behind me. I paced my bedroom floor for nearly an hour, jotting down samples of what I wanted to write.

Braden, I hope you have a very happy birthday.
Wishing you all the best on your special day.
Happy birthday! You only turn 18 once.

I banged my head against my closet door. *Crap. Crap. Crap.*

When Thursday came, I waited in the auditorium after school, begging the universe for a little courage. I couldn't decide what to wear that morning. In the end I went with something different—a shirt with a shade of pink that complimented my pale complexion. At least it matched my white pants.

I held the card in my hand. After spending another hour that morning trying to decide what to write, I simply went with my gut.

It was only a card, I reminded myself when I saw him walk in with Sara. A twinge of jealousy snuck into my core.

Braden and Sara had already perched themselves near the entrance to the ramp hall, their typical spot. She sipped her coffee while he talked about something—probably Paul Simon.

I stood. The seat bounced up behind me, creating a smacking noise, but I was too preoccupied with the card in my sweaty palm to notice. The chatter of the others filled the room; I would have indulged in their enthusiasm if I weren't gulping in air as thick as water.

The ramp hall was five yards away. It must have been zero degrees in the auditorium. Why was I so nervous? He was just Braden. A friend. No big deal.

Cast members messed around with props on the stage while others were scattered in the seats going over lines for the evening's rehearsal.

The shakes had spread from my fingers to all the nerves in my body. The closer I got to him, the more I shrunk. I had to keep reminding myself to correct my shoulders.

Okay. Maybe he wasn't *just* Braden. Maybe I did really like him. Maybe I hoped that the card would mean more than a friendship.

His voice grew louder the closer I approached.

I never would have thought that I would have gotten Braden Gregory a birthday card, but the world was changing. At least, mine was.

Besides Justin, I'd only one time given something to a guy. Matt

Hendrix. A guy whose idea of flirting was barely talking to me for an entire semester because he was "busy with chess club." I had given him a beautiful bouquet of lollipops for Valentine's Day and his response was, "Too bad I can't eat these because of my braces."

I soon found myself standing in front of the ramp hall with two expectant faces turned to me—my attention locked only on one.

"Happy Birthday." My voice broke, but that didn't matter once I saw his bulging eyes.

He pushed himself up and grabbed the card from my hand—the excitement glistened from his starry gaze.

I slid my thumb over my fingertips.

"Leah," he said in his falsetto. "You got me a card!" He flipped it open after tearing away the envelope, which released a swarm of butterflies in my stomach. "Thank you."

"It's nothing," I said, knowing exactly where I'd screwed up.

He did a double take over the card and when the realization smacked him right in the face, he tipped his head back and laughed.

He read the printed message aloud. "Cheers on your twenty-first. Now you can buy me a drink."

When Sara's eyebrows turned inward, I thought it was the end of the world as I knew it.

Then he read my personal message.

"Drug stores suck. No good cards left. But hey, at least I'm the first person to wish you a happy twenty-first . . . anyway, happy birthday, Braden! Leah."

A part of me expected them to start pointing and mocking. Who could blame them? But instead, Braden took two steps forward and, before I knew it, his arms wrapped around me.

I imagined him like the kind of boy who slept in a dusty room and played music in the middle of the night when he couldn't sleep. I imagined him sitting on his bed with a pile of records on his lap, and for a brief second, I imagined myself with him . . . my head resting on his shoulder.

I couldn't wipe the giddy grin off my face when he pulled away.

"You know he's going to expect something from you all the time now, don't you?" Sara said.

I pressed my lips together and looked at Braden who had already been looking at me.

That, I realized, was the end of *my* world as I knew it.

9:14 p.m.

Msg From: Braden

thanks for the card. does that mean u wanna be friends?

9:15 p.m.

New Msg:

It means you got a card for your birthday

9:16 p.m.

Msg From: Braden

so r we friends?

9:17 p.m.

New Msg:

Yes Braden we're friends.

9:20 p.m.

Msg From: Braden

good because i wanted to ask if u'd go to the basketball game with me next friday.

it's a home game. i should only have to work until halftime again.

no rehearsal.

9:22 p.m.

New Msg:

What time does the game start?

9:23 p.m.

Msg From: Braden

after school around 7

9:25 p.m.

Msg From: Braden

leah?

9:26 p.m.

New Msg:

Okay see u then

Chapter 10

I always wondered if Robert would ever show up at The Tree. I never really wanted him to. Seeing him might have ruined the beauty of this paper relationship we had. I enjoyed the mystery—not knowing if he looked like my grandpa or if his voice sounded as old as I imagined.

I wanted to tell Becca and Justin about Robert. I wanted to tell anyone, but I was afraid of what they would think. I considered telling Hillman, but decided against it—the last thing I needed was word getting back to my mom. Even though I trusted Hillman, if I really was going crazy schizo, it was his job to tell her.

Thursday, March 5, 2009

Dear Robert,

I wonder if my dad has suffered alone. I keep remembering his chest rising and falling when I watched him sleeping on the couch... seconds before I turned away. I wondered how a person's chest could rise and fall if their heart was broken. I haven't talked to him since then, but I think about him every single day, hoping he got better.

Robert, I needed to believe that what I was doing was the right thing and the only way to do that was to believe the worst in my dad. It made sense to leave if the person was bad. It just made more sense. Maybe that's why I see the worst in people? Maybe if we move again, it will be easier to let them go.

You're right. Braden was just trying to be kind.

Pen Pal Tina

Monday afternoon came around, and it wasn't quite 3:47 p.m. when I reached the auditorium. I'd been lost in my own thoughts that day and didn't feel like hanging with Becca and Justin until then, so I walked alone to rehearsal. When I opened the door, the air rushed past me in a blast, bringing the scent of wood and a thousand upholstered seats.

The current of students in the corridor paid no attention as I walked into the dim auditorium. The door slammed behind me, shutting out their chatter. Nobody else had shown up yet. The only lights on were a few near the stage. I glanced up—the gigantic room rose so high my footsteps echoed.

I walked next to the wall, looking over the framed photos of past musical casts. Braden was noticeable in a couple of them, being that he was always in the front row striking a playful pose. Drama club wasn't cool enough for framed photos. The only evidence of our cast's existence was in the old programs and school newspaper articles.

I plopped my book bag on a seat in the first row and stared ahead, admiring the large, freshly waxed stage floor—courtesy of choir funds, of course. I walked up to it and ran my fingers over the smoothness. I'd always loved that auditorium. It was home to me, somewhere I felt safe and accepted.

I heard some noise behind the side door when Tamara walked in with the keys jingling in her hand. She quickly waved to me before disappearing backstage. A few castmates walked in after her.

3:47 p.m. approached. Most of the cast was already there by

the time Hillman walked in, calling everyone to sit in the center of the stage.

As soon as everyone was in a circle, Hillman did that thing with his mouth where he was silently counting everyone.

"Does anyone know where Braden is?" he asked.

I didn't remember seeing him, then again, I didn't think our paths had crossed at all that day.

Sara raised her hand. "He wasn't at school today."

I didn't see Braden at all for the next two days. I didn't want to seem overly concerned by texting him, so I let it go. He had this special thing where he went on family business trips a lot. I guessed that was a luxury of that life. They could get him out of school whenever they wanted, and take off to Gatlinburg or someplace cool, using the auto business as an excuse.

I only remembered one time when he was gone for that long. It was toward the end of freshman year and I just remembered being so jealous when I found out the teachers had given him all his homework so he could go on a business trip to Florida.

He missed two weeks of school.

When he came back, he looked rough, almost as if the sun had missed him completely. I always thought trips outside of school were supposed to be rejuvenating . . . then I remembered all his phone calls with his mom.

He must have really missed school when he went away.

I spent that week having lunch in the cafeteria with my theatre friends. The usuals were at The Tree including Scotty who always had his head in the script. Transforming into my brother on stage didn't seem too foreign to how he was becoming offstage, calling me "li'l sis" and backhanding one of his jock friends for asking why he was talking to "unicorn girl."

I thought Scotty might have been into Sara, but when she

would toss her hair back as they sat under The Tree, he didn't look twice anymore. Since being cut from the team, he spent most of his time learning lines.

Rehearsals weren't as fun without Braden, so I found a way to enjoy them.

Helen Keller didn't like being told what to do. As my luck had it, she and Anne Sullivan fought a lot, so Sara and I had to rehearse our infamous kitchen table scene over and over again. That scene was three pages of action to memorize and I got most of the moves down pretty quickly, but Sara struggled.

"Slap me so I can feel it," I finally told Sara after our tenth run-through.

"I will," she said, out of breath. Her cheeks were beet red. I got the sense she couldn't handle much more unless I showed some mercy.

"We don't look believable, right, Mr. Hillman?" I asked.

Hillman sat in the front row with his pen and notepad. He shook his head with his fingers on his temples.

I loved the end of that scene where I got to grab a bunch of Sara's hair and wrestle her under the table. Maybe I had to be a good girl for my scholarship, but Helen certainly didn't have to.

I grabbed her hair when the part came. She squealed and jumped, so I let go.

"Anne Sullivan is not a ballerina." I huffed. "You're supposed to fall to your knees and put up a fight."

Sara gave it her best shot, but I still overpowered her and flipped her over until she landed flat on her back. She panted, staring wide-eyed into the stage lights as if she didn't know what had hit her.

Hillman cleared his throat and pointed to the script in one direct motion. Wrestling Sara like that wasn't part of the action.

I lifted my shoulders and cast an innocent shrug.

At the next rehearsal, we planned how the set would be built. It would be a simple house shown from the inside with a kitchen table where Helen would steal everyone's food and fight Anne.

After rehearsal, Becca, Justin, and I volunteered to pick up paint and supplies from Home Depot. Sara had access to the finances, so she led me to the box office where they kept the goods. She handed me some cash. I signed my name at the bottom of the paper and gave her a sweet wink as I walked away. Hillman would see that I was still the most dedicated member.

"You *had* to drag us into this, Leah," Becca moaned from the back seat. "Couldn't you have picked a night my dad was scheduled to see me? I'm missing *The Amazing Race* for this."

"It won't take long," I said, pulling out the list Hillman gave me. "Three gallons of brown paint, ten wide brushes, masking tape, and a bunch of plastic to cover the floor."

Justin spoke through gritted teeth. "If either of you gets paint on these seats, I will dye your hair green in your sleep."

We scurried through the aisles at Home Depot, marking everything off the list, and as soon as we checked out, we headed back to the school. Becca and Justin helped me carry everything into the auditorium. I needed to give the receipt and change back to Sara, but she had already gone home.

So much for dedication.

I called for Hillman, but he wasn't there either. Becca and Justin stayed behind to get the stage set up for the next day while I searched for him. He wasn't backstage or in the hallways. I figured he was probably in his classroom, so I walked that way.

As I reached for the doorknob, I stopped. I heard his voice, low and steady behind the door. I thought about knocking, but I peeked through the small window of the door instead. I couldn't see anyone except Hillman who was facing the front of the room, and I only caught a quick shadow of the person he was talking to before I turned away.

"We'll get you back on track," I heard Hillman's muffled voice say.

Afraid he would open the door any second, I just left the receipt and change outside of his door and walked away.

Before Justin dropped us off at home, he treated Becca and me to donuts from Quick Stop. I hoped to see Braden's purple minivan, but it wasn't there.

I thought about texting him later, but he might have thought I had no life, just sitting at home . . . listening to his CD after dinner.

By Wednesday evening, I caved.

7:45 p.m.

New Msg:

Hey. No practice tomorrow in case you didn't get informed.

8:22 p.m.

Msg From: Braden

thanks leah

The next evening, I helped my mom count inventory at the hotel. Anytime she was running low on staff, she'd ask me if I'd come help her in return for free snacks from the vending machine.

While counting boxes, she asked me the same question three times, snapping me back to reality.

I clutched the clipboard I was holding.

"What?" I asked.

"Earth to Leah. Did you check off the bar soap?"

"Yeah," I said, checking it off.

All I could think about was Braden, and his Chaplin hat in my closet. I kept forgetting to return it.

After a while, my mom got carried away with computer work, too busy to notice if I stepped out. Knowing Braden lived just down the road, I closed my phone, thinking another text wouldn't help.

I snuck out of the room and waved to the receptionist as I left.

While walking down the street, I practiced what I might say and how I would say it.

"Hey, Braden, just thought I would swing by."

Stupid.

"Hey, Braden, I was just helping my mom at work and remembered you lived down here."

Eh.

I neared his house which was brighter in the daylight—light brown stone, colorful flowers bordering it. His front yard was bigger than I thought. The grass was thick and dark green, and a small rocking chair sat on his front porch with an old-looking teddy bear sitting in it.

I walked around back, glancing around in case someone was outside, but nobody was there.

I heard loud talking coming from inside and noticed movement through the curtains as if someone was walking back and forth. Voices of a woman and someone else escaped through the half-open kitchen window.

"Do you have a better idea?" the woman said.

"God, you are so controlling. Just let—"

"*I'm* controlling? Do you realize how lenient I have been throughout all of this? This is bigger than you can understand. Will you please—"

"Why do you always do that? You always think nobody understands. I'm going through it, too, Mom."

They continued like that while I contemplated running away. If I waited any longer, I would have. I guessed I couldn't have come at a worse time, but if they saw me then they'd think I was eavesdropping.

I knocked on the screen door.

"Just do this, Leah," I said out loud to myself.

The talking stopped. I heard the woman say, "Someone's at the door."

My nerves turned to a shaky fire. Her comment brought my thoughts to my dad. This time, I was sitting at the kitchen table doing my art class homework while my mom and her friend were talking about my dad as if I were invisible.

"He needs help," my mom said. "I can't do this anymore. The guy is a psychopath. He's been sitting behind that door for two straight hours babbling about people coming after him. The drugs are making it worse."

The back door of Braden's house suddenly opened, dragging me from my memories. I looked up.

I thought it was Braden until his brother, Trevor, opened the screen door and stepped out.

"Yeah?" he asked.

"Hey," I said. "I'm looking for Braden."

"Braden's not home." He closed the door behind him, towering over me even after stepping off the porch. "You're Leah, aren't you?"

He wore a collared shirt and blue jeans. I studied his face, particularly his strong jawline. He was fairly thin, but I bet myself his muscles were as hard as bricks. He was taller than Braden, too, with blond hair instead of light brown.

"Have I met you before?" I asked.

"I know most of Braden's people, but I haven't met you yet. You're all he talks about these days. Accent on *all*."

"I didn't know I was one of his people." I rubbed my upper arm. "He wasn't at school all week. I was just wondering."

"With my dad on a college tour or some crap like that. He'll be back tomorrow."

Someone opened the door behind him—a thin lady with short blond hair and gold jewelry.

Trevor raised his eyebrows and formed his mouth into an O.

"Hello?" the lady said.

"I'm gonna finish the dishes," Trevor said, walking back into the house. "See ya."

The woman stepped outside, keeping her focus glued to me. All the while, I couldn't take mine off her either. She made me nervous with the strong, confident way she looked at me, carrying the scent of money though she was dressed like a casual woman on a Thursday evening—blue jeans and a lace top.

I knew it was Braden's mom. She had the same deep-green eyes that made her seem more down to earth than I'd imagined her being.

She looked at me with expectation. My stomach tensed.

"Oh," I said, remembering where I was. "I'm—my name is Leah. I'm—"

"Yes, you're Braden's Leah. I'm Trish, his mother."

Her eyelids were covered in brown eyeliner and the dark circles under them were poorly buried under a thick layer of concealer.

"I think Braden should take a few classes in storytelling because he forgot to mention what a doll you are."

"Oh . . ." I blushed. "Thanks. I . . ."

"You came to see Braden," she finished for me. "Would you like to come inside? I can make us some tea."

"No, thanks. I was just helping my mom at work nearby and thought I'd say hi."

"Well, he's not here, hun."

I was glad she didn't ask me where my mom worked.

"Right. Sorry. Thank you, Mrs. Gregory."

I couldn't tell her that we were supposed to go to the basketball game the following evening. Mothers didn't want their sons to end up with girls like me.

"She's a nice girl, but her parents are divorced."

"She's a nice girl, but her mother is living in sin."

"She's a nice girl, but she doesn't come from an educated family."

As I walked away, I caught Trevor watching me from the kitchen window. The curtain quickly fell in front of his face.

The next day, I saw Braden at his locker. He hadn't noticed me down the hallway yet. I smiled wide and couldn't wait to hear about his college visit. When I started walking toward him, he stepped back, revealing Sara talking to him from the other side. I tried not to overthink it, but I couldn't forget his voice next to me as we'd played his piano. I thought our time together had meant something . . . not just to me, but to him.

It was moments like that when I thought about how I could have lived and breathed theatre, made the best grades of my life, dressed better, and yet still, it was like Sara was designed for guys like Braden.

He laughed at something she said.

I clutched my books and walked to first period.

9:42 p.m.

Msg From: Braden

leah u ready?

9:43 p.m.

New Msg:

What?

9:43 p.m.

Msg From: Braden

im outside

9:44 p.m.

New Msg:

Why?

9:45 p.m.

Msg From: Braden

u said u would come to the basketball game with me.

thats now.

9:46 p.m.

New Msg:

But the game is probably almost over.

9:50 p.m.

Msg From: Braden

leah?

9:51 p.m.

New Msg:

You drive me insane.

Braden parked his van in the school parking lot, shutting off the ignition while The Beatles blasted through the speakers. I hadn't had a chance to ask him about his college visit because he sang along with Paul McCartney for the whole ride.

His vibrato still needed improvement, but I didn't say anything.

"Do you ever wonder how Helen Keller felt the music if she couldn't hear it?" he asked, turning down the volume.

"Is there more than one way to feel music?"

We got out of the van. The parking lot was a ghost town full of empty vehicles. The sound of stomping on the bleachers and cheering as a team scored traveled from the distance. I didn't think our team had a chance anymore.

Big mistake booting Scotty, Garcia.

Braden slid open the side door of his van and shuffled some things around for a moment before plopping a thin book on the seat.

"Has Scotty broken any more chairs lately?" I asked.

Braden shoved some junk under the back seat.

"He's taking it okay. Has to hide his anger so his mom doesn't take more away from him. Canning him for being bipolar was really shitty though. He promised her that he would take his meds as long as he could keep seeing Hillman instead of his shrink."

I ignored the Hillman topic, but was glad to know that Scotty could trust Braden enough to tell him about his sessions. I just hoped Scotty hadn't mentioned me, too.

"He's not taking those pills, is he?" I asked.

"Nope. Not one."

Before I could ask him about the college visit, he gave me a once-over.

"If I'm going to take you to this place, you have to ditch your hat and your shoes." He slid off his shoes and threw them in the van.

"Take me where? We're supposed to go to the game."

I began to refuse, but he pointed to my hat, so I carefully took it off and placed it on the back seat before doing the same with my shoes. The concrete was firm and cold. I stood at least another few inches shorter than him.

"Now let your hair down," he said.

"Why? I like it up."

"No. You don't."

"I really do, though."

"Leah, I want to take you here, but you have to come as you are. You know you don't like your hair up."

With a sigh, I pulled my scrunchie and shook out my hair.

When Braden stared at me, I rubbed my arm, trying to ignore the prickles all over my skin.

"What?" I asked.

His eyes grazed my body and settled on my face. "You're just really pretty."

My temperature rose a hundred degrees before he finally stopped looking at me. After grabbing the thin blue book, he led me across the parking lot. As soon as we passed through the tennis courts, I realized where we were going.

We strolled to the patch of grass between the cafeteria and the north wing. I felt like I was walking into a secret wonderland—a place that would only let you in with a special code.

Then I saw it. Dark-brown bark harboring deep crevices that could go on far into that thick trunk. The thousands of long leaves, limp yet crisp and light green, even under the evening moon. Their abundance protected the many branches that extended outward like a bursting firework.

Though I had been there so many times, this time it looked bigger, more vibrant, more alive. Or maybe it was just Braden standing next to it that had that effect.

I admired The Tree's beauty. I loved the way the leaves danced as the wind brushed through them.

"This is the place I go," Braden said. "The Tree."

He sat down against the trunk while I stood there. His face read excitement and comfort as if he too was entering a magical kingdom where nothing was impossible.

"Braden, can I tell you something?"

He placed the book on his lap and looked at me.

"It's just that . . ." I took a step back. Why was believing in myself so hard? "Maybe it's just a tree and I'm the only one acting stupid about it, but—"

"Woah," Braden sat up. "*Just* a tree? This place is solitude, Leah. When you come here, you're coming to a moment in time. That moment can last as long as you want it to. No deadlines. No pressure."

"This tree is your group's sanctuary. *My* sanctuary is my dog urine-stained bedroom closet."

"So *that's* where you go." He grinned.

I put my hands on my hips, thankful for Braden's ability to take the weight off my shoulders and bomb it to pieces.

"Sit down," he said.

I slowly took a seat beside him. The names etched into the thick bark were still visible under the evening sky.

BG. SH. RR. SW.

Seeing those names made me feel like I was closer to possibility. College didn't seem too unachievable when I was sitting next to that trunk of names, a place where the cool people went to get away from the rush of the world.

I wondered if Robert and his lover had done the same. For once, I was beginning to feel like I could have everything I had ever wanted.

"Trevor said you popped by yesterday," Braden said.

"I did."

"Stalker."

"Hey." I flicked his knee. "I definitely wasn't stalking you. It's just that you were gone for so long. I just wanted to see what was up."

Braden raised half a smile.

"Seriously," I said. "My mom works at the Home Inn right down the road."

"Admit it, Leah. You were worried about me."

"So, college," I said. "Took you all week to check out a school?"

"Took me all week to get over a stupid cold and one long agonizing day on a college tour."

"How was it?"

"Boring. Depressing. Can't accept that my future is already planned."

"I like a good plan. Too much spontaneity is scary."

"Leah, I don't want to be like my parents. The light in their eyes has died over time and I don't want that to be me. I want to stay a dreamer. I want to get out there and really see things. Really live."

"Maybe they are living though. Maybe a part of life is just that people get tired and it shows in their eyes. Doesn't mean they stopped dreaming once they achieved certain goals."

"I don't want to get tired."

I shook my head, picking blades of grass apart.

"I wish I could take you out of this town to show you that there really isn't anything you're missing," I said. "Once you see it, you see it, then what?"

"Then . . ." he sighed. "Then I guess I'll stop driving myself crazy wondering 'what if'."

"Where would you go?"

He was quiet for a moment.

"I'll tell you." He paused. "But first . . ." He lifted the book.

"What's that?"

"*And to Think That I Saw It on Mulberry Street* by Dr. Seuss. I used to read it to my brother when he was little."

"Are you serious?"

"Yeah. I'm going to read it to you now, but you can't freak out on me."

"Why would I freak out?"

When he slipped his arm around my shoulders, chills crawled up my spine and spread through my body. Why did his touch have so much power over me?

I surrendered and slowly leaned into him as he read.

He acted out certain lines, getting louder when the faster parts came, shocking me a couple times. Passion took over his voice, echoing in my head when he would tone it down for the next part.

Nobody had ever read to me, not even my parents. Braden's reading made me feel like a little girl, laying in the grass with my wild imagination. The sky was the limit.

I thought being at The Tree with Braden would be something magnificent, like something earth shattering would happen—glitter would fall from the leaves and I would be transformed into a new, amazing person. I pretended it happened. Glitter covered my body, sparkling and shining like a living dream come true, and I became somebody that everybody wanted to be.

When I eventually opened my eyes, everything had changed. It was calm and quiet. The wind grazed my skin almost like quicksand except it stopped short of swallowing me whole. Instead, it held me just enough to show me that I was safe and everything would be okay.

Braden read softly next to my ear and paused, holding the last page between his fingers.

"Are you going to finish it?" I asked.

"No." He closed the book. "I don't like the ending. I think I'm going to change it."

He looked at me, and I looked into his eyes by accident. We froze there, staring into each other's worlds as if we were about to enter an impossible adventure.

I knew what was coming. A kiss. Was I ready for it?

Just when he leaned forward, I panicked and turned away.

Stage fright. Totally normal.

My hand grasped onto a few leaves next to me and I threw them at his chest. He paused before throwing a couple over my head. I giggled.

He nudged me until I plopped over and we lay on the grass, looking at the sky through the leaves of the branches above.

I could feel the warmth of Braden's hand next to me, and all resistance vanished when his fingers touched mine.

I lifted my hand until it rested in his. He slipped his fingers through mine. How had it come to this? Braden Gregory and Leah Roy. Maybe I hadn't been seeing myself in the light I had always deserved, but somehow, believing in myself wasn't so difficult when our hands were intertwined.

"Where would you go?" I asked, staring ahead.

"Just imagine, Leah." His finger traveled over my palm in a circular motion. "Imagine we are surrounded by trees just like this one, some small, some tall. Imagine all of those leaves above us are from a bunch of trees."

I stared at the leaves, the light of the moon breaking through them.

"Okay, I'm imagining it," I said.

"If this thing between us ends in complete disaster, can you do one thing for me?"

"What is it?"

His hand wrapped tightly around mine.

"Don't lose sight of the forest for the trees."

I inhaled the evening air, imagining trees surrounding us. I could hear cheering from the gymnasium before the song "American Pie" began faintly playing in the background.

I gently rolled my head until it touched Braden's. All the muscles in my face relaxed and as I closed my eyes, any trace of fear within me evaporated.

Don't lose sight.

The forest protected us and, for the moment, I was flying.

Chapter 11

When Braden dropped me off after the game, I was greeted in the kitchen by my mom. She eagerly bragged about how she had found me a suitable psychologist who could help me through my anxiety.

Anxiety.

That's the word she would use when what she really wanted to say was that she didn't want me ending up like my drug-addicted, paranoid, crazy dad.

"She did it," I said, sitting at the desk across from Hillman the following Tuesday morning. "She finally found a psychologist for me. Sucks I won't be seeing you in the mornings anymore."

I shook my head, hoping it would shake off all the bad things I was thinking about my mom.

"Talking to someone more qualified could be a good thing for you, Leah. I can only go so far as a school counselor. And you know you don't need an appointment here. The door is always open."

"You know she gets mad at me because I don't call Beau my dad? Yeah. Then I tell her that I only have one dad. She says 'your dad is psychotic' then I say 'he's still my dad' then she says 'I don't care, he's crazy' then I say 'I don't care either' then she thinks I will be just like him. Anyone who doesn't do what she wants must be a psychopath, right?"

"You are not a psychopath." Hillman leaned forward in his chair. "You are a young woman trying to piece all of this together. That's not easy and it might take you a long time before you and your mother see eye to eye, but the important thing is to respect her as your mother. You don't have to agree with everything she does, but she has a right to live her life as she chooses."

"And me?"

"As long as she's not causing harm to you or your sister."

I tilted my head and leaned back.

"Define *harm*."

When the lunch bell rang, Braden wrapped his arm around my shoulders and hurried me out of the school building.

"What's going on?" I giggled.

The sun blinded me as he pushed the door open and led me down the sidewalk to the north wing. The feeling of his tender yet strong grip around my shoulders got me thinking about how he'd looked as we painted the set the previous evening. He had pulled out the set building plan and led the way. I loved watching him direct the others because he did so without seeming bossy. What made him an even better leader was that he was an example, taking part in the work.

I also loved watching him with a hammer.

Justin watched him, too. Braden's muscles flexed through his long-sleeved shirt, and he sweated so much that he had to peel it off. Justin stared as long as he could before he tossed his tools to the ground and stepped outside for some "fresh air."

Braden stopped me at The Tree and sat me down in front of a plate with a good-looking slice of pizza on it. Scotty and Rachelle gave me a quick "What's up?" before continuing running their *Aladdin* lines. Sara was listening to them, but also on the phone with the Yearbook editor.

My skin sort of rippled with a tingling sensation as I looked around this place that used to feel so distant to me.

"Here." Braden took a seat beside me and opened the folder he had been carrying. He pulled out some sheets of paper and placed them in my lap, then handed me a pen.

I glanced over the papers.

"Fill it out," he said, handing me the opened folder. "The only way you'll know if it's meant for you is if you try."

I looked back down, reading over the content of the folder when I realized it was a college application.

Ball State University.

Life got real in that moment, as if the direction of my future was resting in my lap. I could be a teacher. I could be a doctor. I could be an actress.

I could.

"The first step is filling out your name." He pointed to the blank space.

I can do that. It's just my name.

I wrote my name and filled in the rest of the basic questions. Braden watched me the whole time as if that application decided his future, too.

I read through the papers. Braden handed me the slice of pizza. While I expected it to have this explosive flavor, it tasted the same as the cafeteria pizza.

I noticed the description on the next page. "What's this about an essay?"

"Tell them about you. Something you overcame or an experience you learned from. I'll help you write it if you want."

Something I overcame.

Self-consciousness washed over me when I glanced at the patch of dirt where Robert and I buried our letters. I looked up, wondering if anyone had ever noticed the patch of dirt. I guessed nobody could tell since the thick roots created bumps of heavy dirt that didn't grow grass. It was easy to bury something in that area. Maybe that was why none of them had ever found Robert's letters.

Sara dashed off in a hurry, muttering something about the Yearbook captions.

Part of me felt like a kid who could get in trouble with her parents for hiding something. What if those kids found out I had been visiting The Tree after school? What if they found out I secretly wanted to be like them? Would they ostracize me or treat me like a weirdo who wrote letters to a lonely old man? I wasn't sure anymore.

Something I overcame.

The first thought that came to mind was my dad. Losing him. Losing my old home, my old friends, my old life. Coming to Small Town Nowhere.

"Braden . . ." I looked up, staring into the sky. "Can I really do this?"

He didn't reply, so I glanced at him. He began searching for something in the grass and, for a brief second, I turned stone cold. What if he knew about the letters? I thought I was going to shatter into a million pieces, but then, he lifted a small rock in his hand.

"Here." He handed it to me.

Before I knew it, Braden was helping me push the rock into The Tree's trunk as lightly as I could so it made a clear, smooth mark. We did that over and over again until it was readable. A light-brown **L**—a highlight etched into the dark bark surrounding it.

"L is done," he said into my ear. He wrapped his hands over mine and helped me carve the **R** into the trunk.

I was fully conscious of what was happening, but it still felt sort of surreal like one of my daydreaming sessions. I was there with Braden, not to mention carving my initials into this tree that used to feel so out of reach. Even sitting here after school, it had been a place that didn't belong to me.

"Leah Roy," I whispered so lightly that I was sure Braden hadn't heard a word. I glanced to the cafeteria window, wanting to bring Becca and Justin to The Tree. I was overcome with a strong sense of hope, something I hadn't realized I needed so much of until that moment, and I wanted to give them that same feeling.

I scratched the rock into the bark until the **R** for Roy was as good as I could get it.

"There," Braden said. "Welcome to The Tree."

I looked up. Scotty and Rachelle had been watching and I swear I saw a small smile turn up from the corners of Rachelle's mouth.

"What?" I playfully asked. "No induction ceremony?"

Scotty laughed and leaned back on his elbows. "You don't need anyone's vote to know you're awesome."

I peered up into the leaves, taking in the crisp, cool air. No longer did I have to wait until the last bell rang to go there. No longer did I have to make sure the coast was clear of the cool kids before I could start my daydreaming sessions.

"I feel . . ." I paused and lowered my voice. "Like I can have anything I want."

Braden laughed, grabbing the stack of papers and putting them in my hands.

"You always could, Leah."

The wind picked up. I loved the way it felt against my skin. More than that, I loved the way Braden's eyes squinted under the sunlight.

Spring Break was approaching and I had this exciting idea. Braden and I could take a trip to Alabama to see Helen Keller's house. Since I was playing her part, I figured my mom wouldn't mind me going with a "castmate" in the name of "research." Although it sounded like I was trying to trick her into thinking it was innocent, it actually was ridiculously innocent.

We'd drive straight there, probably stay in separate hotel rooms for a night, see the house, and then drive right back the following day. It hadn't occurred to me until later that Braden might want to make a few stops along the way. In that case, we'd probably be out the entire week of Spring Break.

But I wasn't going to tell my mom that.

Not that she would care, but I didn't want to hear any more of how she'd gotten pregnant when she was eighteen and how it had ruined her life and how I'd be heading in the same direction if I didn't make better choices.

"But we had plans to hang at Justin's that week," Becca complained over the phone.

It was Friday evening. I paced my front yard, dragging my fingers around the only tree we had as I circled it.

"It's not like I'll be gone all next week. Two or three days max, then we can eat chips and salsa, and binge-watch all the movies on our list. I promise."

I heard her sigh through the speaker. The pouting in her voice was prominent.

"Just admit it," she said. "You're in love."

"Are you crazy? I just want to see Helen's house. I'd go with you if you'd stop getting grounded."

"My mom said 'no' because that's the dumbest idea in the world. It's Spring freakin' Break. People go to cool places like the beach and Justin's house, but my own best friend is choosing to see some nerdy tourist attraction with some guy over me. Pain, Leah. Pain."

When I barged through our front door, music was blasting from the living room, which meant my mom and Beau had had a really good day.

Or that they were drunk.

My mom was in the kitchen, swaying her hips while texting. Gracie was in the living room dancing with Beau as Boston played from brand-new computer speakers my mom was finally able to afford.

My mom looked up to me and I waved to her before hurrying to my bedroom. Shutting the door blocked out a little bit of the noise. I plopped my book bag on the bed and rushed to my stereo, nearly knocking it off my shelf when I pressed it.

Just as Braden's mix CD started playing, I heard my mom call me from the kitchen.

The piano began. "Imagine" by John Lennon. It was the most beautiful beginning to a song I had ever heard.

I tipped my head back when I heard her call me again.

"What's up?" I asked, reaching the counter. She was too busy texting to realize I was waiting . . . and waiting . . . and waiting. "Mom?"

I asked myself how people could swallow the bitter taste of alcohol, but I guessed it was like staying in a relationship for the hope that it would get better.

Love.

The worst kind of addiction.

"You wanted something?" I asked.

"Oh, yeah."

She put the phone down on the counter. I could tell I had her full attention then because when she looked at me, she was actually looking at me.

"I wanted to tell you something." My mom lowered her head.

"Me too," I said.

I was already formulating how I was going to tell her about Spring Break when she glanced over the bar at Gracie who was dancing on Beau's feet to "Cool the Engines".

"Me and Beau are getting married."

No pause.

No lead up to the blast.

No warning. No countdown.

Just cold, raw, and real.

I turned my head and, over the bar, I could see Gracie laughing over the music. My body was cold, almost the same cold it would get during winter when they didn't want to turn on the heat to save a couple dollars.

I looked back at my mom. My jaw tightened.

I couldn't believe it. Did she really have nothing more to say? She couldn't have talked to me about this first? It was my life, too. My life would also be affected. Again.

I stormed to my room. I slammed the door behind me, which shook the pictures hanging on my walls.

Her smile flashed through my mind. I tried to block it out. I threw all the blankets and pillows off my bed, kicked my laundry basket, and cranked up whatever song was playing next on the CD.

Jeff Buckley. "Grace."

My mom turned up the music from the living room. I grimaced. It muffled my song, so I turned up the volume. My mom cranked hers and I cranked mine. We did that a few more times until my volume knob hit maximum.

I forced a groan through my gritted teeth, smacking the stereo before screaming and tossing around all the books and knick-knacks in my closet.

Braden's Chaplin hat landed on my feet, so I picked it up.

More changes. Another "family". More explaining why my last name was different. Nothing could ever just *be*. Nothing was ever good enough. There always had to be more.

More.

More.

More!

I slammed the broken closet door, wishing I could transport myself to another dimension. Soon my screams turned into cries.

I put on the Chaplin hat, imagining myself in Braden's world, but it wasn't working.

I covered my ears.

I hated Boston.

thursday, march 26, 2009

"To forget one's purpose is the commonest form of stupidity." Friedrich Nietzsche

there is a difference between being alive and existing. being alive is living. it's feeling the beating of your heart in everything you do, feeling the beating grow faster and faster when you are doing something you love or thinking about someone you love. existing is simply having a heart inside of this shell we live in. it beats sure. it has to in order to keep us alive.

some people know what makes their heart beat. some people will be searching all their life and never find it. they might find it in moments. they might find it in a temporary person or thing. maybe it's the search that keeps them excited or maybe they have to search in order to feel that flare of passion in their heart before it begins to die down. then they will find something else to be momentarily excited about.

stay focused on your goal.

dont waste your time searching tina.

robert

Chapter 12

I left home that night and stayed at Justin's. As I walked out of the house to meet Justin in my driveway, my mom only said, "You should be happy for me."

Becca also came over to Justin's and the three of us spent most of the night sitting in front of the TV with bowls of chips and popcorn spread across the floor.

During the movies, I pulled out my notebook and worked on my college essay. I wrote about my dad, how it felt when I left him, and how that pain had made me stronger. I really believed I was able to adjust to the change of moving to Small Town Nowhere because it didn't hurt as bad as leaving my dad.

The next day, we continued our list of movies, but I felt restlessness overcome me.

It was early afternoon. After the third movie on Justin's list, Becca groaned.

"You guys ever heard of a theatre overdose?" she asked, tossing popcorn into the air and catching it in her mouth.

"Nope. Never," Justin said.

"It's when a person watches *Hairspray*, *The Phantom of the Opera*, and *Dreamgirls* in the same twenty-four hours. Their head gets full of songs until their brain cells morph into dancing music notes. It drives the person so crazy that they finally keel over and die."

Becca lurched and faked dead.

"You sick, twisted creature," Justin said. "*Dreamgirls* may be one of the greatest musicals of all time."

"My list is next," she said. "*The Texas Chainsaw Massacre, House of Wax*, and *When a Stranger Calls*. Originals only."

"Let's get out of here," I said.

They both glared at me.

"I mean it. If I'm ever going to do anything with my life, I need to see this school." I showed them the Ball State application I had been working on. "Let's check it out."

That was all I needed to say. With light traffic, the next two hours were spent gathering snacks from the gas station and riding in Justin's car to Muncie, Indiana.

As we looked for parking, I couldn't help but be mesmerized by the size of the gigantic school. The sidewalks were wide and clean for the most part, each leading to all sorts of different places. It reminded me of a labyrinth, except this labyrinth had bus stops. Cool, colorful buses. The kind that lets you stand up.

Each building had a different name and was dedicated to a different subject; Teachers College, Bracken Library, even a building named after alumni David Letterman. Students wandered in and out of the clusters of dorm buildings that we passed, each of them wearing a look of "I know what I'm doing and where I'm going."

It was scary.

Overwhelming.

Intimidating as hell.

Sure, I had lived in a lot of places, but *this*? This was *huge*. How did anybody find their way around this massive planet of buildings and people?

We walked around campus, feeling slightly out of place. Or maybe it was just me. Becca didn't seem bothered by any of it as she rambled on about how school wasn't for everyone. Justin admired the outside of an auditorium where, luckily, a senior theatre major invited us to sit in on one of their rehearsals.

These people blew us drama club kids out of the water and, as much as I couldn't believe it, the choir kids, too.

We sat through a scene rehearsal for the musical *Hair*. Their trained singing voices and perfect vibratos sent the hairs on my arms into a frenzy. Their volume and confidence reminded me of Braden singing in his van. Maybe they started out singing in their vans, too.

We watched the scene—the three of our faces wide-eyed and fascinated as the cast took their clothes off. Literally. *All* their clothes until they were standing in their birthday suits. I sunk back in my chair, wishing I was wearing an invisible cloak. I knew it was a vital part of the musical, but I felt like I was being caught watching some sort of soft porn and wondered if we would get in trouble for being there. If *that* was how brave I'd have to be to go to college, I wasn't sure I could follow through.

That stage though . . . I couldn't stop thinking about all the people who spent years on that gorgeous waxed floor, performing in countless university shows. Who was I to sit there thinking I could also do it?

But what if I could?

We had lunch at a cafeteria called The Atrium. The food there was better than I ever imagined the north wing food at our school could be; lobster bisque, fresh salad, ice-cold sweet tea. Definitely Grade A.

Sitting there surrounded by all those happy faces, I started to pretend like I was one of them. The feeling made me smile anyway. Maybe in the fall I'd stop here for a quick snack, go to my next class in one of those buildings, and take the bus down to my dorm where all my friends would be waiting to carpool over to the football game.

We took our trays and chose seats next to this huge window that was so clean, I felt like we were sitting outside.

"She's marrying Beau," I blurted.

Justin and Becca stopped chewing for a second.

I just couldn't hold it in anymore. The pressure and excitement all around me forced out what I was almost too ashamed to share with my best friends.

"And my dad is the crazy one. And I'm not allowed to be crazy? What kind of world do we live in where a girl can have three dads and *not* go crazy?"

"Sorry, Leah," Justin said.

There wasn't much more I could say. I looked around the spacious room, taking in the chatter of students who were headed in the right direction.

I could find my direction, too. Maybe Ball State was it.

One thing I knew for sure was that if I wanted to change anything in my life, I needed to start believing.

Chapter 13

Her long nose came to a point, perfect for the big, round glasses that rested two inches below her eyes.

The psychologist.

Exactly what I wanted to do during Spring Break.

As I spoke, she jotted stuff down into her really important notebook. I imagined she was doodling or making a grocery list as I answered her emotionless questions. Mostly my answer was "uh-huh." I'd been saying "uh-huh" a lot with this lady.

"And how is your relationship with him now?"

I wished she was asking about my dad, but the entire session had been about Beau and my unacceptable dislike for him. My mom had prepped her. She must have had this covered by insurance or it wouldn't have been worth it.

I couldn't persuade this lady into talking about what I actually wanted to talk about because my mom's agenda was what Dr. Schwarzkebaber was getting paid for.

Her straight red hair rested on her shoulders when she looked at me.

"Leah?" She adjusted her glasses. "How is your relationship with him now?"

Beau. Caught in the crossfire of my mom and my growing anger toward her. If I separated him from my mom or thought about him as an individual that I didn't have to see every day, I actually sort of liked him. He minded his own business, even slipping me a twenty once in a while when I wanted to take Gracie to the store or to a movie.

My mom had been friends with him for a long time before we moved into his house. He didn't seem bugged by the fact that we were sitting in his living room one day with nowhere else to go, never making us feel like a problem. Only when he was drinking . . . I didn't like him then.

"My relationship with him now is . . ." I examined the psychologist's white skin, realizing I wasn't the only one with a super-pale complexion. "Nonexistent."

"And how has it come to this? You mentioned you both got along in the beginning."

I rubbed my upper arm. Her attention trailed to my hand.

"Yeah, we did. He was a cool guy. Laid-back."

"What do you think happened?"

I thought about it, trying to pinpoint the exact moment, but there was no exact moment.

"Time."

Time always screwed everything up. It was only a matter of time before my mom got sick of whichever guy she was with.

Only a matter of time before I'd never see my friends again.

Only a matter of time before Braden would see I was a walking mess.

I missed talking to Hillman, who actually understood me unlike Dr. Schwarzkebaber or whatever her ridiculously impossible doctor name was.

Next she asked about my relationship with my mom. We talked about that for a while as I remembered the drive to the store when I picked out Braden's birthday card.

"Whose birthday?" my mom had asked.

"A friend." I watched the road. "He likes music."

"You should get him a CD."

"I'm sure he already has everything."

"Okay."

That was it about Braden. The next ten minutes were filled

with awkward silence, so I knew what was coming when we pulled into the drug store parking lot.

My mom slowly stopped the car and turned to me, though I didn't face her.

"You know, you can have your feelings about Beau because he's not your dad, but he's the only dad Gracie knows. You should be happy about that and you should want *me* to be happy."

I pressed my lips together, holding back the burn of tears that were long overdue.

I looked away and put my hand on the door handle. "I want you to be happy."

When I left the car, I shook my head, hoping the tears that fell over my cheeks would dry up in the wind.

I told this to Dr. Schwarzkebaber but she looked right past me. People who didn't listen got this blank look in their eyes, as if they were thinking about what to say next.

I rubbed my arm red, but couldn't switch to chewing my fingernails in front of this lady. Of all the days to forget my jacket. It was so cold in her office that my Dr Pepper was still cool.

"What are you doing there?" She pointed to my arm.

I looked down as if I didn't know what she was talking about. Maybe I should have just chewed my nails like a normal person.

"Oh," I said. "Nervous habit, I guess."

She jotted something into her notebook and continued with her string of questions.

Before our first official dress rehearsal, Braden drove me to Quick Stop to get coffee. As I was stirring sugar into my coffee, Braden explained to me some facts he had learned while writing a paper about Jeff Buckley and the Mississippi River.

He seemed so comfortable, so at ease when we were together, like he had known me forever, but doubt still snuck up on me. I couldn't understand how a guy like him could like a girl who was about to change her last name for the second time.

Was it selfish of me to sit there under The Tree, to give him attention, to show him through my gentle hand squeezes and playful nudges that I liked him, too?

I did though. I really, *really* liked him.

He was no longer Braden Gregory to me. He was Braden, a guy who loved music more than life and whose contagious laugh crippled any bad thoughts I had.

After everyone was in costume, we rehearsed the play as if it were show night.

One of my favorite scenes was in Act Two, when Helen was forced to be in the garden house with Anne Sullivan.

I walked on stage, embodying Helen as I groped around the set. Once Helen's mother and father left her alone with Anne, I began my wild tantrum of kicking furniture, ripping curtains off the window, screaming in frustration at the thought of Anne having the audacity to order me around.

Helen had gotten away with everything until Anne Sullivan was hired to teach her. I tried to connect with how upsetting that must have been for Helen, and how her outbursts expressed that bottled frustration.

As I knocked into the furniture and let out deep screams, I felt for a moment how helpless it was to not be able to express those emotions with words; to not be able to see or point at anyone to blame. All she could do was rebel and attack anything in her way.

As the light went down on Anne and Helen, it slowly raised on Captain Keller, Kate, and James in the house.

Braden transformed into Captain Keller while Scotty became James, only a more southern version.

"I can't understand it," Captain Keller said in his high and mighty voice. "I had every intention of dismissing that girl, not setting her up like an empress."

"Yes, what's her secret, sir?" James asked.

I watched from the dark, hoping Braden remembered all his lines this time.

"Secret?" Captain Keller asked.

"That enables her to get anything she wants out of you? When I can't."

As James turned to leave, Captain Keller grabbed his wrist.

Scotty's face morphed into anger, yet a subtle look of emotional pain crept into his expression.

Captain Keller shouted, "She does *not* get anything she—"

James yelped in pain while Kate, played by Riley, intervened to calm down Captain Keller.

"He's afraid," Captain Keller said, throwing James away from him. "What *does* he want out of me?"

"My God, don't you know?" James cried. "Everything you forgot when you forgot my mother."

At that, James transformed back into Scotty. The scene paused as Scotty turned away and pressed the back of his hand over his face.

I knew he had started to cry then, but we weren't supposed to break character.

The silence and Scotty's soft whimpers seemed to last forever in that moment. Nobody was allowed to help him. Nobody was allowed to be real. Worst of all, he had to suck it up, turn back around, and continue the scene.

I watched from the dark of that part of the stage. I smiled, proud of Scotty and knowing how strong he was for powering through it.

"Leah?" Braden touched my shoulder. "Everything all right?"

Everyone in the cast was packing away their things to go home after rehearsal. I sat thinking about Scotty.

"Leah?" Braden said again, sitting in the seat beside me.

I looked at him, not caring if he could see all the little red veins in my tired eyes.

"I was seeing Mr. Hillman," I said.

He raised his eyebrows. "That explains why he's been humming show tunes during class."

I tapped his hand and shook my head.

"No, you dork. I mean, I was seeing him. As my counselor."

"Well, he is a counselor. That's what he's there for."

"Braden . . . when I stopped by your house the other day, I wanted to think I was just checking up on you. I didn't want to think I was some girl who couldn't bear the thought of you being gone for so long. It was weird not having you here. I know I have Becca and Justin, but with you it's like I can breathe deep and everything will still be okay. I didn't want that to be over, not even for a few days."

I thought I would have this naked feeling after telling him that, but I didn't. Instead, I got the feeling that maybe he felt like the naked one by the way he slouched and grew quiet for a while.

"Come with me," he said, taking my hand.

The back door slammed. A gush of the evening wind rushed past us. The last of the cast members were leaving in their cars.

It was pretty dark for that time—the stars were already peeking through. Braden was still holding my hand when he stopped in front of The Tree. The thick leaves rustled in the wind. I remembered the way his hand felt over mine as we'd lay there looking at the night sky the other night, his touch warming my skin.

I squeezed my jacket cuffs when Braden knelt beside the trunk.

"You see this?" He pointed to my initials. "Trees can live for thousands of years. When you chop one, you can tell their age by how many rings you see on the inside. Even when we're gone, your name will live on as long as The Tree does."

He rose.

"I don't know why you can't see it, but you *are* awesome, Leah," he said. "You're Leah Roy. You can go to college. You can do anything you want, be anyone you want. So what if you see Hillman?" He pointed to the names in the trunk. "We all need someone to talk to. You think you're the only one who has something to feel ashamed about? You think you're the only one who feels worthless sometimes?"

I looked at Braden as he walked back to me, reading honesty in his eyes. He slowly reached for my hand and threaded his fingers through mine while I glanced over the initials—those hopeful dreamers who wanted the same out of life as I did.

Chapter 14

During down time at the next dress rehearsal, I sat in the back of the auditorium and worked on my college essay.

I was eleven years old. The sun hadn't come up yet, so I wasn't really sure what time it was. All I knew was how tired I was because all night I'd been staring at the ceiling.

My mom whispered for me to hurry up while my sister slept next to me. My mom held a bag containing the rest of our things—toothbrushes, soap and all that. While my dad was working late the night before, my mom and our neighbor had organized a rental truck and made enough sandwiches to get us through the drive.

I'd known about the plan for a few days. Sometimes I wished my mom had never told me. I was supposed to look at my dad and act like everything was okay, act like I wasn't about to break his heart. When he came home from work, I'd look at him with glazed eyes. He'd ask me what was wrong, and my mom would glare at me.

I didn't hurry that early morning. I just got out of bed and adjusted my pajamas, trying to go somewhere else in my mind, but the reality of that day clung to me.

My mom held my sleeping sister in her arms and signaled for me to be quiet as we walked out of the room. My dad had fallen asleep on the couch the night before. We walked past him, careful not to step on the part of the floor that creaked. He was sleeping on his stomach wearing black shorts and a dark-red shirt. I'll never forget that.

Sometimes, I would wonder what they were fighting about the times when I'd wake up to them yelling at each other. Did all parents do that?

There were things I didn't understand, things that were too big, too complicated for me to comprehend. All I knew was that my dad loved me the way I needed him to. Maybe he wasn't the best provider; maybe he didn't treat my mom right; maybe he really was sick. All I knew when I went to bed at night was that my dad's smile was honest.

Apparently, he wasn't honest though. He was too dangerous to live with, ready to fly off the handle at any moment. My mom tried to explain all that to me when I asked her why we were leaving. I didn't know that dad. All I knew was that his heart beat like mine, he bled red whenever he got hurt, he laughed when he was happy, and he cried when he was sad.

I thought about how when he woke up in a couple hours, he was going to be really sad, and it was all because of me.

I didn't get a say. Nobody asked me if it was okay. Would my voice have been heard anyway? Would we have stayed if I protested, if I cried, if I screamed and said, "I don't want to make anyone sad."?

My mom carefully turned the doorknob and led me out of the apartment. I turned around. She whispered for me to follow her, but I hurried back to my dad and stopped before the couch.

I wanted to wake him up. I wanted to scream and hug him and never let go, but I didn't do any of that. I didn't. I just looked at him... watched his breathing for a while.

I could hear the anger in my mom's loud whispers. God, I didn't want to go.

I looked at my mom who was holding my sister with one arm and motioning for me to come with the other.

I looked back at my dad and laid my small hand on his

back, watching it rise and fall. Warm tears slid down my cheeks, but I made no sound. I kept telling myself it was only temporary, but I had this sharp pang in my gut. I knew that pang. It was always right.

I didn't know how I did it. I'd never be able to explain the places I had to go in my mind to be able to turn and walk away from my dad, knowing it could be the last time I'd ever see him.

I did though.

Three potty breaks and ten hours later, we arrived in Tipton County.

The next morning, I waited for Braden at his locker, but he didn't show up to school.

At The Tree, I only talked to Scotty. Sara wasn't there and Rachelle was studying for a Chemistry test. I was glad most tests were over for the year. All we had left to worry about were the final exams in the last week of school and those were only for the students who scored a D or an F in any of their classes.

Scotty went on about how his mom had been trying to talk to him, but he refused to entertain her with one word. He had gotten in trouble for destroying the locker room, but his mom was able to negotiate his punishment with Principal McCoy. She loaded Scotty with yard work to pay the cost of repairing the lockers and he had to spend basketball practice repainting the locker room walls.

Before rehearsal, I attached my completed essay to the back of the college application and sealed the envelope. Justin drove me to the post office a couple blocks away. When I sent the envelope off, all I could do was trust that I had done the best I could.

Vulnerability... scarier than fear itself.

During the intermission break, Becca put on a fake mustache

and pretended to be Captain Keller. In her best Darth Vader voice, she said, "Leah, I am your father."

I shook my head and laughed.

"Not even close."

"Act Two, Scene One," Hillman shouted from a front-row seat.

We all scurried back to our spots. Tamara had to shout Braden's lines that evening. Hillman didn't like it when someone missed rehearsals this close to the opening show night, but I assured him that Braden had all his lines down.

We ran through the scenes. Hillman shouted, "Stop!" more times than he would have liked to. Mostly on Scotty.

"Try using your chest voice and lose the southern accent," he must have told Scotty about forty times over the course of the rehearsal. "I know the Kellers are from Alabama, but nobody will be able to understand *that* thick of an accent."

"You have any idea how much I've had to sing this week?" Scotty said at one point. "I'm giving you everything I've got."

With the *Aladdin* show weekend approaching, the wear and tear of theatre was starting to show in the choir kids. Even Rachelle gripped her fists a little too tight when Hillman called her out on missing one of her cues.

"Rachelle can take my spot for a while," I joked, glancing at Sara who had taken enough beatings from Helen that day.

During one of my scene breaks, I retreated behind the stage curtain and texted Braden.

5:04 p.m.

New Msg:

Hey, you okay?

5:06 p.m.

Msg From: Braden

hey leah

yeah.

felt a little crappy this morning so i just stayed home

miss anything good?

5:07 p.m.

New Msg:

Nope. Just some announcements about buying tickets for Aladdin before they sell out.

5:08 p.m.

Msg From: Braden

guess you better hurry

5:09 p.m.

New Msg:

Oh you think I'm going?

5:10 p.m.

Msg From: Braden

if you don't the Genie wont have any power

5:11 p.m.

New Msg:

Okay.

5:12 p.m.

Msg From: Braden

I can buy the ticket if you want.

5:13 p.m.

New Msg:

Shut up.

5:14 p.m.

Msg From: Braden

im still in bed btw ;)

Chapter 15

Justin, Becca, and I took a trip to Harold's Pharmacy downtown, just a short walk down the sidewalk from the salon. It was the oldest pharmacy in Tipton County. What made it special was that it also sold thrift clothes and cheap office supplies along with the best barbeque chicken in town. If you didn't know Harold's Pharmacy, they'd probably kick you out of Tipton County.

I loved the old glass door and how pictures of Tipton County from the early 1900s hung along the walls as we walked in. The place even had that old smell, until you got to the little kitchen that served barbeque chicken and homemade root beer floats.

Justin treated us to some food and then ordered us root beer floats. He followed behind as we walked through the small women's clothing section while I checked my phone for any texts.

"Gimme your phone," Becca said.

I jerked my phone away, almost knocking over a top-heavy rack of clothes.

"Screw you. Look at your own phone."

"You got dirty pictures in there or something? Geez, all you ever do is text."

"Even if I had dirty pictures, they would be for my eyes only."

She stepped over to me, nearly spilling her root beer float as she started rifling through her bag as if looking for something.

I didn't buy her act. "Stop it, Becca," I said, stifling a laugh. "I know you're up to something."

"What?" She leaned closer, holding out her root beer. "Grab this and finish it for me. My mom would kill me if I wasted food."

As I reached for the drink, she snatched the phone from my other hand.

"Hah!" she hollered. "Did you really think I wouldn't finish this delicious drink?" She flipped open my phone. "Braden. Ooooh, Braden. I knew it."

"Give it back."

I grabbed it from her. I had wanted to tell her everything, but Becca wasn't exactly a boyfriend kind of girl. She once jerked off a guy behind the bleachers as a favor to him. She was nice like that. He was a virgin and Becca was not, so a little handy was her way of showing him she liked him. When he asked her on a date after that, she never talked to him again.

She probably thought I was wasting my time with Braden.

"Are you two like an item or something?"

"No, I . . ." I didn't look at her. "I don't know."

"Then how come this is the first time I've seen you in, like, weeks."

"Please, it hasn't been weeks. Days maybe. I'm sorry. I just—"

"You like him," she said.

I bit my lip. I couldn't help it. I must have looked like a silly little girl gawking about her crush.

Becca sighed and looked away. Knowing her, I could imagine the thoughts probably running through her mind like "Get real, Leah" or "Braden? Seriously?"

Instead, she turned to me and rested her hand over my shoulder.

"Promise me this isn't going to ruin our plans for prom night."

"I promise," I said. "You, me, and Justin. Riding in on four wheelers wearing our super-duper camouflage suits."

"Then I think you should go for it," she said. "He seems like a decent guy and I like to see you this happy. You're less of a pain in the ass. Justin agrees."

"Never said that," Justin shouted from the aisle across, as he scanned through a small stack of used DVDs.

Becca laughed, then it got quiet again. I fiddled with my phone.

"What if it's all a joke?" I asked.

She gave me a side glance. "Oh please, Leah. This isn't the movie *She's All That*. You're already *all that*."

Thursday, April 9, 2009

Dear Robert,

I want to run sometimes. It would be my choice then. I would get to decide when it would be the last time I saw someone and I would actually get to say goodbye.

But then what?

Would all those judgmental parents prove right about me? Would I be searching forever and ever like my mom?

He makes my heart race like you said. When I'm around him I don't feel like myself. When he looks at me or touches my hand, I feel like every part of me is glowing.

I'm also terrified.

If I run from this now, I won't be the one left in the dust... but it feels too good to be with him.

Who would want to run from that?

Pen Pal Tina

When *Aladdin* premiered that Friday, I was the only one of my friends to go to the musical.

Braden graced the stage as Genie, singing with a slightly improved vibrato, I had to admit. Despite his faults here and there, he was still the most perfect Genie I had ever seen.

I knew then why Mr. Steele had cast him for that part. It wasn't because Mr. Steele was friends with his parents or because Braden was some musical prodigy. It was because he engaged the audience and filled the auditorium with his voice and charisma, pouring his personality into the character, bringing him to life like a vibrant soul dancing away all that was wrong in the world.

Once, I caught him glancing into the crowd. Breaking character was forbidden for me, but I guessed it was different for Braden. When it was his moment, it was *his*—nobody could take it away.

At first, I thought he was looking for me. I sat in the second row, last seat, wearing a dark-brown shirt which might have been difficult to spot under the blinding stage lights. I waved so he might see, but he continued searching the audience until his next line.

Watching Braden on stage did something to my stomach that I had never felt before. My body turned into a heater, boiling me from the inside out even when I took off my jacket. All those years we had been in school together and I never really noticed him. I had seen him, but never stopped to actually look at him, hear his inviting voice, or notice how his body sort of curled when he laughed.

Seeing him on stage magnified all those beautiful little details I had come to adore about him, especially how he could move so freely and own every second of his spotlight.

I watched him almost as if in a trance, captive under a gaze that gripped my entire body. I surrendered all excuses I could find to protect myself from the pain of loving someone. I wanted to run on stage. I wanted to run up there, wrap my arms around him, and hold him forever.

If I knew one thing for sure, it was that I fell in love with Braden Gregory at that very moment.

After the show, I stood in the background and watched him

from the corner of the lobby as the cast walked out for the meet and greet.

A lot of his friends nudged his shoulder and spoke a few words. I waited to see his parents, but as time went by, no one came.

Once the crowd dispersed, I couldn't hold my feet in place any longer. I walked right up to him and pulled him into a hug, actually feeling the strength of his body and how he also melted into me. I didn't want to let go, ever.

He invited me to the cast party with him, but I had promised Becca I'd hang out with her after the musical. I couldn't keep letting her down and I also needed to process what was going on with all of my emotions.

I held his hands, wishing him a good time at the cast party.

Braden Gregory - Most Likely To Break My Heart.

Soon the room looked empty enough for it to be acceptable to walk away, which is what Braden did after gently squeezing my hands.

I had never had sex before, so the thoughts taking over my mind were making me feel hot and fuzzy between my legs. All I could think about was stripping the clothes off his body and doing things I only ever saw in movies. I imagined him on top of me, licking me from my lips down to my breasts, touching me until I couldn't resist the urge to get on top of him. I wanted to know what he looked like naked, what he felt like, what he tasted like. God, I was losing my mind.

I started feeling guilty for not celebrating with him. He had worked hard on his role and he deserved to have a memorable night. If that night turned into what I saw in the movies, then I was ready for it. *All* of it.

After the meet and greet, I stepped outside and texted Becca that I was going to be a little late.

Just a little late.

Maybe a lot.

She would understand.

The cast party was in one of those big houses behind the high school. A lot of students were still walking there after the meet and greet. I had forgotten which popular kid lived there since there was often talk of parties at that house. I could just walk past the tennis courts, across the baseball field, and be in Tipton County's very own Beverly Hills.

I waited until most of the cast had left the school so I didn't look like the nerd who showed up early.

It was easy to find the party because it was the only house with every single light still on at that time of night—a giant box of a house with a mini box right next to it called the pool house. That pool house was damn near the size of Beau's entire house.

Loud music blasted through the front door as choir kids poured out, laughing with giant red cups in their hands. I decided to take the shadowy walkway between the house and pool house instead.

People jumped half-naked into the wavy, oval-shaped pool while others clustered around the massive back patio playing beer pong, dancing, and some even sloppily singing songs from *Beauty and the Beast*.

"Leah!" Scotty shouted from the other side of the pool.

He stood with a few other guys wearing Letterman jackets while Scotty was still shirtless and in his Aladdin pants.

I gave him a small wave, hoping nobody noticed me standing there looking as awkward and out of place as I felt.

"Hey, where's your queer friend?" some guy shouted from across the pool.

Hoping I'd heard him wrong, I tried to ignore the guy pointing in my direction and laughing.

"Tell him I wanna give him a big, wet smooch!" he said.

More laughing ensued. Giving in to people like that would have only given them what they wanted. Attention.

When I turned around, I spotted Rachelle—still dressed as

Princess Jasmine—leaning against the side of the house, burning me with her eyes. She chatted with someone before turning her attention back to me again. I wished I knew what her problem was, but I hadn't done anything to her. Not that I knew of anyway.

"Hey," I said, approaching her and her ever-so-glad-to-see-me glare.

"Looking for Braden?" she asked.

"He said he'd be here."

"Sorry. Out of luck. He doesn't come to these things anymore."

"Skip out on *this*?" I motioned to the backyard where nearly naked jocks ran and belly flopped into the pool. I couldn't say I was surprised about naked jocks and underage drinking, but I also couldn't imagine that being Braden's scene.

"He hasn't been to a party all year."

All year?

Maybe it wasn't his scene, but surely he'd at least show up for a while.

It grew awkward standing there with her. I could have cut the tension with a knife though I still didn't understand why she was so short with me.

From across the pool, I thought I heard a faint voice ask, "Is that unicorn girl?"

I stopped breathing for a moment. My heart thumped up to my ears.

Then I heard Scotty's loud voice calling him a "homophobe" and telling him to knock it off or he'd stick a uni "corn" up the guy's ass.

Before Scotty could make his way over to me, I threw out some lame excuse about needing to get home, and then took off before anyone noticed the old paint stain on my jeans or the hole in my jacket.

10:45 p.m.

New Msg:

You home?

10:47 p.m.

Msg From: Braden

hey leah.

at cast party.

this place is killer.

10:48 p.m.

New Msg:

. . .

You're at the cast party?

10:50 p.m.

Msg From: Braden

yup

booty call?

10:51 p.m.

New Msg:

You wish.

10:54 p.m.

Msg From: Braden

it could work.

trevor and my parents are at the cabin tonight.

10:56 p.m.

New Msg:

You're such a dork.

btw didn't they know you had a musical tonight?

10:59 p.m.

Msg From: Braden

ill pick you up in ten minutes

"Ugh, it bugs me when she does this." I slammed the door to Braden's van. "It'll be like this all night long. She's crazy. The woman is crazy."

My mom had come home with a bunch of her friends at the same time as I'd made it home after the cast party.

The music was still booming from my house as Braden backed out of my driveway.

"What's happening in there?" he asked. "Looks like a rave."

"She's throwing a party with all her friends. They'll get wasted until they finally drop at four in the morning. I just wanted to sit in my room, listen to music or something, but do you think she asks me what I want? No. Never. She rules my life."

"I wish my parents would host raves."

"I wish she'd at least warn me. It starts off with a couple card games, but after the alcohol kicks in they get obnoxious, and start banging on my door, wanting me to come out and dance with them."

"Did you tell your mom you were bailing out?"

"Do you think she would notice?" I jammed my seat belt into the buckle.

Braden looked ahead, focusing on the street as he drove.

"I wish she'd acknowledge that it's my life, too, not just hers. She could've at least asked me how I felt about her getting married again. I mean, that's huge."

"Wait, your mom is getting married?"

I put my fingers to my temple. I hadn't told him, too embarrassed.

"I'd rather live in a ditch than change my last name again." I glared out the window, barely noticing the cars passing from the other lane. "I'm eighteen, so maybe I won't even have to."

It grew quiet and we were soon at Braden's house.

My phone buzzed in my pocket when we got inside. I expected a text back from Becca, but it was my mom calling.

"Gosh, it's her. She's probably drunk."

Braden walked over to me.

"You going to answer?"

"There's no talking to her when she's like that."

I waited for the buzzing to stop, then I opened my phone to a glowing screen of unread texts.

> 11:24 p.m.
>
> Msg From: Mom
>
> get ur ass home
>
> where ru
>
> u cant just be happy for me
>
> come dance

I was surprised she could even spell.

"You okay?" Braden asked.

"I have to be. It's the only way I can keep going."

"Well . . ." He headed to the record player. "Not the *only* way."

My phone buzzed again, so I threw it onto the chair.

Braden put on a record from a band I had never heard of.

"School is in session. Intro to Simon and Garfunkel. Feast your ears on one of the greatest duos of all time."

As soon as "The Sound of Silence" began, I vowed to believe everything Braden would ever tell me about music.

"That's so beautiful," I said.

He then went on to tell me about their history, switching to different songs. His eyes lit up at the parts he liked. When he tried to sing like them, I told him he should always sing in his falsetto.

I really did like his falsetto.

Then he switched the record to The Beatles.

"You know 'Help', right?" he asked.

"I never really listened to them much until you made me that CD. I like them. Old-school rock and roll before the hair metal."

Braden began singing a few lines before going over to the piano.

"No way," I said. "You can play this song, too?"

He sang along while hitting the keys. I couldn't tell whether he was playing right or not, but it blended well with the music.

"Crank it," he said.

I turned up the volume on some sort of amplifier and let my hand trickle over the record player.

I accidentally tapped the needle, skipping into the next song.

"I know this one!" I shouted over the music.

Braden played while I sang along to "Hey Jude."

My body swayed to the rhythm. I unzipped my jacket and tossed it onto the chair, leaving me in my old white shirt. I gently shut my eyes and tilted my head back, letting my arms rise into the air. Somehow liberated by the music, I was the kind of person I had always wanted to be.

I sang louder, dancing faster as the music heightened. Braden stopped playing and stood up to sing with me. He joined me in a dance that I wasn't even sure could pass as dancing—it was fun anyway. We both sang loud with Paul McCartney, feeling like The Beatles ourselves.

Before I knew it, Braden pulled me toward him. His hands traveled down my back, wrapping around my waist. I didn't have a chance to get nervous under his touch, so when his face came forward, my eyes closed. I then felt the warmth of his lips against mine. The moment could have lasted one second or it could have been an eternity. I wasn't certain. All I knew was that I never wanted it to end.

It didn't matter that he came from money or had a great house or all these popular friends in school. Nor did it matter that I barely had money for lunch or new clothes. We were just people, two people who connected, who understood each other, who might have actually loved each other.

When he parted from me, I opened my eyes to the deep-green ones staring into my world. He smiled and I giggled back. He pressed his lips against mine again, my breasts pressing into him as he pulled me closer. He lifted my hand in the air, folding his fingers into mine while together we swayed to the music—all the while our lips never parted.

Just then, a light hit the corner of my eye.

A light beamed through the front window and Braden turned his head in that direction. He hesitantly parted from me and then hurried to the record player. Within seconds, everything was quiet other than the car pulling into his driveway.

"Shit, it's my dad." Braden closed the curtains. "Come on."

He grabbed my hand and rushed me into his room.

"Stay in here," he said, switching his light off. "Don't come out till I get back."

My chest pounded.

"I thought you said they were at the cabin? How will I get out of here?"

Braden glanced between me and his bedroom door.

"I . . . I don't know. Just wait a minute."

He left the room.

I hadn't realized how much my knees were shaking, nor how much I enjoyed the rush of excitement until that moment. I hid out of sight next to Braden's bed, trying to hone in on any conversation, but I could barely hear.

If worse came to worst, I could just hop out the window, run down to the hotel, and ask for a room. The receptionist was cool. My mom would end up making me work to pay for it though, but it beat getting Braden into trouble.

The loud words being exchanged were hard to make out.

"Why didn't you tell us it was tonight?"

"You've had my schedule all year."

"The dates . . ."

There was more heavy mumbling.

"Next time, young man."

"There won't be a next time."

The back door slammed.

I heard footsteps outside, then nothing more.

After a minute, I got up and tiptoed to the door.

I shrieked when Braden surprised me in the doorway. "What's going on?"

"Just my dad," he said. "They needed more of Trevor's insulin or something. He never takes enough. I don't know, I keep telling my mom to stop putting him in charge of it."

"You okay?" I asked, reading the defeat in his face.

"Yeah . . . totally killed the moment though, huh?"

I felt my cheeks filling with heat. "Kind of."

We stood there in the doorway. Braden looked around while I glanced at my feet.

"Want to listen to another record?" he asked.

I followed him back into the front room, smelling the leftover scent of his dad—a mixture of oil and chalk, or whatever garages smelled like.

On the chair, I noticed my phone buzzing again, so I picked it up. Before I resisted again, my finger opened the call and clicked the speaker button.

"What, Mom?"

"Where are you?" she asked in her best slurry attempt at a complete sentence.

"I'm with a friend."

"You need to get your ass home. There are people here celebrating our engagement and my own daughter is too good to be with them."

I looked at Braden whose phone was also buzzing. He motioned to it before picking it up.

"I'm not coming home now. I'm with someone," I told her.

"Get your ass home."

"No. I'll be home later."

"Get your ass—" I shut the phone, feeling the snap to the core of my bones.

Crazy, huh. I must be the crazy one. Well, maybe crazy is okay.

I heard Braden on the phone.

"Where are you guys?"

There was loud babbling from the other end.

"Okay, stay there. I'll be there in five minutes."

"Don't tell me it's your mom, too?" I said.

"Not exactly."

The main street glowed in the old yellow-orange light from the streetlamps as we neared the gas station next to Taco Bell. The only places open at that time of night were Walmart and Taco Bell —the two coolest hangouts for anyone with a bedtime after ten o'clock.

I spotted Princess Jasmine twirling under the gas station sign. Aladdin bowed to the cars that honked as they drove by. I couldn't help but let out my laughter as we drove up beside them. Scotty was pretending to roll out the magic carpet until he saw us. He pointed. Rachelle looked and they both laughed.

Braden rolled down the window and motioned for them to get in.

I looked at him.

"Yup," he said. "The aftermath of Smirnoff. If you don't watch them, they end up like loose animals flying around town on their magic carpet."

Scotty threw the back door open and shouted, "Braden!" He paused when he looked at me. "Leah?"

"Hey, Scotty," I said.

Rachelle slid into the back seat. To my surprise, she leaned forward and grabbed me in a hug.

"I love you guys," she said.

She squeezed me so tight, I thought my eyes were going to pop.

Scotty slammed the door.

"Took you long enough," he said, leaning forward. "We didn't know if you were gonna show up. I was about to run back to the party and pick up my new ride, but I'm too fucked up to drive."

"It's literally been five minutes, Scott," Braden said.

"You didn't show up tonight, dude. Everyone was asking about you. It's not the same doing quartet parodies without you. And Leah took off faster than I could blink."

I looked at Braden. He glanced at me, then looked away. I had known something was off, but hoped he would be the first to tell me.

"You said you were at the cast party," I said softly. "You weren't. I went to surprise you."

He was quiet.

"You missed it, man," Scotty said. "Right in the middle of the party, Mr. Steele showed up for like twenty minutes or somethin'. When his car pulled up, we threw all the beers and booze into the closet. I kept guard. Everyone was tryin' to keep a straight face and walk in a straight line till he left. Pretty sure he knew we were hammered."

Rachelle leaned forward. "What're you guys doing out?"

I could smell the alcohol in her breath.

"My mom's having a party at home," I said.

"What's wrong with you guys?" Scotty asked. "We've got dud number one skipping out on cast parties and dud number two skipping out on her own house party. Y'all are losin' it."

"I have an idea," Rachelle said. "I say we go to Leah's house and crash their party. It's about time we throw our own cast party. You guys in?"

"It's my mom's engagement party," I said. "I'm kind of pissed about it."

"More of a reason to crash it," Rachelle said. "Seriously, it's senior freaking year. Time to let loose."

The thought of all of them seeing the inside of my house, smelling all the cigarette smoke, knowing I didn't live in Tipton County's Beverly Hills made me think twice. Then I looked at Braden. His eyes lit up when he cracked a smile. He didn't live in Beverly Hills either.

"Oh! My! God!" one of my mom's friends shouted as she opened my front door. "Looks like somebody called a PARTY GRAM!"

She pulled Scotty and Rachelle inside. The music boomed so loud, I could barely hear Braden next to me as we walked in.

"Add some black lights and glow sticks and it could be a rave," he said with a grin.

There must have been at least twenty people in that small room. My mom hurried over to me, smiling, no sign that her anger had ever existed. She thanked me for finally showing up.

"And with strippers!" she cheered.

She ran over to the computer and selected a new song.

"This one's for you, Leah!" she shouted before clicking play.

"More Than a Feeling" by Boston. My favorite song by them.

She grabbed Rachelle, admiring her costume and stage

makeup. Rachelle jumped right into a dance with my mom and Scotty, while some of my mom's friends joined in.

I peeked over the bar and saw Beau at the kitchen table with the only other two men at the party—they each had a beer and were playing cards. Beau waved to me.

I mouthed "Gracie?" to him. He mouthed, "At a friend's."

I nodded and turned to Braden.

"Guess this would be a good time to give you back your Chaplin hat," I said.

Braden looked away. "Uhh . . ." he said, "maybe not this second."

When I looked back, Scotty was standing on the coffee table, belly dancing for a bunch of hollering women. One of my mom's friends rolled up a dollar bill and placed it behind the band of his Aladdin pants. Rachelle danced in a circle with my mom and some other women, starting a train around Scotty.

"And you wanted to miss this?" Braden asked.

I laughed with him. We watched as the attention went straight to Scotty's head, turning him into Shakira on steroids.

I glanced up to the loose ceiling fan that was wildly spinning around. My head was light. Weight left my shoulders and disappeared into the fan above.

Braden lifted my hand into his.

"Where did we leave off?" he asked.

He pulled me closer until my body was gently pressed against his. We danced through the song, even as the train of hollering women blasted past us.

"Boston is my favorite band," I said into his ear.

"What?"

"You asked me once what my favorite band was." My head rested on his shoulder. My hand in his. "It's Boston."

Chapter 16

Our final dress rehearsal came.

Curtains closed. Lights down. The cast and crew gathered in their positions backstage. Actors in the opening scene, including Braden, took their places on stage. Everything was dark and quiet, except for Hillman in the empty audience shouting, "Lights up!"

Curtains opened on cue as the light guys turned on the spotlight.

We went through the first play rehearsal without much mess up. Hillman only had to call out lines to a couple people, Rachelle being one of them. She had missed her cue and I heard her cuss under her breath.

I preferred drunken Rachelle.

I was proud of Braden for getting all his lines down despite his absences. Scotty blasted through his, too. All that extra time he had proved helpful.

During the kitchen table fight scene, I eased up on Sara. I could sense her gratitude in the gentle way she delivered her lines.

Perhaps there was something to the whole "opposites attract" thing. If I'd had the life I wanted, then maybe Braden and I wouldn't have been together. I might have blended in and he would have never noticed the girl wearing the unicorn shirt.

During intermission break, Braden surprised me by pulling me behind the stage curtain. He wrapped the large, heavy material around us until no light broke through and all I could hear and smell were his sweet breaths. I giggled against him until he paused. I felt him looking into my eyes.

His fingers trickled their way from my hairline down to my chin where he lifted my face to his. Slowly, his lips touched mine. His hand cupped my cheek, the other wrapped around my waist, pulling me closer. My body melted into his and I savored his taste on my tongue, wishing it would never fade away.

Stage fright. Gone forever.

After rehearsal, Becca could hardly get a word out of me. Braden invaded my mind, my conversations, my time.

She stopped me on our way to the parking lot. Braden was ahead of us, talking to Scotty.

"I know you like him, Leah, but don't forget what happened after you fell for Matt," she said. "He broke your heart."

I tried to change the subject, but she kept giving me that concerned look.

"Matt was gay," I told her. "Braden is . . . *totally* not gay."

When the first show night came, Justin offered to drive me, but I told him I'd catch a ride with Braden. Gracie had finished drilling me on my scenes after I promised her five bucks if she'd follow me around the house saying my cue lines.

Before Braden arrived, my mom was applying some makeup in the bathroom. It reminded me of when I was a little girl, watching her do her makeup before she went out. She used to keep the basket under the bathroom sink and I'd go through it once in a while, wondering if I'd be as pretty as her when I grew up.

"Hey." She rubbed in some foundation. "Ready for tonight?"

I leaned against the doorway, watching as she dipped her finger into the concealer.

Since the party, she had been extra nice to me. It was as if my presence at the party made her feel more connected to me. Was my support always that important to her? If so, would I have tried harder to show her that I cared?

"If ready is being nervous as hell, then yeah, I'm good to go," I said.

"I've barely seen you the last few weeks. When I did, you had your head in that script. I don't know how you do it, but you have a lot of drive. Must be in your blood."

I looked at her as she went on, soaking up a rare moment when I actually felt noticed by her.

"We're going to get there a little early so we don't miss the good seats. Beau is bringing the camera. I'll try to record as much as I can before the batteries die on us. Crappy thing. I'm hinting to Beau to get me a new camera for my birthday." She winked. "I'll use the old one for the rest of the show if there's enough storage space."

Beau was wearing his only nice shirt. He wished me luck as I passed him on my way to the front door. Gracie gave me a hug and sent me off.

Braden was parked in my driveway and looked up when he saw me coming.

"Hey," I said, hopping in the passenger seat. I closed the door and buckled my seat belt. "I know I'm supposed to be, like, completely nervous, but I'm starting to feel a normal kind of nervous."

He backed out of my driveway. "Well, you've got me beat."

"How?"

"I need to stop home and deal with something."

His phone flashed in one of the front cup holders.

I rolled up my sleeves. It was a hot day, so I turned up the air conditioning and turned to Braden. I noticed his forehead had broken out in a sweat and a subtle look of dread passed through his face.

"My parents are coming." He sighed.

As he drove, the wind blew in through the half-open windows, cooling my face faster than the air conditioning. I glanced between Braden and the road in front of us.

"That's a good thing," I said. "You want your parents to be there, don't you?"

He was silent. His face drained with worry. I could tell his thoughts were overpowering any words he might have wanted to say, any words he might have wanted to believe.

When we reached his house a few silent minutes later, he slid out of the van in a nervous rush. I didn't know whether to stay or follow him to the back door. I eventually got out of the van and immediately heard shouting from inside.

I had never heard Braden shout before. It wasn't a pleasant sound. It carried a sort of brokenness, as if he were pleading for something on the verge of tears.

I walked around the side of the house to the back door. The shouting continued.

"You told us different," his dad yelled, his voice even more broken than Braden's.

I saw them through the back screen door. Braden's face was red, and his hands were thrusting in the air as he yelled for his parents to just listen to him.

In between shouting, his mom intervened with "now calm down" and "listen to your father."

When Braden's dad got in his face, I rushed to the back door and jerked it open.

Everyone stopped and looked at me. Before his parents could say anything, Braden hurried over to me, grabbed my arm and led me away. He said nothing else to his parents and nothing more to me other than, "Let's get out of here."

My mind wandered to many different possibilities, including the horrible thought that his parents didn't care about his play. I struggled to find the words to say on the way to the high school. Braden was lost in his thoughts, letting out a long sigh every couple minutes.

"You did amazing on this show, Braden," I reminded him, hoping it would release a smile from him. It didn't.

When we arrived backstage, I got my costume on in the girls' dressing room and slipped on my black flats while the rest of the girls scurried around me, pushing their way toward the mirror to put on their makeup.

I tried piecing together the bits of yelling that I'd heard at Braden's house, but it didn't make sense. All the while, I couldn't forget the sound of Braden's voice as he practically begged them to listen to him.

I teased my hair a bit and applied some foundation about five times darker than my actual skin tone, before adding some eyeliner and blush.

When I looked in the mirror, mixed emotions churned inside me. I found it difficult to concentrate when all I could think about was Braden, worried and wishing he would stay strong throughout the show.

How could they do that, suck away his energy knowing he needed it tonight?

I met Braden in the hallway. He stepped out of the boys' dressing room in his striking Captain Keller suit. No bow tie.

"Braden." Hillman stopped us as he made his rounds. He motioned to Braden's face. "What's going on here?"

"What?" Braden asked with an innocent tone. "I just finished it."

"Your makeup is way too light. The audience will never be able to see that. They'll think you're the youngest father of the 1800s." Hillman turned to me before heading off. "Please double his age."

I tugged Braden's hand and pulled him into the boys' dressing room, which was nearly empty of cast. Boys seemed less particular about makeup.

I pulled the box of stage makeup forward and got to work. He needed a darker coat of foundation and a little eyeliner. The hard part was drawing in the wrinkles.

"Why was your dad so mad?" I tried asking him, but he kept making a bunch of silly faces while I filled in his creases with eyeshadow.

"Knock it off," I said, giggling inches from his face.

He made the tightest frown so I could work around his mouth, but I could barely stop laughing.

"Braden, I'm trying to concentrate."

Even though he tried to make fun, there was unsteadiness in his deep breaths, and the way his gaze wandered when we were done.

Hillman shouted that the lights were going down in the audience, which meant we had to get backstage fast.

Cast members hurried to finish whatever last-minute touches they needed. Some wished good luck to whoever they passed by on their way backstage.

Out there, the chatter from the audience was dying down. Backstage, the cast and crew scurried around, whispering loudly for everyone to take their places.

Braden was in the opening scene, so he had to get out there. Before he left, he turned to me.

"I know it's killing you because I look so strikingly sexy, but I can't kiss you yet," he said. "I'm a method actor."

I smirked and poked his side. He wrapped his hands over my upper arms and rested his forehead against mine.

"You're the most talented person I know," he whispered to me. "This is your night, Leah."

He parted from me and smiled. I watched him walk onto the stage; each step he took transformed him into Captain Keller.

Before my first scene came, I remembered how nervous I was during auditions, how badly I wanted the part.

My moment had finally come. I walked onto the stage. When the lights came up, it was as if my stage fright had never existed.

In my first scene, Helen wrestled a maid to the floor and grabbed the scissors from her hands. It was more work for me to be the angry, frustrated Helen because my own anger and frustration had faded over time.

After the scene, I glanced at Braden backstage; gratitude simmered inside of me. When the show would be over, I knew I could let go of Helen, therefore letting go of an old part of me. I could enter a new chapter of my life, a fresher, healthier Leah, and I couldn't help but credit Braden for that.

As the play progressed, I stood backstage and watched a scene between Braden and Sara—the scene Hillman had auditioned Braden and I together with. Somehow, Sara's blinding smile didn't send my fingers curling into a fist anymore. I still felt a hint of jealousy when I saw them together, but something told me that she could smile all she wanted and the only thing Braden would see was me.

I watched Braden through his next scene. He'd sometimes look into the audience, not caring that he wasn't supposed to do that. He was Braden. He could do anything he wanted, and I loved that about him. I noticed that his demeanor had changed. He wasn't as lively on stage as he had been during rehearsals. Something faded in his stage presence and his line delivery was as weighty as his cautious movements, like he was using the last ounce of energy he had to get through the scenes.

When the lights came up on me again, I suddenly knew why Braden had broken character during *Aladdin*.

He was looking for his family.

I knew that because it didn't take me long to spot my mom, Beau, and Gracie in the front row. I was supposed to be blind, so technically it wasn't breaking character if my eyes fell over the audience. My mom had the camera up, the red recording light flashing.

I wondered about Braden's reaction from earlier, why his family coming tonight had made him so upset.

I soaked up every ounce of frustration I had left in me and poured it into the kitchen table fight scene. My hands left red marks on Sara's cheeks and I guessed she had been practicing her slapping when she returned them to me. Her muscles must have embodied whatever frustration she had been hiding behind that perfect smile.

My, how the tables have turned.

I would never forget the breakthrough moment in the play.

My body filled with a rush as Sara smacked the sign language into my palm, shouting, "Yes!"

I thrusted my hands into the water pouring from the water pump. I heard the "oohs" and "ahhs" from the audience as I spoke Helen's famous first words, "Wah. Wah."

My body burned.

My heart raced.

Two months of practice and preparation came down to one moment.

I emerged from the four walls that used to confine me, returning the sign language to Sara's palm, spelling out the word "water".

Sara shouted as I imagined the real Anne Sullivan had.

"She knows!"

I fluttered my eyes wildly around, moving my hands as if everything I touched could be scalding hot. Though I pretended to be blind, I could see and feel everything.

The color shined in everything I looked at. I could see the lines in the wood all over the set we had built, the chipped paint on the green water pump. My eyes burned under the bright stage lights.

I saw my mom in the audience.

I saw her smile.

Roars of approval erupted from the room in the form of whistling and clapping.

Helen Keller, I hope I made you proud.

My mom wasn't much of a hugger, but at the meet and greet, she gave me such a squeeze it made me moan.

I took pictures with some cast members and their families. Even Sara's mom slipped over to me.

"You're a natural," she said with a smile even brighter than Sara's.

Becca's mom was there, too, walking through the crowd as Becca's dad followed behind, speaking something in Vietnamese. Becca hugged them both, her face gleaming with joy.

Gracie clung to me and asked me how I did my makeup, while one of her friends asked me if I really was blind.

After a while, my mom found me again.

"Hey, we're heading out," she said. Beau stood beside her with his hands in his pockets. "We're going to Applebee's. You coming with?"

Going out with my family on a night like this was much different than other times. On the rare occasions when we went out to celebrate, I knew there wouldn't be any drinking or yelling. As much as I wanted to go with them this time, I glanced over my shoulder to Braden who was talking with his parents.

Before I answered, Hillman popped in and quickly introduced himself.

"You've got a talented one here," he said.

My mom and Beau both looked at me, smiling.

"Leah's always had a lot of drive," she said.

"Well, you must be very proud."

"We sure are," she said, nodding.

I felt my belly fill with butterflies.

Hillman congratulated me and made his rounds to other parents.

"The cast party's tonight," I said to my mom and Beau over the chatter. "I probably won't be home until much later."

"Is that hottie from our party giving you a ride?" my mom asked.

"Are you talking about Shakira Scotty or Braden?"

"That one." She pointed to Braden who was walking through the crowd of people.

He was alone, forcing a smile as some cast members patted his back.

I soon retreated to the dressing room and changed out of my costume, wiped off my stage makeup, and chatted with Becca and Justin before they left for the cast party at Riley's house.

Hillman congratulated me again and told me what a joy I had been to work with the past four years. I was so wrapped up in the show that I hadn't fully processed the fact that it was my last high school play. I didn't want to think that any moment could possibly be my last walk down the dressing room hallway.

I knocked on the boys' dressing room. Most of the cast had left for the party. Braden was supposed to be my ride there, but I couldn't find him.

I called his number, but it went straight to voicemail.

I searched the auditorium and backstage with no luck, asking if anyone had seen him. A crew member mentioned he had left by the back door a while before.

The night breeze sent a chill down my spine as I let the back door close. I rubbed my arms and looked around.

I figured he'd be by The Tree, but no one was there.

Moisture filled the air. I looked up to a few dark clouds.

I trailed the sidewalk next to the north wing leading to the main parking lot. It was drizzling. A few families were walking to their vehicles from the auditorium, noticing me and quickly congratulating me on a great show before the rain picked up. I blushed, thankful they couldn't see how worried I must have looked under the night sky.

I checked behind me to see if he was in the small crowd walking to their vehicles.

No Braden.

When I spotted his purple minivan, I let out a sigh of relief.

I didn't see anybody inside when I approached. I opened the passenger door, but he wasn't in either front seat. It wasn't until I slid open the side door that I noticed his feet on the back seat.

"Hey, you asleep?" I asked.

He didn't move.

"I hope you weren't waiting too long. Thought you were still inside."

No answer.

"Braden?" I asked, leaning forward. "Is this about your parents?"

When he didn't respond, I shook my head, ignoring the pang in the pit of my stomach. I kneeled on the middle seat and looked over.

"Braden, wake up." When I nudged him, his copy of Dr. Seuss' *Mulberry Street* slid off his chest.

He didn't move. When I turned his face toward me, my heart stopped. A freezing cold shook my body when I saw the white foam plastered on the side of his mouth.

I don't remember much after that because it all happened in quick scenes.

My scream.

My calling for help.

People running toward me.

The dark of the night. The ambulance sirens and bright colors.

Strangers from the parking lot comforting me. Braden being pulled from the van by paramedics.

I heard, "There's a pulse!"

All I remembered thinking about was *Mulberry Street*, clutching it to my chest so nobody would take it away.

friday, april 17, 2009

"We are afraid to care too much, for fear that the other person does not care at all." Eleanor Roosevelt

other peoples thoughts and judgements only have power when you give them significance.

you want to change your life. you want to do wonderful things.

don't let anyone distract you from your goal tina.

we all want to run from something.

robert

I walked to the hospital after the ambulance had taken Braden. Took me thirty minutes, but I would have walked all night if I had to.

It rained. A lot.

I was soaking by the time I showed up. The staff told me his parents weren't allowing any visitors.

I called Scotty from the waiting room. He was the first person I could think to talk to. I didn't want to embarrass Braden by telling anyone else, especially not knowing what had happened.

Scotty showed up like a lion about to attack his prey, blasting through the hallway in a heavy run.

"Let me see him!" he shouted.

Hospital security ran after him; a few ran forward to catch him. They were able to hold him against the ground long enough for him to calm down, threatening to call the police if he didn't stop.

"That's my best friend!" Scotty repeated.

I started to cry as I ran over to him. I didn't care if anyone was looking. I cried and tried ignoring the pleading way with which Scotty begged to see Braden.

"Scotty," I said, leaning down on the floor with him.

One security officer was kneeling on Scotty's back while the other held his arms down.

"They'll let us see him eventually. Come sit with me. Please."

After a few minutes of back and forth, trying to convince him not to knock out the officers, he stood up in a calm manner and followed me to the waiting room. But, of course, not before he lunged forward at the officers, causing them to jump back in a quick scare.

"What happened?" he asked me, still breathing heavily. "You found him in his van? Was he awake? Were you able to talk to him?"

All these questions were answered by a simple, "He was sleeping." That was all I knew and all I wanted to believe. He was just sleeping and needed some help waking up.

We waited. And waited. I asked the receptionist countless times if we were allowed to see him, but all she told us was that his parents still didn't want visitors.

Scotty offered to drive me home and I accepted. We promised to give the other an update as soon as we heard anything.

Blisters covered my heels when I got home and peeled off my wet shoes. I didn't tell my mom or Gracie what had happened. They didn't ask. They probably assumed I'd been at the cast party all night.

I just wanted the night to be different. I wished Braden would have sat up and read *Mulberry Street* to me. We could have left that night and driven all the way to Alabama if he wanted. It wouldn't have mattered where we went or what we did. Anything but *that*.

I'd sent Braden countless texts—all went unanswered.

The next day, Scotty called me with Rachelle on the other line. Rachelle, who was close enough with the family to hear things, gave news that Braden was better. He would spend another day in the ICU before they released him. Due to the incident, Hillman thought it would be best to cancel our final show. I couldn't have performed anyway.

I could barely focus on school that week. Sitting in class was like sitting under water, listening to mumbles and feeling like I could just sink to the bottom.

Becca and Justin wanted to hang out, but I blew them off for the safety of my closet. I lay there after school, staring up at the ceiling with the CD playing, wondering if Braden was doing the same thing.

Monday, April 20, 2009
Dear Robert,
He is significant. His opinions, ideas, thoughts, words, feelings are all significant. I can't imagine a world without him.

He scared me recently. I thought the absolute worst. He's okay though. I hope. Not just for me, but for all the people who love him.

If I go to Ball State, say I do, what would that do to him if he chooses a different college or doesn't go at all? What would it do to me? The thought of being without him is terrifying. I want to spend every second with him. I want every moment we are together to last forever.

Even when it seems like my world is crashing down, thinking about him makes my world a little more livable.

Is this normal, Robert?
Or is this all just craziness?
Pen Pal Tina

It was a Thursday morning. I thought he would be back sooner, but he'd been gone almost two weeks. There had to have been something nobody was telling me.

"Braden!" I shouted when I saw him at his locker.

He turned around, a huge smile forming on his face as I ran toward him. He opened his arms and took me in with a tight squeeze.

"Leah," he said into my ear.

I held on to him. He felt thin and fragile.

"You didn't answer my texts. I called a million times."

When I pulled away, I could almost see tears glazing his eyes. He looked like he hadn't slept in days.

"You lost weight." I scanned his body with my hands on his shoulders.

He just stared at me.

"What happened?" I asked. "I tried to be there. I argued with the nurses. Scotty almost got arrested. What's going on? Why didn't you call back?"

"Yeah, sorry about that. My parents took my phone."

"Why?"

"Because I didn't tell them I stopped taking my pills."

I couldn't take my eyes off him. "What pills?"

The first bell rang. Students scurried around us.

He took his time grabbing a couple more books.

"Braden, are you diabetic like your brother or something? You have to tell me what happened."

Maybe I sounded like a moron. I didn't know anything about diabetes, but I had to ask.

He paused and looked down. His expression deepened when he turned to me.

"It's no big deal. I just sort of had a bad reaction when I started taking them again."

"What did the doctors say?"

He glanced around the hallway of moving students. "That everything's okay and not to worry."

His eyes fell back on me. I could tell from his expression that he wanted nothing more than for me to drop it, but I couldn't.

"What pills?"

"Leah." Irritation passed through his face. "It's nothing. Trust me. My parents are pissed enough that I lied. Scotty's mad at me, too, for not calling him back. Just let it go."

"I waited to hear from you. I worried the entire time. Do you know what that felt like not knowing anything for so long? And how did Rachelle get news before I did?"

"Just drop it already."

"Would *you* just drop it if you found me in the back seat like that?"

"Leah," his voice rose. "You don't know what you're talking about. You don't know anything."

He slammed his locker and walked away.

Chapter 18

I t was our last drama club meeting for the year.

Braden had been short with me that week. Even when we had lunch at The Tree, he barely talked to anyone.

Sara had stopped coming almost completely. The Yearbook Committee had become a greater priority. On Braden's first day back to school, she'd asked him how he was, but that was it. I knew her disinterest in what had happened bothered Braden, but I wished he could see all the people in his life who did care.

"Can I have everyone's attention?" Hillman said, coming into the auditorium with a notebook. "I have some news that hopefully more than a few of you will be interested in."

Hillman paused, scanning over all of us as if we were a breath of fresh air.

"It's been a pleasure working on this production with all of you. Some of you will be leaving and will be greatly missed. Those of you I have gotten to know this year, I hope you will return."

I squeezed Braden's hand until he gave me that reassuring smile.

"It's not certain that we will have the finances to continue with drama club next year, but we are working on it. Most of you know that every year I give away an Honorable Mention award to the person who has shown the hardest work, discipline, and who really went the extra mile." He held up a stack of certificates in his hand. "This year is different. I want to honor all of you with this award for your hard work and dedication. You all truly deserve it, and I hope you go off to do great things with your future."

We all won.

Somehow that didn't seem fair.

I guessed that was better than losing to Sara.

After Hillman handed out the certificates, everyone started to disperse for the end-of-semester tidy up. Becca left to the side of the stage where she started organizing some old prop boxes.

"Hey," I said. She sorted through plastic swords and daggers. "Can you believe it? I mean seriously. We *all* win? Sara hasn't even been here a full year."

Becca shrugged her shoulders, keeping her focus on the props.

"I guess," she said.

"You guess? She's hardly earned it."

"Stop taking it so personally. I'm sure she just saw the opportunity and took it."

I watched her for a while.

"Is something wrong?" I asked.

Becca huffed before finally putting a dagger down and looking at me.

"You keep talking about Sara like she's so bad, but aren't you guys, like, friends now? Aren't you a part of her little group?"

I wanted to protest, but she kept going.

"Besides, the award wasn't guaranteed to you. You just *wanted* it. We all want a lot of things. We don't always get what we want. Geez, Leah, you seriously need to learn how to lose a little."

"How can you say that?"

"And damn, stop talking about Sara as if she's the worst person in the world. At least she's consistent."

"But . . . Hillman knew—"

"You were so worried about the choir kids taking over drama club," she said. "If it mattered that much to you, then you shouldn't have gotten so wrapped up in Braden Gregory. It's *your* fault. Not Hillman's. Not Sara's. Not your mom's, for God's sake. Share your win and get over it."

Becca went back to rummaging through the prop boxes as if I was never there.

My body hunched under the weight of her words. It wasn't so much the sting of her attitude that hurt. It was my own guilt for being such a neglectful friend. I wasn't a bad friend. She knew that. We even had plans to crash prom together.

As I walked away, I turned once to see if maybe she had come to her senses, but she remained focused on the props.

From the stage, I looked down to where I'd been sitting and saw Braden there, talking with Scotty.

Chapter 19

"I'm in! This is actually happening. I can't believe I got in!"

"Of course you got in," Braden said. "They'd be idiots not to take you."

He hugged me in my driveway after dropping me off from school. My mom and Gracie had been waiting on the steps with a letter.

"I'm going to Ball State," I said. Part of me almost couldn't believe it. All I had to do then was sign and mail in the confirmation form.

"You have the world in your hands now," Braden said. "You can do anything you want."

I paused, swallowing my excitement in front of him.

"Thanks so much for helping me with this."

I hugged him in front of my mom and Gracie. I wanted to show them how important he was to me, how much he had impacted my life. Part of me wished Becca and Justin were also there to celebrate. Since our visit to Ball State, I knew they would be happy when I told them.

It felt like everybody had a plan.

Everybody except Braden.

When we talked, he'd often stare off into the distance. To distract him, I'd poke him occasionally, and he would reassure me that everything was okay with a peck on the cheek. I wasn't used to this new Braden—this Braden who wouldn't share what was really on his mind, who acted like life would draw his cards.

That evening as we lay under The Tree, we watched the moonlight slowly replace the sun's pink and orange aura.

"It's not too late to apply," I told him, resting my head next to his.

He was silent. I heard his breaths next to me.

"How are you feeling about everything?" I asked.

"You want to know so much, Leah."

I frowned.

"*Everything* is a lot," he said with a smile in his voice.

I wished he would finally face my question instead of dancing around it. The nagging thoughts in my head persisted no matter how much I tried to avoid them. I wanted to talk to Braden about what had happened to him and it hurt that he wasn't ready to share that with me. I wanted to know more, but his silence made it obvious that he needed more time.

"One day we have to take that road trip," he said, holding my hand. "We have to get out of this town and see what else is out there before everything changes."

Braden rose from the ground. "But first . . ." He pulled something from his pocket and showed me two thick white tickets.

"Go to prom with me?" he asked, as his grin stretched across his face.

It had always been the plan for Becca, Justin, and me to go to prom together, but since we hadn't been talking much, I didn't expect to go anymore. When Braden asked me, I could barely contain my excitement as I squealed and jumped into his arms.

The next day, my mom took me to a decent store in town and shopped with me for two hours until we found the most perfect silver dress priced under forty dollars. It fit perfectly around my frame, and the best part was the shoulder straps which wrapped around my upper arms revealing a cute amount of cleavage.

On prom day, Braden showed up at my house wearing a black suit with a shiny green undershirt. He reminded me of a prince holding a beautiful white rose corsage, which he wrapped around my wrist.

My mom had just gotten home from work, so she hurried to grab her camera and took pictures of us until the storage was full. She said she wanted copies of his pictures, but Braden explained that his parents had been too busy with Trevor's track race to take any.

Prom night was being held at a warehouse downtown. On our way there, other students were driving in Oldtimer cars. I didn't know what any of them were called, but they had these cool wings on the ends which weren't made on newer cars anymore. They fit in perfectly with the downtown vibe, blending in as if we were living in the '50s.

As we neared the building, we saw the disco lights circling in the air. The booming music vibrated Braden's van.

We walked in as others were also just arriving. The giant room was loud . . . exciting . . . totally not what I expected. The theme was old-time rock 'n' roll—colorful streamers and disco lights lit up the dance floor as blaring music bounced against the walls. I thought it would be like something out of a movie where all the girls slow danced with their hands on their dates' shoulders and everyone drank the punch.

Instead, the punch had been spiked and everyone was either dancing or dry humping. You couldn't tell the difference.

I was Braden's world that night. He acted as if nothing else mattered, dancing with me to every slow song, holding me as if the world was ending. I held on to him during our slow dances, taking in the faint scent of his aftershave. Even though the room boomed around us, I could still feel the beating of his heart.

After our dance to Elvis' "Jailhouse Rock," I took Braden's hand.

"Come here." I led him off the dance floor to our table. I pulled out a few college applications from my purse.

"Here." I handed them to him and had to talk loud over the music. "You'll have to check them out, but I think they would be worth applying for."

He looked over them but didn't open any. He sighed, already shaking his head in disapproval.

"These seem like really good colleges, Braden."

What he didn't know was how I couldn't imagine leaving him knowing he was dealing with problems he wouldn't tell me about. I sensed he still wasn't ready to talk about this though. I wanted to believe he had a plan, but I wished he understood how worried he was making me.

"Leah," he said, placing the applications on the table.

"I know you've been having a hard time lately and I know college is the last thing on your mind, but what if you change your mind over the summer? What if you want to go to college with me?" I pointed to one of the applications. "This is the one you helped me fill out. Ball State. I know it's nothing like what your parents probably dreamed for you, but we can go together. I can help you figure this out."

"I'll figure it out. Trust me. I always do."

Justin hollered at me.

"Go hang out," Braden said. "I need a break anyway."

When I went to see Becca and Justin, Braden stayed at our table, gazing off into nowhere. I thought he would hang out with his friends for a while, but he brushed them off when they tried to take him away.

Becca ignored me most of the time. I got the hint that she was still mad about us not showing up in four wheelers and camouflage, but how could I talk to her when she acted like she hated my guts?

I danced with Justin to a Panic! At The Disco song until I ran out of steam. The punch was too strong to drink, so I gulped some faucet water.

It was dark outside when we left prom, but all the lights made it feel like daytime. Braden and I were hand in hand, walking out with sweaty faces and some glitter stuck in our hair. Most prom goers rushed to their cars to get to the after-prom party.

Braden squeezed my hand and I looked up at him. His face was dim under the streetlamp shining down on us.

"So, after-party?" I swung my hand in his.

"I was thinking something else."

Before I could respond, a few of Braden's friends called to him while jumping over to us.

"You comin' out?" Scotty asked, crunching an energy drink.

Braden shrugged his shoulders and searched for an answer in my expression.

"No," Braden said. "I think we're gonna skip tonight."

"Aw, come on. It's the after-party!" Scotty said.

Braden's friends dispersed, but Scotty stayed for a moment to talk to him. From the corner of my eye, I noticed Becca and Justin talking by his car before Justin made his way over to me.

"Hey," he said, lifting his voice.

The exhaustion of hours spent dancing showed under his eyes. Sweat replaced his hair gel and seeped through his suit.

"Hey," I said. "Whew, Justin. A little deodorant next time."

"Don't even. My sweat smells like roses. I had a blast tonight."

I tapped my foot against the pavement while Braden sent Scotty off.

"No after-party for you, I hear?" he asked.

"I don't think so."

"Hey, listen," he said once he noticed me glancing at Becca. She waited next to his car. "Don't take her too seriously. I know you don't mean it, but . . . it's not easy feeling second best. Not even for me. It's difficult for her to accept this thing going on between you and Braden. Our Becca doesn't do well with change."

"That makes sense." I tried to find some hope in what he said. I wanted to explain myself, but something told me that words wouldn't work this time.

"Anyway," Justin said. "Just because she's mad, doesn't mean I am, too. Let me know when you want to hang. I'm sure she'll come around."

I hugged him before he skipped over to Becca.

Braden and I watched Scotty and the rest of his group leave the parking lot. He waved to them and when they drove off, there were just a few vehicles left from some of the chaperones who were closing down the warehouse.

"So, what I was thinking . . ." Braden took my hand. "The Tree?"

I hopped in his van and enjoyed the slow, smooth ride to the school. Every so often, I'd glance over and wait until he gave me that sweet, reassuring smile.

Once we were at The Tree, we snuggled beside each other as if the weight of the world was easier to carry together.

I tasted moisture in the air. Braden wrapped his suit jacket around me.

"We're graduating soon," he said.

"It's so weird. This was like our last hurrah for our high school careers. Honestly, I always figured you'd go to prom with Sara."

Braden sighed. "Sara isn't who I thought she was. I ignored my feelings from the start though and just hoped she might have actually liked me for me. I feel like she used my friendship to get ahead. She doesn't even act like she needs me anymore now that she's found her clan."

"I kind of figured she was that way. I hoped she was, anyway. I didn't want to like her. She was too nice, too shiny, too involved in everything."

Braden shook his head and repositioned himself in the grass.

"I felt obligated to like her because I get so much pressure from my mom. It was the same with my last two girlfriends."

"You had girlfriends?"

"Sort of. Not really. Taylor Beckwith and Lilian Murphy."

"How did you sort of not really date two of the most popular girls in school?"

"Our friends kind of decided that, but it was never anything official. It was Taylor my freshman year and Lilian my sophomore year. Only for a little while though. We just hung out a lot. My mom knew their moms so whenever she would ask me if we were dating, I'd just say yes. I knew it'd make her happy."

"Did you like them?"

"I liked them, but I wasn't really in love with them or anything. They were the kind of girls I was supposed to be with, girls my mom expected me to be with. Like Sara. They just weren't my kind of perfect. Meeting you, going to prom with you, was the best choice I've made in a long time."

His words took the air right out of my lungs.

I thought about my stringy hair, my old clothes. I thought about my mom getting married again, our family's chaotic past, and where my future might have been headed based on all of that. If that was all perfect to Braden, then I didn't want to be any other way.

"Graduation." I lifted my hand into the air and traced the moon with my finger. "Sometimes I wonder if I can do this college thing. I wonder if my mom has always been right. Maybe I'm not cut out for all of that."

"You have to go to college," Braden said. "You said it would mean everything to you. You can make it come true." He looked up into the sky. "I'm the one who can risk screwing up. I know my parents will always be there if I make a mistake. I just feel like there's something I'm meant to be doing with my life."

He lifted his hand from next to mine and traced the span of the leaves on the branches above us.

"Sometimes," he said, "I just imagine the forest. I imagine being surrounded by thousands of trees."

I imagined it . . . thousands of trees surrounded us. We were protected by hope, by possibility.

We lay in the grass beside each other. I giggled when he started quoting lines from *Mulberry Street*. He spoke as if he were reading it to a class full of kids.

I grabbed some loose leaves beside me and tossed them into the air, feeling the gentle touch as they fell over my face.

When I sat up, I watched Braden stare into the sky and felt all his hopes and dreams glistening in his gaze—those same eyes that had captured me right from the day I'd watched him sitting in that very spot.

I tucked my hair behind my ears and leaned down until my lips grazed his. He lifted his palm to my face and pulled me closer until we were laying, kissing side by side. His tongue touched mine, rousing every cell in my love-drunk brain, and until then, I didn't realize how much my lips had been craving his.

What was it about moments such as those that could make fear disappear? I could have kissed him at the edge of the highest cliff, about to fall over, and I wouldn't have cared.

As our lips parted, my eyes remained closed and I held on to him. The wind rushed over us. His fingers folded into mine until I drifted to sleep.

I woke up to Braden shaking me. A drop of rain fell on my nose.

"Leah . . . Leah," he said in a hushed tone. "Leah, listen to me."

I wiped the rain off my nose and leaned up on my elbows.

"Braden . . . what's going on?"

The night had deepened into a dark hole. Thick clouds covered the moon and rain trickled down as I sat up. My vision adjusted to Braden sitting in front of me, his face nearly touching mine.

"Just hear me out." His expression was serious. "We can get out of here. We can go somewhere, just the two of us."

I said nothing, trying to take in what he meant.

"We can do whatever we want, go wherever we want. We can go to L.A., Vegas, Nashville, the Mississippi River. We can travel the states, see places we've never been able to see. We can go to Helen Keller's house like you've been wanting."

"Braden, we only have, like, two weeks left of school. We can't skip out right before we graduate."

"It's senior year. You can afford to miss a few days."

"But *you* can't. You have to be home. Take it easy. Don't you have to take medicine?"

I managed to make out his face in the dark, his eyes pleading like the depth of his voice.

"I have cash savings. I have a credit card. We have my van right here. We can do this road trip the right way, not wait out the next two weeks in this school or wander around this small town."

"I don't want to just leave. My sister, my mom ..."

"Your mom's too busy to notice. You said so yourself."

"I can't just leave without saying something."

"I'll take you home to let her know. What do you say?"

More raindrops hit my face. I had never done anything crazy like this before. I was always staying in line, doing what was expected of me until I had resented others, even myself for holding back. Right then, I wanted to feel whatever it was that Braden felt. Carelessness? Impulsivity? Freedom?

"Just for a week ... okay?"

"Just for a week," he said. "We'll be back before graduation. We can go up north. We can go south. We can see places we've never seen."

"And if it goes well, what, do we run away forever?"

"We can do whatever we want, plan our own lives the way we want them to be. Leah, listen to me. I need this. I need to get out of here." His hands were cold against my upper arms. "Come on, Leah. Don't lose sight. Come with me."

"This is insane. We don't even have a plan."

"Why plan? What's the point? Just go for it."

"Okay." I couldn't believe I said it, but it felt right. To live, to seize the moment with the person I loved felt like the cutting loose I had always needed.

Braden helped me off the ground. The wind came in spurts with rain as we hurried to his van. Once inside, he started the engine and looked at me.

"Where are we going first? Alabama? Tennessee?" he asked.

A rush of excitement filled my belly.

"My house," I said. "I need to say bye to my sister first."

I looked ahead, but before I could think of anything else, bright white lights flashed through the rear of his van. A loud horn went off. Heavy rain had covered the back window when I turned around to check.

"Who's that?" I asked as a larger van pulled up beside us. Braden stretched forward to get a better view from my window.

"Braden, who is it?"

The curiosity in his eyes dissolved when the realization hit him. A darkness fell over his face.

"I'll be right back." He opened his door.

Before I could push the question, he shut the door and walked around the front of his van. I cracked the window to get a better view. This van was black, newer, and bigger. Once I saw Braden get in, I saw a woman from the inside car lights.

Braden barely looked at her. Although she spoke loudly, I couldn't make out anything she was saying under the heavy rain.

I glanced at the clock. We had only been sleeping for a couple hours. We still would have been at the after-party if we'd gone to it.

My fingers clutched the door handle. I wanted to come to Braden's rescue so he wouldn't get in trouble. I wanted to explain whatever needed explaining until the woman glared at me through the rain-streaked windows which separated us. I remembered that face—his mother—and meeting her at his house, only this time, her eyes looked black.

From the distance, Braden didn't look like my Braden at all. His head was down, hand raised to his face. Somehow—looking at him through the windows—I knew why he had been acting so closed off. He was trapped.

Maybe me being in his life was hurting him more than it was helping. Maybe Braden would be better off if I got out of his way. His family knew him better than I did; they knew things that I didn't. They knew a Braden that I didn't see after school let out and everyone went home.

I needed to set him free.

saturday, may 16, 2009
"There is only one happiness in this life, to love and be loved." George Sand
can you think of any other happiness? when someone loves you those walls crashing down around you become doors that lead to amazing places.
perhaps love is crazy. lets say it is. will that make you stop loving him?
you cant be in love and scared at the same time. if you separate the two you will see that fear is just an obstacle. everything you want is on the other side of it. some people are strong enough to overcome that obsta-cle. others not so much.
you are tina. yes you are.
robert

"**S**he found your jacket at my house," Braden said as he dropped me off at home that night. "And then someone ratted us out that we weren't at the after-party and now I'm screwed for life since I lied to her."

That was all he would tell me when he dropped me off after his mom caught us. He just gave me the jacket and left my driveway.

I thought about Braden that weekend, carrying a heavy weight in my gut—the sense of doom that came before something bad happened.

I flipped open my phone almost every minute to see if he messaged back, but he didn't text me until Monday morning.

> 8:05 a.m.
>
> Msg From: Braden
>
> hey cant give you a ride this week

I walked to school that Monday. School was buzzing with the chatter of students.

I searched for Braden when I made it to the hallway, but he wasn't at his locker.

Monday, May 18, 2009
Dear Robert,
Something happened this weekend. I tried to face my

fear of loving someone, but maybe I was being reckless. I think Braden got into a lot of trouble because of it. Maybe he wasn't supposed to go anywhere after prom since what happened to him. Now I don't know what to do.

You think I'm strong enough, but Robert, I wish you could hear my voice, how it shakes when I'm nervous, how soft and fragile it is. Fear is what I know. It's been my life going from one home to the next, meeting one person after another.

Leaving.

I don't want to leave anymore, especially when people need me. What would Becca do without me? Gracie? Braden?

Braden.

My biggest fear.

Pen Pal Tina

I walked to The Tree before the first bell rang. Thick gray clouds smothered the sky. Nobody was there so I buried the letter in a plastic bag and covered it with a heavy layer of dirt.

First period flashed by. My stomach fluttered when I saw Braden pass me in the hallway on his way to next period.

"Hey!" I said.

"Oh, hey," he said, whipping past me. "My next class is in the north wing. Talk to you later, okay?"

Without another word, he left. I went into the bathroom to check if I had something repulsive on my face or in my hair.

Nothing.

During science class, Braden popped in to deliver something to my teacher. I waved to him, but he quickly looked away and left the classroom. I glanced around with red cheeks, hoping nobody had caught that moment of sheer embarrassment, but they whispered.

Oh, they whispered.

During lunch, I wouldn't have been able to eat if I'd tried. Instead, I walked to The Tree, but Braden wasn't there. Nobody was.

I headed to the glass doors of the north wing, but before going any further, I saw Braden sitting at a table with Scotty and a couple other boys. I stepped back so he couldn't see me through the set of doors.

Braden's chin rested on his fist while the others talked. I tried reading his expression—something in between exhaustion and worry. He had no food in front of him either.

Maybe it was none of my business, but I had to know what was wrong, and if he had gotten into some sort of trouble because of me, I had to fix it.

Before I pushed open the door, I bumped into Rachelle who was walking in beside me. She dropped a few coins on the ground, so I picked them up and handed them to her.

She glowered. "Just leave him alone, Leah."

I looked at her. Her dark-brown eyes were big and round, surrounded by black eyeliner and thick mascara.

"Braden," she said, answering the confusion on my face. "Leave him alone. He's having a really hard time and doesn't need you making it worse."

I stepped back.

"How am I making it worse? He won't even talk to me."

"Good."

"Good? I don't know what's going on. I know he got in trouble, but that doesn't explain him avoiding me."

"His *real* friends know him. His *real* friends care enough."

"What's your problem, Rachelle? I never did anything to you."

She put her coins in her wallet and zipped it shut.

"Braden's one of my best friends. He needs his friends right now, not some girl who's trying to satisfy her little crush on him."

"I just want to make it right," was all I could think to say.

"You can't." She opened the door. "If he doesn't want to talk to you, then just accept it and move on."

The door closed behind her causing a wave of frustration to pulse through me. She sat down next to Braden and put her hand on his back.

Rachelle's warning voice echoed in my head. How could she possibly think I didn't care about Braden as much as she did? I should have been the one comforting him, not her.

Becca and Justin were in line to get their food when I walked into the loud cafeteria. I waved.

They reluctantly waved back, Justin a little happier than Becca.

I found an empty table in the back and spent the rest of the half hour by myself.

Braden avoided me for the rest of the week, pretending he didn't see me when we passed each other in the hallways. During lunch, Scotty and Rachelle sat with him in the north wing. Nobody was at The Tree anymore. It stood alone—lonely and unwanted. I sat under it just to give it a bit more life, just to let it know I still cared.

Days went by with nothing to do but sulk and listen to my mom plan for her wedding. I hoped Braden would show up at the wedding, but that hope quickly dissolved. I listened to the CD just to drown out my thoughts of him and what I could do to make the situation better.

I answered more of Dr. Schwarzkebaber's questions as emotionlessly as they were delivered.

"Are you looking forward to your mother's wedding?"

"No."

"Why do you think that is?"

"I don't know."

"Will you be involved?"

"Yes."

"What will be your participation?"

"Being her daughter."

I wanted to talk about Braden. I wanted to tell her that I thought he was in trouble. I wanted to ask her what I could do about it, but she wasn't being paid to talk about my problems.

I reread my college acceptance letter at least twenty times, trying to imagine what Braden would tell me.

Do it.

Take a chance.

You deserve the best.

Doubt flooded my mind; it took over my body. I had to lie down, breathe, and remind myself that I was at home in bed and nothing had changed.

Nothing yet.

Most people would have killed for an opportunity like mine. The feeling of freedom—barely able to sleep from the excitement of college. I wanted that feeling back.

When the last bell rang on Friday, I had ten minutes until the bus left. I hurried out to The Tree and uncovered the new letter, not even realizing how much air I had been holding in my lungs until it all came rushing out. When I plopped into my bus seat, I pulled the letter out of the plastic bag and unfolded it.

friday, may 22, 2009

"A fool sees not the same tree that a wise man

sees." William Blake

how can your fear be some boy? you are young and free, just like angela was. the possibilities are endless! if she stayed here because of me, i would have only slowed her down. everyone has to take responsibility for their lives. that includes you. if you stay around this town for anyone other than yourself you are making a mistake. i cant hear your voice but i bet you have one. i bet you are smart, talented, determined, and everything good. you have to put that to use not waste away in this town for some boy.

go to college.

stay a dreamer.

robert

I found myself on autopilot that evening, hanging up decorations in the hotel's conference room while my mom talked to her coworkers about how many chairs to set up and what time food should be served. I stapled another ribbon into the wall, checking my cell phone again just in case Braden might have texted.

I'd sent him several messages during the day. I just hoped someone was reading them.

10:15 a.m.

New Msg:

Sorry for everything. Let me fix this.

1:43 p.m.

New Msg:

Do they know it wasn't your fault?

4:06 p.m.

New Msg:

I'm worried about you. I wish you would just
talk to me.

I should have pimped them up a bit before sending them. Anything to show his parents, if they were reading them, that they had it all wrong.

After stapling the last piece of red ribbon, I hopped off the chair.

This was all so cheesy, I thought, looking around.

My mom was organizing the table situation with her friend, too stressed to notice if I stepped out.

I closed my phone, thinking another text wouldn't help. I needed to talk to him. I needed to talk to somebody.

When I got to his house, I knocked on the back door. Someone moved behind the window curtain before the door opened.

"Oh . . ." his mom said, opening the screen door. "Hello again."

Her hair was down. Perfect. Straight. Freshly highlighted. She wore a light-blue cardigan and white pants.

"Hi, Mrs. Gregory."

When she stepped outside, the screen door clicked shut. She folded her arms as the wind blew.

"As you might know, Braden is grounded. He's not allowed to see friends for a while."

I nodded, swallowing hard.

"I know. That's kind of why I came here."

She tilted her head.

"I know I should have come to you sooner." I swallowed again. My throat dried up. "My jacket was here because Braden was helping me. I wanted to get away from this annoying party my mom was having. I would have done the same for him . . . you all were at the cabin . . . we didn't do anything stupid. I'm not all that exciting, if it helps. We just stayed inside, listened to some music. That's it. What happened on prom night, you know, that wasn't Braden's fault either. We just lost track of time. Honestly. We ditched the party to hang out at the school and we fell asleep in the grass and then it started raining and—"

"Darling, I wasn't born yesterday, if you can't recognize that from my crow's feet." She smiled a little, revealing the wrinkles around her eyes. "I know how these things work. If he wanted to spend time with his girlfriend, he knows we don't have a problem with that."

His girlfriend.

"This has nothing to do with you," she said.

"He said you found my jacket. That's why he got in trouble."

"I found your jacket, but that was not the reason he got in trouble. I have a problem about the lies he's been telling us. Since last year, Braden and his father have been to several colleges to decide which one would be the best choice for him. Braden was supposed to apply to each of them.

"I started to become suspicious after I had asked him several times for any letters he received back from the colleges," she went on. "He would always tell me that he'd get to it, but I never saw anything in the mailbox. So, I called the colleges and none of them had knowledge of him ever having applied."

I looked down, feeling so guilty, feeling as if I had somehow caused his disinterest in college.

"How did you know where we were . . . after prom?" I asked.

"That night, I realized he had been lying about sending in applications. I called him, but he didn't answer his phone. It was getting awfully late and . . . well, you heard about Braden's hospital trip after his play. I was worried as any mother would be when he wouldn't answer my calls. I drove by the after-party and one of your classmates told me you'd both stayed behind."

"Didn't you see my text messages though? I know he lied, but doesn't he deserve a chance?"

"Hun, how would I see your text messages to my son?"

"He's grounded. You have his phone."

She gave a confused smile. "No dear. We're strict, not stupid. Braden has never been grounded from his phone. He needs it to contact us. What if there's an emergency?"

"You haven't had his phone at all?"

She shook her head, confusion in her expression.

He had been lying to me, too.

I zipped my jacket. Gusts of wind invited raindrops.

I went there in hopes of fixing whatever was going on. I wasn't sure I'd get the opportunity to talk to his mom again and I wasn't sure I'd ever have the courage to face her again either, so I took my chance.

"Mrs. Gregory, I don't exactly come from a rich family or a classy one either. My mom is getting married for the third time. I grew up moving from one crappy apartment to another until we ended up here. I had babysitters in parts of towns where I wasn't allowed to go outside alone. I know I'm not up to your standards, but I really care about Braden. I don't know why he's been lying. I just want the best for him and I feel horrible . . . I feel like I had something to do with this."

"How on earth could you think that? Whoever Braden chooses to love is his choice. Certainly, as his mother, I would want him to be with someone who makes him happy."

Before I could respond, she continued.

"What I do know is that you don't exactly understand everything. He has been quite off balance lately and this isn't the first time he's lied to us. He needs to focus on college and what he needs to do with his life instead of flying by the seat of his pants. Braden is full of incredible potential; he just hasn't been doing anything with that potential.

"He's certainly had days where he has been in brighter spirits.

I'm sure you've had something to do with that, Leah. Unfortunately, he lied, and as a punishment he is not allowed to be with friends for a while.

"He knows he can still talk to you all in school; he can even call or text you if he wants. He just has to be home after school. Those are the rules if he wants to live under our roof."

"Right." I felt like a giant fool. "I understand."

"Leah, I don't know what Braden has said about us to make you think we are so horrible, but when Braden is off punishment, I'd like to have you over for dinner. Would that be all right?"

"Yeah, I . . . that would be nice. Thank you."

"And Leah?"

Before I turned away, I stopped.

"Thank *you*," she said. "For calling the ambulance."

I wanted to smile, but I couldn't shake the next question I wanted to ask.

"Why weren't you guys at his musical? He had a big part. He was really amazing."

"We were given the wrong dates on purpose." She shook her head. "Braden didn't want us there."

More lies. Or maybe she was lying. I felt like I didn't know anything anymore.

I just walked away, sensing her attention on me until I disappeared around the corner.

I hated when my gut was right.

As soon as I got home that night, I crawled into bed. The blankets relaxed over my heavy body, but they couldn't protect me from the rejection that crept into every fiber of my being.

He was allowed to talk to his friends during school.

He wasn't talking to *me*.

I shut my eyelids, trying to force sleep, trying to think of anything else other than Braden and the possibility that he was breaking up with me.

Chapter 21

By Saturday night, I needed Braden more than I ever had. It was the night my life would change.

Again.

I'd helped my mom with her makeup that evening. We'd gotten along, laughed a little as she sat on the edge of the bathtub. I tried to force a smile whenever she looked at me as I applied her eyeshadow. She wasn't much of a makeup person. She really looked beautiful though, especially dressed in white for someone who normally wore sweats and loose jackets.

When we arrived at the hotel, I took my seat in the front row next to Gracie. It was nice being next to Gracie, to soak up all the joy in her sweet smile as she watched our mom walk down the aisle.

During the ceremony, I heard a voice from the chair behind me.

"Hey, stranger."

I turned and saw Justin wearing his excited grin.

"What are you doing here?" I whispered behind my huge smile.

"You know I have a soft spot for weddings." He winked. "Besides, you know I'd be here for you no matter what."

Gratitude filled my heart.

I watched as my mom said those vows and promised her life away. It didn't exactly put me in a lovey-dovey mood. Maybe it would have if this was her first marriage or the marriage of somebody else's mother, but not mine. It was hard to believe in love that night. Not only because Braden was distant, but because I wished love was a promise someone made to one person forever.

My mom looked stunning. Beau looked happy, like he'd won the best prize in the world, as he grabbed her hand and walked down the aisle. Everyone clapped.

The reception room—lined with shades of red and white ribbon—filled with people. Most of them I recognized, others were fresh faces. Red and white flowers rested in the middle of each table. My mom's favorite 80s music blasted from the DJ's booth in the back corner.

Happy, buzzed faces surrounded us either sitting and watching, or dancing and shouting. My mom was one of the faces dancing and shouting.

I couldn't help but think that Scotty and Rachelle would have fit right in. Beau actually looked like he was having a good time with all those people, most of whom were his family members.

The others were mom's friends because most of our family members were still living in Big Town Somewheres. I hadn't realized just how sociable my mom was until then.

She needed people in her life. She needed the support. I guessed that's what happened when a person was left to do it alone. I doubted I would have done a better job than her if I was in her shoes.

I was glad Justin was there. He danced with me to "Baby Got Back". When he started twerking, I doubled over and, for the first time that night, I laughed until I cried.

I shot Beau a thumbs up when I saw him dancing with my mom. They were just two people in love. I knew my mom didn't plan for her life to go the way it had. I was sure when she was a little girl, she'd sat in her room and imagined marrying the man of her dreams and living happily ever after. Sometimes things just didn't go according to plan, but at least she didn't stop believing in love.

"Wanna go up and dance?" Gracie asked me.

I was checking my phone again while we took a break at our table.

"Not really." I frowned.

"Becca?" Justin asked, nodding his head toward my phone.

"Sort of."

"Come on, Gracie." Justin grabbed her hand and pulled her to the dance floor. "Let's show these old folks how it's done."

I smiled, tapping my phone with the tips of my fingers.

I rose from my seat, pulling down the bottom of my red, knee-length dress.

While they were dancing, I left for the bathroom. Alone in there, I dialed Braden's number—a number I was sure I'd always remember for the rest of my life.

It rang but eventually went to his voicemail, which was always full. I called again, slamming my finger into the buttons as if that would make him feel how frustrated I was. It rang before going to voicemail again. I grunted and smacked the phone shut.

How could he do this? After all the time we had spent together, all the feelings we'd shared, how could he ignore me?

I paced the bathroom for a moment until a couple of women came in. One of them recognized me though I had no idea who she was. She congratulated me.

I managed to slip out of the reception room without being noticed.

I stormed all the way down the street. There was a half-moon floating in the sky and I scowled at it for no reason. Sometimes it just felt good to be angry.

I plucked my heels off and slammed my feet onto the cold pavement; my bottled anger escaped through the pain of those little street pebbles poking my skin.

I didn't know what the truth was anymore, but I wanted it. What was he thinking? That he could avoid me from now on? If our relationship was over, then I needed to hear it from him.

My shoes swung in my grasp, hitting my wrist. My red dress looked like blood in the dark of the night.

When his house came into view, I saw his front room light on and imagined him sitting there listening to record after record, not caring that somewhere in the world, someone was hurting because of him.

I stomped all the way to his back door and jerked the screen door open until it banged against the house.

My fist pounded the door.

"It's the weekend so I know your family is at the cabin tonight! I know you're here!"

I banged on the door faster. I then stepped over to the window and hit the glass with my palm.

"Answer the door, Braden! I know you're in there!"

I kicked the door with my bare feet as hard as I could.

Suddenly the door opened, and I shoved past Braden until I was standing inside his dimly lit kitchen. I'd forgotten how old the house smelled, like that of loose dust and vanilla-scented candles.

He wore a white shirt and jeans. No shoes. No tie. No smile.

"What are you trying to do, Braden?" I threw my shoes onto the floor. "Was this all just a joke to you? The poor, pathetic unicorn girl? If it was, just tell me. I can take it."

His focus strayed.

"You are such a hypocrite." I flailed my arms. "All you ever talk about is not doing what other people want you to do, but here you are in your true colors. Not doing what *you* want." I stormed closer to him. "You can't treat me like this. You've been avoiding me since prom night and you're an idiot if you think I'm going to believe it's not you doing all this."

"It's not," he said with a low voice.

"I talked to your mom, Braden. She told me she never took your phone, that she never told you to stay away from me. You're only grounded from hanging out after school. What other lies are you going to tell me now?"

"Leah, it's not what you think."

"You can't ignore me forever. If you want to break up with me, then be a decent human being and do it already."

He grabbed his hair, redness flushing his face. "What is it with you, Leah? Why can't you just leave? Why can't you just move on, lose my number, forget my name, forget I ever existed?"

"That's what you want, isn't it? This whole time you've been trying to break it off, ignoring me like I'm a child."

He stepped closer to me until we were face to face. I read sorrow in his eyes, a pain that didn't belong to the Braden I thought I knew.

"I used to hate you," I said. "You were such an arrogant jerk. The kind of person I never wanted to be. You did this to me. I'm here because of you. *You* started this. *You* end it."

He shook his head as if a gun was pressed against his temple.

"You know what," I said. "Maybe you are the stupid rich boy I always thought you were. Maybe your life is too easy. Why can't you just put me out of my misery and break up with me already?"

"Because I fucking love you!" he shouted, stepping back. "You ruined everything. I had a plan, Leah. Why can't you just let me be the shitty person I am and let me go!"

Not knowing if I'd heard him right, I dropped my arms to my sides. I found myself standing in a shaking body while my anger slowly morphed into pity.

"So now the truth comes out," I said softly. "Fine. If you wanted me gone all along, then I'll finally go."

I turned to leave but Braden grabbed my upper arms and pulled me into him. His lips planted on mine with a passion that zipped down my spine.

I pushed him away. I pushed him again. I pushed him harder until his back slammed against the wall.

Now he was *my* focal point.

My magnet caught his eyes and I held them captive under my gaze. I stepped forward and pressed my mouth against his, grabbing his shirt until my nails pushed into my palms. His hands reached behind me, unzipping my dress from the back. He jerked it off my body and, in that moment, I decided that if hating somebody felt that good, then maybe I'd hate him for the rest of my life.

I wrapped my arms around his neck, feeling the strength in his muscles as he picked me up until my legs hugged his waist. I could feel his desire for me in the way his hands squeezed up and down my upper arms, pulling me in closer as if he'd been craving this moment. The hot trickle of his lips on my neck forced my mouth slightly open and as soon as he lifted my chin, his lips owned mine. As his candied tongue danced with mine, he moved his hand up my belly, relishing the softness of my skin as he reached higher. The juice over his lips—an elixir lubricating our movements as he pressed me harder against the wall. His sweet breaths filled my lungs, emboldening the soft growl from within me.

He brought me into his room. Each step had me burning for his hands over my body. I don't know what had come over me as we fell onto his bed, but all traces of resistance left me when his eyes claimed my body. I let out a soft moan, sure it had turned him on even more when I felt him grow harder against me.

His hot breath sent my back into an arch as he kissed me down to my breasts. When he parted from me, I peeled off his shirt, revealing the soft skin of his chest which I grazed my hands over. He unclipped my bra and flung it to the floor.

While I expected to be nervous as his eyes traveled up and down my naked body, I wasn't.

I slowly unbuckled his pants. Surrender. His every kiss, every touch owned me and, better than that, he owned my heart. He rose between my legs and studied me for a moment. Nothing short of pure, hot-blooded passion burst through his eager eyes and I realized I had never loved myself as much as when he looked at me that way.

"God, you are so beautiful," he said.

I returned the sureness in his expression, hoping he wanted me for as long as I wanted him.

Forever.

He leaned over and gifted me with a light, adoring kiss.

In a quiet, poetic tone, he said, "I love you, Leah."

I heard him . . . every word like slow motion and, though every ounce of me wanted to say it back, the words remained on the tip of my tongue.

I could tell by his next kiss that he didn't expect me to say it back.

My heart raced as I enjoyed every second of his body with light groans as he took his time. The weight and heat of his body set my nerves aflame. I moaned into his ear when he licked my neck all the way down to my belly. As he rose, his fingers traced my bottom lip until his lips took their place.

I clutched his back, pulling him to me until our bodies slowly became one. Running my hands through his hair, I exhaled, wishing the sensation of him inside me would last forever.

It was a moment I hadn't planned in my mind. Most girls had thought about how it would be for the first time, but I'd never imagined it would be like that; passionate, tender . . . more than I could ever dream.

He moved above me, pressing his fingers into my sides as I took in his breath, tasting his sweet tongue on mine. Waves of shivers rippled across my skin. It was his touch and the way he loved me that trickled through my flesh, wrapping my body in a blanket that could keep me warm for the rest of my life.

My vision was blurry and unclear, something I thought only happened to girls who were desired by boys.

I was the unicorn girl. She wasn't a "chick" or a "babe." She was quiet and anxious, hoping that maybe one day she would be lucky to be desired.

Braden took over my mind. He took over the feelings I had about myself, beliefs that I always thought were true until he proved me wrong. Not only did I realize that I was wrong about myself, but I wasn't alone in the world I had confined myself to.

His lips fell over my eyelids, my nose, and my lips. He rested his forehead against mine until I was overcome with a sureness that these feelings we shared were true and real.

"Did you know that Jeff Buckley was about to record his new album around the same time he drowned in the Mississippi?" Braden asked.

We were still in his bed hours later. We held hands in silence, the only sound coming from the record player next to his bed.

"His band was on their way to Memphis when he died. He was found in the river just days later with his clothes on. All except for his shoes."

I guessed I was supposed to have some kind of response to that, some kind of awed fascination.

"And you're telling me this . . . why?"

"John Lennon signed an autograph for a fan. Later, that same fan shot him five times. Killed him. And the crazy part is, as soon as he was pronounced dead, the song 'All My Loving' came on the radio."

"Sure. *That's* the crazy part."

I watched Braden think before finally looking at me.

"Jimi Hendrix. You know Jimi Hendrix, right?"

I nodded, though I couldn't name a song to save my life.

"He died when he was twenty-seven years old. How about that?"

He paused and I could tell he didn't expect a response. I realized he'd just mentioned most of the people on the CD he'd made me.

"These are things you should know," he said with a serious expression. "The good die young, Leah. It's painted in history. I wonder if anybody would care so much about them if they were still here."

It was quiet for a few seconds, the room a little colder than before.

"Life is like a riddle," Braden said. "Once you figure it out, you're old and ready to die. Agreed?"

"No."

While he studied my face, I tried to hide the fact that his bluntness was making me nervous.

"No?" he asked.

"Life is like . . . a box of chocolates."

"Leah Roy. You never cease to impress me."

"We went to Gatlinburg once. My mom's boyfriend . . ." I caught myself. "My mom's *husband* took us to that cool Bubba Gump restaurant. I don't really think life is like a box of chocolates, though."

"What is it then?"

"Life is . . . what we make it."

Braden rose slightly and put on a soft record. I couldn't shake the feeling that he was avoiding something.

I thought about the night after the show when I'd found him in the van. The pills he had lied about. All the times he hadn't texted me back and blamed his parents.

"What, Braden?" I asked against his shoulder. "What is it that you can't tell me?"

He lay down. I closed my eyes and rested my head on his beating chest, hoping I could give him the strength to open his heart to me.

"Your mom seems like a nice person," I said. "I don't understand why you told them the wrong dates. Why wouldn't you want them to come to your shows?"

"My parents are good people. They really are. It's just that, if I knew they were in the audience, I'd freeze under pressure. I wanted to be free with the character, make mistakes on stage, feel like I didn't have the weight of the world on my shoulders."

I began to understand why he didn't want his parents at his musical.

"I'm not a liar," he said under his breath.

I looked up at him. He concentrated on the ceiling, but his glazed eyes were tinged with guilt. His heart melted into his voice, unveiling the sound of a perfectly imperfect human.

"I thought maybe if I lied by omission or convinced myself I was doing the right thing, it wouldn't be that bad. I should've known I was being an idiot. I just wasn't ready when you came into my life. I got scared of losing you, of losing more control over my life. I just thought it would be better if this thing between us stopped before it went any further."

I'd been wanting to talk to him about the future and I hoped he'd finally be receptive to what I had to say. "Braden?"

"Yeah?"

"I've been thinking a lot . . . you know . . . about college and stuff. With everything that's been going on, I've been thinking I should stay."

I wanted to know what he thought. I hoped his response would show some kind of concrete plans he had for himself. His confidence had always given me courage in ways I didn't expect.

"I can still graduate," I said. "I can get my diploma and find a good job this summer, but if you aren't sure about your future, I can't just go and leave you behind."

He remained quiet. My curiosity evaporated when I felt his labored breaths.

"It's okay," I told him, holding my head to his chest. I wasn't sure I was ready for the truth. I wasn't sure it even mattered among all the love I felt for him at that moment.

"Braden, I don't have to understand everything. I'll be there for you no matter what. I always will."

Chapter 22

I walked to The Tree that Sunday morning. It took me about twenty minutes, and included an almost near-death experience on the highway, but I made it.

Sunday, May 24, 2009

Dear Robert,

I know what you mean and I want to believe I can make something of myself, but I just don't think I'm cut out for this sort of thing—you know, the college life and actually having money. I grew up seeing my parents struggle. Pretty much everyone I knew struggled. My scholarship will help with tuition, but I'll still be paying off loans for a long time. Would it even be worth it? How long would I really last out there? Besides, I just don't think I can go even if I knew I would be okay. People actually need me here.

I know you think I'm giving all of this up for some boy, but he's not just some boy, Robert. He's... more than that to me.

Fear would be to run, right?

Facing it would be to stay.

I hope you understand.

Pen Pal Tina

I buried the letter in its plastic bag and rested my back against The Tree. Wasn't a day named Sunday supposed to promise a little bit of sun? Clouds filled the sky, but I found beauty in the way they sheltered the earth.

I sat there hoping that Robert would show up this time. With the last day of school on Wednesday fast approaching, I wasn't sure how often we'd be able to communicate that summer. I hoped he would come out of nowhere and give me all the answers to all the questions I had.

Why was living so hard? Why did people fall in love? Why did love sometimes hurt?

An hour passed and no Robert, so I got up and walked back home.

Braden hadn't shown up to give me a ride that Monday morning, so I ended up walking after missing my bus.

The atmosphere changed when I made my way into the school. I walked down the hallway to my locker. Some kids stopped talking in their groups, staring at me as I passed them. Some whispered, but I couldn't catch what they were saying.

After getting my books, I shut my locker and began walking to my first class. That's when I slowed down and stared back at all the kids staring at me.

"What?" I said.

They continued whispering. It wasn't until I continued walking and neared the main office that I began to realize why.

Everyone behind the office glass window seemed so far away. Scotty sat in front of a police officer who held a clipboard and jotted things down.

A couple more officers were talking to some choir kids.

The sound of my heart reached my ears until every sound around me became nothing but a loud thump, one after the other.

A truth tormented me—a truth I didn't want to face. Scotty looked at me through the glass. His expression deepened and confirmed what I refused to accept.

I looked down the hallway to where Braden's locker was. Police were pulling out books and crumpled papers and putting them into a bag.

When I turned around, an officer stood before me holding a pen and a clipboard.

"What did they expect me to tell them?" I paced Hillman's classroom. "What were they expecting? A confession or what? I. Don't. Know. Where. Braden. Is."

"They kept badgerin' me. Like I was a criminal or something," Scotty said, sitting at a desk next to Rachelle.

We were the only ones in the classroom after school that same day.

After missing the bus, I'd called my mom for a ride. After I told her what had happened, she came into the school and threatened the office staff. She even banged on Principal McCoy's door, but luckily for him, he wasn't there.

"Next time you want to have the police interrogate my daughter, you call *me*!" she yelled before storming out, clutching her purse to her side. I had to admit, it made me proud to call her my mom.

She told me I had five minutes before she would be back from the gas station. I needed to talk to Hillman.

"You guys have been his friends for a long time," Hillman said, leaning against his classroom wall. "You really have no idea where he might be?"

"Not a clue," Scotty said. "I found out this morning. My mom told me that his mom had called her, totally freakin' out. She said when they came home on Sunday, he was gone and hasn't shown up since. They called the cops but since he's eighteen and all, the cops didn't do much until today."

"I've been trying to call him all day, but it goes straight to voicemail," Rachelle said.

I buried my head in my hands and pressed my fingers against my temples. "What should I do?"

They stared at me.

"Seriously, what should I do? I can't just go home and pretend nothing happened, like he's not out there somewhere."

"Think about it." Hillman rose. "Where would he go?"

I thought about that, but I certainly wouldn't have gone anywhere obvious. At least not now anyway. I'd be too easy to find.

"We thought you might know where he is, Leah," Rachelle said.

Scotty chimed in. "We just figured you might've heard him say something."

"Believe me, I wish I did."

I looked down, thinking about the road trip he wanted to take —all the places he could be. Just then, the world seemed like a really big place.

"What if he doesn't make it to graduation?" Scotty asked.

Hillman sighed. "Then that's Braden's decision. Just make sure that you all are there. Leah, if it helps you, why don't you go talk to his family when the time is right."

Before I met my mom in the parking lot, I hurried to The Tree, hoping Robert had written back. I uncovered the plastic, practically ripping it from the dirt. It was heavy and the only letter from Robert that had ever come in an envelope.

I didn't open it. I just put it on my shelf, hoping time would make its contents something better than what I began to suspect.

The next day, I went to get groceries with my mom after school. On our way home I asked if she could drive me to Braden's house.

"I don't want you getting involved."

"But I need to talk to them. Maybe there's a way I can help find him," I said. "I need to give this back anyway. It's Braden's."

I held *Mulberry Street*.

"What in the hell is that? Dr. Seuss?"

"Yeah."

"Leah," she sighed. "You only know what you know. You aren't a superhero. Let the cops figure this out."

"Please, Mom. I won't be long. I promise."

"You don't know what's going on with these people. It could be drugs. You don't know what their deal is."

I tilted my head.

She rubbed the steering wheel with her thumb. "How long will you be?"

"Five minutes. I swear. He lives right down the road from the hotel."

She cocked an eyebrow, but I resisted the urge to smile.

"I guess I can check a few things at work while you're there."

I had no questions planned, nothing I really wanted to say other than, "Where could Braden be?"

There were no vehicles in the driveway other than his dad's orange Mustang in the open garage and . . . Braden's purple minivan.

I squeezed the book in my hands. My heart skipped a beat. I ran to the back door and banged on it until it opened.

"Braden," I said.

But it wasn't Braden.

"Trevor," his brother said, slipping his hand into his pocket.

"Where is he? Is he home?"

Trevor shook his head.

"But the van . . ." I pointed.

"He left it here. Left everything here. His phone, van, clothes. We have no idea where he is."

As I caught my breath, I noticed how much older Trevor looked than fourteen.

"When we came home on Sunday, he wasn't here. My parents called everyone they know, everyone Braden knows. He wasn't with any of them."

Trevor raised his eyebrows, opening the door for me to come in.

"Are your parents home?" I asked.

"They're at church organizing a search and flyers and whatnot."

Once we were inside, he let the screen door shut.

"They think he ran away?" I asked.

"I don't know. They overreact to every little thing. It's kind of what they do." He shrugged. "They need to let him be. They couldn't be pushing him more away than if they grabbed him by the shoulders and kicked his ass."

"Where do they think he might be? Did he leave anything behind? A note or something?"

Trevor led me to Braden's room. It looked the same as I remembered.

"And his van?" I asked. "Nothing?"

The air blew a warm breeze into our faces as we walked outside. It was the perfect day to sit at The Tree and dream about life, but there was no life to dream about when Braden wasn't there.

Trevor opened the van door.

"Fuck . . ." he said. "What a slob."

I forgot just how messy Braden left things.

I lifted *Mulberry Street* in my hands, remembering him reading it to me.

"He always loved that book," Trevor said with a laugh.

I pressed my fingers over the old, peeling cover. I attempted to give it to Trevor.

"You can have it," Trevor said.

"No. No way. He used to read this to you. He told me."

"Yeah, centuries ago. I doubt he's ever going to read *Mulberry Street* to me again. It's yours."

I squeezed the book. "I just don't understand. How could he run away from home? Especially right before we graduate?"

"He probably wants to prove something to my parents. College means everything to them, but not to him. Not yet anyway. My parents are pissed because they can't really do much about him being gone since he's an adult and everything."

"Maybe he just left for a while."

"I know you were here," Trevor said. "I heard my parents arguing with Braden about your jacket and why he didn't tell them anything anymore and blah, blah, blah. After that, Braden told me more about you and how you hated his guts in school. He said you were the coolest girl he'd ever met. Real and stuff. He told me a lot."

For Braden to think I was cool just by being myself . . . I couldn't hide a small smile after hearing that.

"You guys must be close," I said.

"Yeah. Because of him, my parents let up on me a lot. The diabetes doesn't help, but they *try* to let me do my own thing."

I glanced at the van. There was that bottle of aspirin near the back seat. I remembered seeing it when we left the basketball game.

I leaned forward and picked it up, but quickly noticed it wasn't a bottle of aspirin or Tylenol or anything like that.

"What's this?" I looked at Trevor. I scanned the print on the label.

He sighed. "Those are his antidepressants."

I shook my head. Trevor had it all wrong. Braden wasn't depressed.

"Sometimes he falls into this darkness and can't get himself out of it," he said.

I shook the bottle. It was half-full.

Trevor looked around before stepping closer to me. "He barely takes them. He just tells my parents he does so they'll get off his back. As long as they believe he's taking his pills, they can live easier."

"Why doesn't he just take the pills to feel better?"

"When he takes them, he becomes a slower version of himself.

He's not really motivated for anything. I think he hates that the most. Maybe he sort of feels out of control when he takes them. He hated that psychotherapy, too. All his sick days from school . . ."

"What—"

"Yeah. He'd want to stay home when the deeper depressions hit. He stopped eating. He slept all the time. That's how my parents knew he stopped taking his pills. They kept him home to keep a better eye on him, sent him to a psychotherapist at the clinic. He promised he'd take the pills if he could pick his own therapist. He'd get better for a while, then stop taking his pills and fall into that hole again."

I thought back on those phone calls I overheard him having with his mom in the empty school hallway.

I looked at the bottle again.

I remembered finding him in his van, how my heart sank, how his face looked under my shadow. He'd promised me it was no big deal.

"Trevor . . ."

I wasn't sure what I wanted to say or maybe I wasn't sure I wanted to believe it.

"Yeah?"

"He never told me what happened after show night." I squeezed the bottle. "He never explained it."

Trevor looked away. Impatience crawled over his face.

"Look, he promised me it'd never happen again and I believe him."

"What would never happen again?"

He grew quiet and barely looked at me. He rested his back against the van and rubbed his shoulder.

"He sucked down pills. A bunch of them. Spent days in the ICU. Like I said, he promised he'd never do it again."

My stomach turned. I didn't want to believe he could have attempted suicide, but looking at Trevor's face, I couldn't deny it.

Trevor was quiet as I read a bit of hope in his eyes.

"Hey," he said, letting out a nervous laugh. "He'd always say that I'm the one with the needles and he's the one with the pills."

"Do you know where he could be?"

"Not here. That's for sure."

When I saw my mom's car pull up against the driveway, I pulled out my cell phone and handed it to him.

"Add your number," I said. "I'll call if I come up with any ideas."

I sat at my bedroom desk, sorting through all the texts Braden had ever sent me. I found no clues.

A suicide attempt.

Braden was strong; he had things to live for, people who needed him, who loved him. How could he ever forget that, even for a second?

I know Trevor didn't seem worried, but I was the one who found Braden in the van. I watched the ambulance take him away. What if I hadn't found him in time?

Graduation would be on Sunday. That gave me five days to figure out where he could be and, most importantly, find him.

I pulled out a scrap of paper and made a list of all the places he could be.

Friend
Family member
Hotel
Camping
Parking lot
Amusement park
Secret hideout
Hitchhiking

Lost

    Such a stupid list.

Why would he leave me with so many possibilities? Maybe he was staying at a hotel right now. Maybe he was at my mom's hotel. She had left again to run errands, so I called her and asked if she could have someone look. When she called back, she said that there was no one by his name staying there.

    If I were going to leave, I would go somewhere farther away. I called all the hotels within a twenty-mile radius and asked if they had a guest by the name of Braden Gregory or a Gregory anything.

    Nothing.

Friend
Family member
~~*Hotel*~~
Camping
Parking lot
Amusement park
Secret hideout
Hitchhiking
Lost

There was only one amusement park near our area. Maybe a cheap thrill was all he needed. If he was there, he would have surely checked into a hotel, but when I called there was no one by his name staying there either.

    I also called all the campsites. Unless there was a place off-the-grid, then he wasn't camping either.

Friend
Family member
~~*Hotel*~~
~~*Camping*~~

Parking lot
~~Amusement park~~
Secret hideout
Hitchhiking
Lost

A secret hideout could be a possibility, but there was no mention or clue to anything cool like that in his texts. If it was a secret, then there was no way I could know about it anyway. The only place I knew was The Tree.

A parking lot?

Seriously, Leah.

Braden was too spontaneous to stay at a parking lot. Plus, he had no vehicle.

Friend
Family member
~~Hotel~~
~~Camping~~
~~Parking lot~~
~~Amusement park~~
~~Secret hideout~~
Hitchhiking
Lost

Although I wouldn't catch him hitchhiking, it could've taken him *somewhere*. The only way to find out if he was hitchhiking would be to put up flyers at almost every exit in Indiana.

I had to get out there.

I scanned over the list of options, hovering over "Friend". Unless he had another friend that none of us knew about, then there was no way he could be with someone else.

~~Friend~~

Family member
~~*Hotel*~~
~~*Camping*~~
~~*Parking lot*~~
~~*Amusement park*~~
~~*Secret hideout*~~
Hitchhiking
Lost

Lost.

If there was one thing I had learned from all the times we moved, it was that sometimes a person had to get lost in order to find themselves.

~~*Friend*~~
Family member
~~*Hotel*~~
~~*Camping*~~
~~*Parking lot*~~
~~*Amusement park*~~
~~*Secret hideout*~~
Hitchhiking
~~*Lost*~~ *DEFINITELY LOST*

My genius led me to the following possibilities:

~~*Friend*~~
Family member
~~*Hotel*~~
~~*Camping*~~
~~*Parking lot*~~
~~*Amusement park*~~
~~*Secret hideout*~~
Hitchhiking

~~Lost~~ *DEFINITELY LOST*

Unless someone were to come and pick him up, he had to have hitchhiked wherever he went. I couldn't prove that though. It also didn't seem like something he would do, but he lived right by an exit and could have found a ride on Sunday morning before his family came back from the cabin.

I pored through all his texts again, analyzing every word he wrote.

If suicide was a possibility, I didn't want to find out. I needed to know he was still out there, waiting to be found.

I grabbed my cell phone and called Trevor.

He answered after only two rings.

"Trevor?"

"Hey, Leah. Sup?"

"I'm sitting here thinking. I need your help. Is there anywhere you think Braden might have gone? Anyone he would have gone to? Think hard."

He was so quiet on the other end that I could hear him breathing.

"Yeah. Centuries ago when our grandpa lived closer. Nobody's kept in touch with him though."

I tapped my pencil on my list.

"What about Braden? Do you think he has?"

"Cops have probably already been to his house and if Braden were there, we'd know by now."

"But he has to be somewhere. He has to be with someone."

"I wouldn't worry about it. My parents are obsessed enough. They probably sent cops to the moon by now."

"Your parents didn't call me."

Trevor lowered his voice. "My mom just got home. She's been a wreck. I told them on Sunday that I'd called you already so that they could focus on other people. I know he's not with you. Figured you'd call us if he was."

I let my fingers glide over my list.

I was quiet as if his parents could hear me, too.

"What's his first name?" I asked.

"Who?"

"Grandpa Norris . . . your grandpa."

Trevor took a moment before answering.

"His name's Robert."

Thinking I heard him wrong, I asked again. "Did you say his name is Robert?"

"Yep. Robert Gregory."

"And you're absolutely sure he doesn't live close by?"

"He moved down south after my grandma died a few years ago. It was a big deal to my dad. I remember him being really upset and talking to my mom about how he wished he would've been nicer and—"

"Hang on."

I peered at my list, then at the stack of letters underneath my lamp. I grabbed one, read the bottom, grabbed another until I had gone through all of them, until the last unopened envelope was in my hand.

All the names were the same.

Robert.

"Leah?"

"Yeah, I'm here."

I heard Trevor sigh from the other end. "Braden will find his way. He's my brother. I know him. I think it'd be best if you just let this go."

"Why?"

"Look, I've already said too much. He will find his way."

"What're you talking about?"

". . . he made me promise, Leah."

"Trevor . . ."

"Just let my brother go. Let all of this go, Leah. Do it for him."

Then Trevor hung up on me.

sunday, may 24, 2009
"Never give up on something that you can't go a
day without thinking about." Winston Churchill

I read the quote from the letter, biting the end of my pencil until the wood peeled off. Flakes of yellow paint covered the letters and I wiped them off before reading the quote from the last letter again.

Tears threatened my eyes, but I refused to let them fall.

Not this time.

Not yet.

I pushed the last letter out of the way, ignoring the rest of the contents in the envelope.

Braden said that his grandpa was the smartest man he knew, that he always did his own thing. He said that his parents didn't let him visit anymore.

"What are you doing to me, Braden?" I clutched my hair. "What did you make Trevor promise?"

Suddenly, my heart picked up speed. I scanned the letters, rereading all the quotes at the top . . . Grandpa Norris was the smartest man Braden knew.

Maybe there was no connection to the letters at all. Maybe there was. Maybe Robert took Braden with him, and if not, then maybe Robert had a clue to where Braden might be.

Chapter 23

When I got to school Wednesday morning, I headed straight to the library. It was the last day of school and there wasn't much left to do aside from busywork in each class.

I typed his name into the search bar.

Robert Gregory

A lot of searches came up, so I narrowed it down to towns around ours. Ten contacts.

I called each phone number. Some didn't answer and the ones who did had no connection to the Robert I was looking for.

I did another search. His name came up hundreds of times throughout the states, but there was no way I'd have time to call all of them. It was then when I noticed his name next to Shelbytown, Alabama.

Alabama. Braden had mentioned Alabama. Even Trevor said his grandpa had moved south.

It clicked. I sat up in my chair and looked around as if everyone else felt it, too.

I looked over the other three Robert Gregory names around that town, but each had a middle initial. I called the phone numbers. One answered, but no luck. The other two didn't pick up the phone. I stared at the Robert Gregory name with no middle initial and no phone number. It seemed fitting given everything Braden had told me about his grandpa being different. Maybe he liked to live a little more off-the-grid. It was a small chance to take, but a chance, nonetheless.

Braden's grandpa was Robert Gregory. He lived in Alabama.

Braden even included it in the road trip he wanted to take. Braden was most likely with his grandpa in Alabama. If not, then his grandpa was possibly the only person who might know where Braden was.

I jotted down the address. I wanted to make flyers for Braden, but didn't have much time left before first period began, plus I didn't have a picture of him.

I had to get out there as soon as possible.

I planned my trip during classes. It would take roughly eight hours to drive, plus any stops I needed to make for gas and food. I would need to get there by Friday, enough time to bring Braden home and get him ready for graduation.

I could help him.

I could save him.

He would see that he wouldn't be coming home to the same old thing—he would be coming home to whatever future he wanted for himself.

I would need a hotel, too, and money for it.

Shit.

I needed a car.

Shit.

When the last school bell rang, I wanted to feel what the other kids were feeling as I walked down the hallway. Relief, sorrow, dread, excitement, anticipation . . . maybe all of that at once.

As I stepped to my locker, a few drama club members waved at me. Everyone was hugging and saying goodbye as if they'd never see each other again.

I opened my locker and put the rest of my notebooks and folders into my book bag, which had never felt so light. The teachers told us that would happen . . . four years would go by fast and college would go by even faster. I hoped that Ball State would have such a nice theatre club.

I couldn't believe it was all over.

I wished I could go back in time, just to hold on to one of the nice moments for as long as I could, savoring the memory until I had to let go. But then I realized, I would always want just one more moment.

I closed my locker for the last time, glancing to Braden's down the hallway. I couldn't think about never seeing him in those halls again, nudging me, waving at me, hollering my name when he saw me.

"Hey, you," I heard a voice say behind me.

For a split second I thought it could have been Braden, but when I turned around, his high voice matched his bright orange hair.

"Justin." I dropped my book bag and grabbed him into a hug. "I'm sorry."

He drew his head back to get a good look at me. "You okay?"

"I didn't know what I was doing. You and Becca and drama club and . . . I feel like I lost everything that was important to me."

"You didn't lose me." He grinned.

I let go of him and shook my head.

"It's all over, Justin. School . . . drama club . . . all our salon shenanigans . . . the dances . . . the games . . . I should have been a better friend. I shouldn't have let anything stand in the way of that."

"Except one thing," he said.

I looked at him.

"I wasn't expecting to like Braden," I said.

"You guys are a cute couple. If I could have picked someone for you, it would've been him."

"I was being selfish though."

"A little." He winked and caressed the hair over my shoulders. "I love your hair down. You should have worn it like this before."

I patted my hair.

"About Braden," he said. "You okay?"

"I don't know yet, but I will be. I'm leaving tonight to find him. I think I might know where he is."

"Woah, tonight?"

"Long story," I said. "I really wish I could say bye to Becca. I called her so many times."

"I know where she is," he said.

I slung my book bag over my shoulder and hurried with Justin to the parking lot.

So many kids were crying. Most were jumping on top of their cars and hooting and hollering "Freedom!" as if high school had been prison.

I saw Becca standing next to Justin's car. Her head was turned down and she looked sad. Still a little upset, but sad. It reminded me of the first time I'd met her in sixth grade science lab. She'd looked down at the frog we were supposed to dissect together, her bottom lip stuck out as she refused to even pick up the scalpel.

Justin put his hand on my shoulder.

"A lot of us are going to drive around town to celebrate. We were going to kidnap you and bring you along for the ride."

"But . . ." I said.

"She's still your best friend, Leah."

I waited until Becca looked up and caught me watching her. She tilted her head to the other side and shrugged.

I started walking her way. Justin followed behind. When I stopped in front of her, I knew she had been crying. Without another thought, I leaned forward and grabbed her into a hug; her arms wrapped tightly around me.

"Enough with the melodramatics, ladies," Justin said.

When we parted, we both wiped tears from our faces.

"I'm sorry," she said. "Really. Braden's a good guy. I just missed you."

"Me too."

"How're you holding up?"

"Honestly? I'm terrified."

"He'll be back. He's probably just burnt out from high school. We still gotta do graduation. Bleh."

"I need to find him."

"The police have been questioning everyone all week and they still haven't found him."

"I might know where he is," I said.

"What?" Becca's eyes popped.

"But I need a car." I looked at Justin.

"Sorry, hun." He smacked the top of the car. "This baby belongs to my momma this weekend. She needs it for work. Plus, it's due for summer tires."

I grunted, hating that I had a license I could never use.

"There's no way my mom is going to let me take her car," I said. "She doesn't even know I'm leaving."

Becca looked at me. "Leaving? When? Where are you going?"

"As soon as I can. I need to make it to Alabama before graduation. There's no way I'm letting Braden miss it."

"All the way to Alabama? By yourself? Are you insane?"

"You know I'd do the same for you."

"Then I'll go with you," she said.

I glared at her.

"Seriously, I'm coming with you. I just don't have a car or anything with an engine, but we'll figure it out."

Justin cleared his throat. "Excuse me? This is a road trip we're talking about and nobody bothers to ask me?"

I looked at him, amazed at these friends I almost left behind.

"Okay, so now that we have a party established, where are we getting a set of wheels?" Becca asked.

I glanced around the parking lot. I couldn't take my mom's. Becca didn't have a car. Justin's was out of the question.

I saw Scotty a few rows down texting next to his Range Rover. That might have been the only thing he hadn't smashed against a wall in a fit of rage. It was worth a shot.

Becca and Justin hurried with me.

I explained our plans to Scotty and how I thought I knew where Braden was.

"I gotta run it past my mom first," he said. "But if you really wanna do this, if we can really find Braden, then I'm in."

I jumped and squeezed him around the waist.

Someone jogged toward us. I noticed it was Rachelle by her blown out hair.

"Scotty," she said, holding something up. "You left your sweater in Hillman's room."

"Leah thinks she might know where Braden is," Scotty said.

Rachelle looked at me with hope.

"He might be in Alabama. Do you know his grandpa?" I said.

"I don't know anyone in Alabama."

"Leah, me, Scotty, and Justin are going there," Becca said.

"When are you leaving?" Rachelle asked.

"Now," I said.

"Woah, like *now* now?" Scotty asked. "We're supposed to blast our horns around town."

"Why don't we do the town drive," Becca said. "We can take off first thing in the morning. Plus"—her voice lowered—"I'm having dinner at my dad's tonight."

"Oh," I said. "That's awesome, Becca."

I knew how much work it had probably taken for her to get to a place where she could spend an entire evening with her dad, and as much as I wanted to leave that night, I didn't want to stand in the way of anyone else's progress.

"Look, you guys," I said, dreading the idea of waiting. "That's really sweet that you all want to come, too, but I'll just take off by myself. I'll see what I can do about a car. You guys don't have to change your plans because of me."

"Leah, we all want to do this. Right?" Justin asked, looking at everyone until they all nodded. "Let's get prepared tonight, get a good night of sleep, and take off first thing in the morning."

I paused. Concern took over my face.

"Don't worry," Becca said. "We wouldn't make it to Alabama

tonight anyway. You can't drive that late. Try to sleep well, then we can drive straight through tomorrow."

"I gotta get some clothes, pack some stuff. I gotta run by the bank," Scotty said.

Damn.

Money.

"Everyone should bring some cash," Justin said.

"Then I'm coming, too," Rachelle said.

I didn't know whether to smile or run for cover because a road trip with them could end well or in total disaster.

We followed behind the train of vehicles leaving the parking lot, everyone beeping their horns and shouting, "Class of 2009!" from their car windows. I sat in the back seat of Justin's car while Becca rode shotgun. Scotty followed behind us in his Range Rover with Rachelle and a few others. When I turned, I saw Rachelle actually laughing and waving at some cars which passed them from the other lane.

As we drove downtown, other cars honked and gestured in support of our "freedom" with the middle finger or a flexed fist. Though high school had its ups and downs for my social class, I began to think that maybe every social class had a roller coaster ride. Even the nerd squad driving in front of us looked more relieved about the end of school than the jocks were. One guy stuck half his lanky body out of the sunroof and cursed Tipton High to hell . . . and a few other things.

Becca turned around and rested her chin over the headrest.

"What do you think?" she asked. "Should we cut loose and live a little?"

I rolled down the back window and stuck out my head, closing my eyes against the wind. I pushed myself a little further out until I could wave at Scotty and Rachelle behind us. They pumped their fists. I looked forward as we drove the main street of Tipton County, passing the gas station where Braden and I had picked up Aladdin and Princess Jasmine.

I'd always had to leave a place against my own will, but this . . . this time, leaving would be my choice and I still had time to make that choice.

Becca shouted, "Hell yeah!" as Justin pressed his hand against the horn.

I let one of my arms fly free against the wind, allowing my eyes to close as images of Braden flashed by.

Chapter 24

My hands wrapped around the steering wheel the following morning, the breeze cooling us through the open windows.

Rachelle and Justin gossiped about some dancing show in the back. Scotty took the middle seat while Becca rode up front.

We had been on the road for over an hour, stopping once for snacks, and after a long, almost heated discussion, everyone agreed that the first stop would be Kentucky.

Since then, they had been going on about which major in college made the most sense regarding money and job opportunities. Rachelle and Justin both wanted to minor in theatre. Apparently, showbiz wasn't a great Plan A.

Scotty's attention was on me as I drove the speed limit on the interstate. I hadn't driven much since getting my license the year before, so it took me a while to trust the Range Rover, which might as well have been a Transformer.

At first, Scotty had refused to let me drive. Something about not wanting scratches on his precious ride. I couldn't explain that driving would distract me from thoughts of Braden . . . thoughts I wanted to avoid. Scotty finally handed me the keys after Becca threatened to kick him in the balls.

Though I refused to believe Braden would do anything to himself, just the fact that he had before scared the hell out of me. Anytime I thought about it, I'd press my foot against the gas even if I still didn't fully trust the Range Rover.

"What about you, Leah? What's your major gonna be?" Scotty asked, leaning between the front seats.

I still hadn't sent in Ball State's confirmation form.

"Maybe child development," I said.

"To do what?" Scotty asked.

"I don't know. Maybe be a counselor. Maybe a teacher."

"Who actually *wants* to be a teacher?" Scotty said. "You'd be in school for the rest of your life."

I stifled a laugh. "I think I'd be good at it."

"I think you would, too, Leah," Justin said.

"Sure," Scotty said, "but it's not gonna make you rich."

"Probably not," I admitted. "It would make a difference anyway, even if I was able to help one kid."

"Suit yourself," Scotty said. "I wanna be rich. I wanna make tons of dough."

"A job in sports medicine will just fall into your lap," I said.

"I know I'll probably have to flip burgers for a while, but I don't care. How 'bout you, Becks?"

Becca woke up from her daydream and rolled her eyes.

"Don't know, don't care," she mumbled.

"You have to care about somethin', Becks."

She turned around in her seat. "Nobody calls me Becks, and I don't really care what I end up doing just as long as it pays better than flipping burgers."

"Nice." Scotty smiled at her. "Hey, you like sports?"

"They're all right," she said.

"Hah!" Justin shouted. I saw him through the rear-view mirror, leaning over as Rachelle stared out the window from the opposite side. "She likes sports just as much as a kid likes their vegetables."

"I like sports," Becca said. "I watch the Super Bowl every year."

"You only watch it for the half-time show," Justin said.

"I only watch it for the half-time show, too," Rachelle chimed in. "We don't really do that kind of football in Mexico. My family watches a lot of soccer. I've never understood the point of a bunch of big dudes tackling each other either. The half-time show though . . . that's the best part."

"All right," Scotty said. "If Becca can prove that she's seen one baseball game this season, I swear I'll dye my hair purple."

And just like that, another heated discussion.

I shook my head, keeping my focus on the road. Chills spread through my body when we passed the state border. Every inch we drove was an inch closer to Braden.

I thought about the day before when Becca and Justin had dropped me off at home after the school drive. I'd hurried to take a shower, clean up my room, and pack some clothes and Robert's letters in an old duffel bag I had. It only smelled a little like dog urine. Or maybe I'd just gotten used to the way the house always smelled.

I called Scotty to remind him about printing the flyers. He had a photo of Braden, and Rachelle was working on the flyer design. We would make stops along the way and post them in hotels.

In the morning, my mom had knocked on my bedroom door before I left. It surprised me because she'd never knocked before.

"I'm going to be gone for a couple days," I said, turning off my TV. "Some friends and I are going to Alabama to look for Braden."

She just looked at me for a moment, as if she already knew I would be leaving.

"Who's driving?"

"I don't know yet. Maybe Shakira Scotty. It's his van."

"What makes you think Braden's in Alabama?"

"I'm not sure if he is. He's got this grandpa he used to talk about, so I think if I have the right guy, then he might be with him."

"Why not just call?"

"I can't find a number. It's just an eight-hour drive anyway . . . There's still enough time. Braden has to graduate with us."

She nodded her head and glanced around my room.

"What about your appointment with Dr. Schoenhofer?"

So that's the psychologist's real name.

"Is that today?"

"Tomorrow morning."

I tapped my fingers against my thigh.

"I'll call and postpone it," I said.

My mom was quiet for a while, glancing around my room as if it was her first time in there. She walked over to my broken closet door and looked over all the pictures I had taped around the frame. I wasn't sure whether to break the silence until she finally did.

"Wow, I remember this." She slid her finger over a small photo of tiny me petting a goat. "This was that petting zoo we visited in Buffalo. You were so little."

She glanced over a few more, taking her time before turning to me.

"We've lived in a lot of places, haven't we?"

I nodded, giving a half-smile.

"You had to make a lot of new friends." She turned to the pictures with one hand on her hip, chewing her lip.

It got quiet in the room again. I thought I would normally be uncomfortable with it, but there was this conversation happening in the silence that lingered between my mom and me. I imagined her voice in my head . . . apologizing. She was sorry for thinking I could ever be like my dad. She was sorry for having put me through so many changes, so many that I would never want to leave Small Town Nowhere even though everyone in that town wanted out. She was sorry for ever . . . *ever* hurting my feelings.

She turned back to me and dropped her arm, free from her own thoughts.

"Well, be safe." She sighed. "You need anything?"

"Actually . . . yeah," I said. "We're all chipping in, but I don't have any cash."

She went to her bedroom and came back with a small wad of money.

"Here." She handed it to me. "We're not going to use it all for the honeymoon."

"Thanks," I said, surprised. "I'll give back whatever we don't need."

When the Range Rover arrived, I opened the front door, but before I left, I turned around. I slid my hands over the Nike hat on my head. I slowly pulled it off, replacing it with Braden's Chaplin hat.

I caressed the gray jacket over my arms, the way its material warmed my skin, making me feel safe. My fingers grazed the zipper before pulling it all the way down. I slid the jacket off and left it on one of the living room chairs while my hand rested over it for a moment. I closed my eyes before letting my hand slide down as I turned away.

I heard my mom shout from the kitchen, "Be careful!"

I smiled and walked out the door.

As the conversation in the van quieted, I grabbed the CD from the console.

Becca looked at me. "Did you make that yourself?"

"Not exactly."

I popped it into the CD player and turned to track two.

The vehicle grew quiet, the only sound coming from Jeff Buckley in the speakers.

"What the hell is this?" Scotty asked.

"Shut up, Scott," Rachelle said. "It's good music."

"This is the kind of mind shit Braden would force us to listen to on our wrestling trips."

"What's wrong with it?" I asked.

"It's depressing as hell. We need somethin' to jump to."

"It wouldn't kill you to listen to something thought-provoking for once," Rachelle said.

"Well, I'm not taking it out," I told him.

"Seriously, we're on a road trip," he said. "You expect me to believe this is all you brought? Where are you hidin' the party music?"

"How about this?" I flipped to track nine.

The music came on and everyone's posture shifted.

"I can settle for that," Scotty said.

Scotty started singing when the vocals came. Though he was no Bocelli, he wasn't too bad. Soon Rachelle joined. She wasn't exactly in tune, but Justin pointed up to let her know to raise her voice another octave; a benefit of having been both a choir and drama club kid.

Braden had implied I was an idiot for only knowing this one song of Paul Simon's, but as it happened, so were the others. Maybe he had tried to school them, too.

Becca and I looked at each other and giggled.

Justin joined them in singing "You Can Call Me Al."

Becca and I sang, too; our voices grew louder until we were almost shouting the lyrics. I thought about Braden and how his vibrato would have sounded better than all of ours put together.

Never in the past four years, sitting behind the school cafeteria window, would I have thought that the five of us would be friends. Scotty and Rachelle had been like store items kept behind a glass— the really precious stuff that could only be accessed with a key. Now, they were people I knew I could count on. I then understood why Braden liked them so much.

Scotty smacked the seats in rhythm, and Justin jammed with Rachelle with as much room as they could muster around Scotty. Becca laughed hard for the first time that day and I . . . well, I thought about Braden, knowing how much he would have loved to be there.

Chapter 25

T hursday, May 28, 2009
   Dear Braden,

I'm sitting outside of the Slugger Museum here in Louis-ville. It looks pretty cool from here. The others are inside, but I can't have a good time without you. You would like it here. You could play the guitar. People would stop and listen to you. I don't think you'd make enough tips around here, but it'd be cool for a while anyway.

There is so much to do, but I just want to find you. I want to know that you are okay.

We posted at least a hundred flyers around Louisville. I know that's not much, but even if just one person meets you, they will never be able to forget you.

I don't blame you for wanting to do what you want. For so long, I wished I could be someone else. I guess I never thought someone like you needed to get out. I always assumed you were happy with your life. I always thought that happiness came from having money and involved parents, but I was wrong.

I want to know what's going through your mind. Maybe you think you are doing something noble, but Braden, this really sucks.

I need you. I can't get through this summer without you.
Leah

"So where have you been so far?" my mom asked over the phone.

I could tell she was busy at the stove. Something crackled and she muttered a curse word.

"Just left Kentucky. Driving through Tennessee now. We went to the Slugger Museum. The others wanted to stay another day and check out more stuff, but I promised them we could go to a cave on the way back if they agreed to leave now."

"Oooh, Kentucky. We've never spent a lot of time there."

"I think you'd like Louisville. It makes you feel like a tiny ant surrounded by a bunch of ginormous buildings."

"You having a good time?"

"I didn't think it would be this exciting, but there are a lot of places to see and nobody has killed anyone yet."

"What's next?"

"We're deciding on whether to make a stop in Mississippi or Georgia. It's still being debated."

I lifted the phone from my ear so my mom could hear the bickering in the back seats.

"Go to Georgia," she said.

Thursday, May 28, 2009

Dear Braden,

We're at the aquarium in Georgia. This place is amazing. You could play guitar here. I can picture you looking up at all these creatures swimming around us. It really makes me realize how small we are in such a big world.

We posted a hundred more flyers. Only a hundred left now. Scotty didn't have a lot of printer paper left, so hopefully three hundred finds you.

Scotty is hilarious. He's posing in every picture, thinking he's Robert Pattinson or something. Instead of sports medicine, he should consider being an actor.

They're taking so many pictures, but I refuse to take one without you.

This was all your idea. We're here now, out of the bubble.

So when are you coming back?

Leah

"Hungry!" Scotty moaned, laying dramatically across Rachelle's lap, his massive feet kicking the back of my seat. "Dyyyying."

"Suck it up, Buttercup." Becca smacked his legs down. "You should've eaten something other than a tiny power bar and an energy drink when we stopped."

"I'm getting kind of hungry, too," Justin said. "Plus, I need water to hydrate this skin. Did you know I found a cystic zit on my forehead last week? A. Cystic. Zit. I almost died."

"You guys, we are not stopping," I said. "We all agreed to drive until we get there. Just try to go to sleep or something."

"I cannot sleep in here. Too cramped," Rachelle said, attempting to stretch her arms.

"Use me as a pillow, darling." Justin patted his shoulder which was way out of reach next to Scotty.

"We only have two more hours to go. We can do it," I said.

"Liar," Rachelle moaned. "It's more like three hours."

They didn't know what I knew. Braden made Trevor promise something.

"Leah, we need a hotel," Justin said.

"Get a hold of yourselves," I said, trying to make light of things. "Just three more hours to go. You can handle it. We can get a hotel after we get there, I promise. Then you can feast and sleep for the rest of the trip if you want."

Scotty sat up. "But if we drive three more hours, it'll be like one in the morning when we get there. You really think you can knock on an old dude's door that late? Don't old folks go to bed like right after dinner?"

I looked at the clock. Blond boy might have had a few brain cells after all.

"But I can still check out the house and see if Braden is sitting outside or something."

"Psycho," Scotty sang, stretching out each syllable.

"Leah, you're exhausted," Rachelle said. "If you would've just let someone else drive for a while, maybe you could do it. It's been a long day and you aren't a superhuman. You need sleep. You need fuel. Braden will be there when we get there."

"Graduation isn't until Sunday," Becca said quietly. "I know you want him there. We all do, but safety first."

"And food!" Justin said.

Rachelle hollered, "All in favor of stopping this madness, say 'I'."

I lost.

We picked the nearest motel. There was a Waffle House right next door, so I offered to check in while they took off. Becca insisted I come, but I wasn't feeling that hungry anyway.

I booked two connecting double rooms and lucked out on the extra rollaway bed without a charge.

When I got to my room, I took a shower, allowing the water to run over my body as if it was washing away all my fears. I told myself he was okay. I promised myself he was.

Although I wished Trevor hadn't said anything, if he hadn't then I may not have been staying in a Georgia motel, looking for the person I loved.

After putting on some fresh clothes, I plopped on the bed where my duffel bag was and pulled out the envelope from The Tree.

I took the letter out and read the quote at the top. I stopped. Trying to read further felt like a betrayal. I had to stay positive.

Keeping my hope strong could somehow change what I dreaded was written in the letter.

My throat burned. Tears almost came, but I was too parched to produce any. I started humming "You Can Call Me Al."

It was true. You couldn't be upset during that song.

I pulled out a piece of paper and a pen.

Thursday, May 28, 2009

Dear Braden,

Just like me, you also wanted a better life, but I guess the grass isn't always greener on the other side. Except here. In Georgia.

There are trees everywhere, Braden. It feels like I'm surrounded by possibility. I feel what you want to feel so bad and if you come back, then we can feel this way together.

I thought that maybe if I wrote to you, then you could see everything you have to live for, but I don't even know if you will ever read these letters.

There is only one of you in this world. One. The world needs you and only you can give it everything you have to offer. Braden Gregory cannot be replaced.

I hope you are with your grandpa when we get there tomorrow.

If there is any chance in the world that you can feel how loved you are, then I hope you choose to stick around.

Leah

There was a knock at the motel room door. Becca walked in carrying a couple of Styrofoam boxes and two water bottles. "Hey."

I folded the letter and put it in my duffel bag.

I smiled. "Is that food I smell?"

"Did you really think I was gonna eat without you?"

She came over to the bed and sat on the edge.

"I got you these greasy chicken tenders with fries, coleslaw, and extra barbeque and honey mustard."

"You rock."

I grabbed the box and munched on some fries, not realizing how hungry I was until then.

"What do you think so far?" I asked. "They aren't as horrible as we thought, right?"

"Rachelle and Scotty? Naw. They're not so bad." She dipped a biscuit in the mashed potatoes. "That dumb jock is starting to grow on me."

"How'd I know that was going to happen?"

"I didn't say I like him or anything. I just think his overflowing testosterone and incredible lack of intelligence is endearing. That's all."

I wrinkled my nose at her. She tossed a bottle of water to me.

"He asked me to a baseball game," she said. "He didn't believe I'd go. He said if I go to a game with him, he really will dye his hair purple. I couldn't pass that up."

"Smooth."

As we ate, we talked about how Justin would be attending university for theatre and a major in art, while at the same time finishing his training program at his mother's salon.

"He's going to have it made," Becca said.

"Agreed. He will put us up when we're older."

"Penthouse suites, maid service, glam squad. We chose a good friend."

Becca put her food on the table when she was finished and sat with her legs to the side.

"Hey, there's something I've been wanting to get off my chest."

I looked at her. "You're not pregnant, are you? Because that would be record-breaking speed. Does Scotty know?"

She smacked my ankle. "Knock it off."

I sat my food on the nightstand and took a swig of water.

"I don't really know where to start," she said. "I'll just start with saying that I never had a problem with Braden. I actually like him. Didn't think I would, but he turned out to be cooler than I thought.

"I felt like I was second to him. When he came into the picture, it's like I didn't matter anymore. I was always your go-to person when you wanted to talk or hang out, so when I realized how important he was becoming to you, it really pissed me off. I mean, you ditched me to go to that musical cast party . . ."

"Becca, we can forget about this. Really. I screwed up, too."

She fidgeted with the holes in her jeans; her face read regret.

"Promise you won't hate me?" she asked, looking up.

"What?"

"Just promise you won't hate me," she said. "Promise."

I tilted my head, sitting up a little straighter. I wondered what could possibly make me hate her.

"Okay," I said.

"Leah . . ." her voice quivered. "I told Braden's mom about you and him skipping out on the prom after-party."

The hairs on the back of my neck rose. "What?"

She looked down and shook her head.

"It got really late. His mom showed up and asked where you guys were." She paused to swallow. "It was our night, you know? It was supposed to be me, you, and Justin crashing prom night . . . camouflage . . . four wheelers . . . the whole bit. I was so pissed when Justin told me you were going with Braden. When I saw how mad his mom was, I thought I'd take my shot. I told her he stayed behind with a girl."

"Why would you do that? Do you have any idea how much trouble he got into?"

"I felt bad right after I said it. Maybe if I hadn't said anything, we wouldn't be looking for him right now. I'm so sorry, Leah. I'm sorry and I hope you know me enough to know that if I could take it back, I would in a heartbeat."

I thought back to Braden's mom showing up next to us. I saw

Braden's face, him getting out of the van and walking over to her, his expression while she scolded him.

Becca tilted her head. Regret weighed on her frown. "I'm sorry."

I rubbed my arm.

"Becca," I said. "That was a really crappy thing to do."

"I know. I was stupid and jealous and stupid."

"What do you mean jealous?"

She glared at me. "You don't get it, do you? It's so hard being your friend sometimes. You're pretty, you're smart, you're talented. You are everything anybody could hope to be at our age. You kick my ass in drama club, blow me out of the water with grades . . ."

I was quiet as she went on.

"All of my crushes liked you. I could always tell. Like Jase Cumberworth our freshman year. He wanted you the whole time. He even told me he liked you. And Miles Green last year. I gawked over that short little stoner so much even though I knew he had googly eyes all over you."

It was supposed to make sense to me, but it didn't. I never thought good friends could let jealousy affect their bond, especially ours. I hadn't given a lot of thought to the way other people perceived me other than what they might have thought if I tripped or got my sleeve slammed shut in my locker. I guessed I thought it would feel good to have someone be jealous of me. But it didn't. It really sucked, especially when it was my own best friend.

"Maybe I would have done the same thing," I said. "I can't sit here and act like I wouldn't have. I know that if I came and apologized to you, you would forgive me."

Becca leaned over and hugged me.

"I really am sorry," she said. "You don't think that pushed him to go, do you?"

I thought for a moment, remembering how seemingly little I actually knew about Braden. I even wondered if I had pushed him away. There must have been something I could have done. I could have paid more attention. I could have asked more questions when I saw that his parents didn't show up for *Aladdin*. I could have hammered into his head how important college was, how he deserved to go despite the pressure his parents put on him. He needed to know that I was there for him, that I cared, that he didn't have to feel pressure around me.

"If it wasn't that, it would have been something else," I said. "It wasn't the only thing he was in trouble for . . . it wasn't the only thing he lied to his parents about."

"Shitty home life? I get it."

I rested my back against the headboard.

"I just wish I knew what he needed."

Chapter 26

I woke up with light beaming into my eyes. I shielded my vision enough to see through the window that the sun was up.

"Shit. No!"

I kicked the covers off and ran to Becca's bed. She moaned when I smacked her back.

"Wake up! We're late."

I ran to the other room and nearly pushed everyone off their beds. Except for Scotty who wouldn't budge.

"Get up! We're late, you guys."

They groaned.

"Come on, Mom, five more minutes," Scotty begged.

"You have exactly that to get ready and be in the van. If Braden doesn't want us to find him, I'm not risking another second he will leave his grandpa's before we get there."

I rushed to my room and put on some jeans and a white shirt, almost tripping over my bag. Becca was ready with her bag in hand.

I zipped my duffel bag and put on the Chaplin hat.

As soon as I checked out, Justin was practically crawling out of his room.

"Hate you, Leah. Totally hate you."

Becca was already in the front seat. Soon Scotty came, then Rachelle whose hair was puffed out like a chow dog.

"How could we have slept so long?" I turned on the ignition and checked the time. "It's almost eight thirty in the morning."

"We only slept six hours? No wonder I feel like a zombie," Scotty said.

Once we were all in the van, I let the music play on low while Scotty, Rachelle, and Justin drifted back to sleep.

"Granola bar?" Becca asked, sliding one out of her bag.

I shook my head.

"He's either there or he's not," she said quietly. "If he's not, we just have to keep looking. Someone should recognize his face from all the flyers."

The next few hours floated by like a dream. I barely remember being present at the wheel, never mind how fast I was driving. All I could think about was Braden, sitting next to him in front of the piano as he taught me "Hey Jude," except this time our fingers glided across the keys in perfect melody.

It was a little after eleven when we finally arrived.

The house stood alone, small and unkempt, surrounded by trees.

So many trees.

The lawn looked like it hadn't been mowed in weeks, and old leaves filled the gutters. There was a rusty blue truck in the driveway with the paint chipping off. The place was isolated, the only neighboring house a mile down the road.

I stepped out of the van, smelling the fresh breeze as it nearly blew Braden's hat off my head. The sun hit in just the right places, reflecting off the old truck near the shed.

I could see why someone would want to live out there. The privacy . . . the silent sounds of nature . . . the birds singing in the trees. Oh, the trees. There must have been thousands surrounding the house—the perfect spot for Braden.

Justin and Rachelle were still sleeping, but Scotty and Becca came out with me.

"So, Braden likes the boondocks, huh?" Scotty said.

An axe was stuck in a tree stump. I wondered whether Braden would have liked that. Braden's voice echoed in my head from when he'd told me how the rings in a tree could tell how old it was.

What if he'd never been there at all? All these thoughts came rushing to me. What if he'd left already? What if we were too late, just hours too late?

When we got to the door, I couldn't raise my hand to knock. I felt the rush of nerves like right before a play audition, except this was real life hitting me hard.

"Leah, it's okay," Becca said. "Just knock."

Scotty offered to do it, but I insisted.

I felt Braden. I felt that he was still close, waiting for someone to find him.

I looked up and let my fist knock on the door. Shortly after, the door opened.

Robert Gregory—a brunet Chuck Norris. Braden wasn't joking when he said how fit his grandpa was for a seventy-something-year-old. A black short-sleeved shirt fit snugly around his torso. His veins were prominent on his upper arms, and his muscles bulged as if he were constantly flexing.

He had a full head of thick dark hair, and teeth that shined when he smiled at us. His tan skin had already seen a lot of sun for that time of year. I would have pegged him for a fifty-year-old if it weren't for the depth in the way his crystal green eyes looked at us.

"Men are not prisoners of fate, but only prisoners of their own minds," he said upon opening the door. "You kids familiar with Franklin D. Roosevelt? He was an interesting man, that one. Always had wise things to say." He stepped back and welcomed us in. The place smelled of dog food and laundry detergent.

"I gather you all know me, but I don't know you in the slightest. Not personally, that is. Care to introduce yourselves?"

I glanced around the small living room. A few puppies grunted in a small box in the corner. Framed photos hung neatly on every wall and a soft-looking taupe couch sat in front of a small fireplace.

Becca started, pointing to herself. "I'm Becca. This is our friend Scotty and—"

"I'm Leah." I gave him my hand and he took it with a gentle, yet controlled shake.

"A very warm welcome to you all. Would you care for something to drink or nibble on? I was just about to brew up some coffee. Nothing like fresh hot coffee after a late morning workout."

"That'd be nice," Becca said.

"Sure," Scotty nodded. "Thanks a lot, sir."

"Sir? What am I, an old man? I plant my own vegetables right there in that garden." He pointed out the window. "Pluck 'em out and cook 'em right onto my plate. Repaired most of this old house with these two hands. Now, do you think an old man could do that?" He laughed. "Call me Rob."

Becca went to the puppies and Scotty followed. I stood awkwardly in front of Robert until he motioned for me to come with him into the kitchen.

"You have a nice place," I said. "Cozy."

"Didn't do too bad, did I? Been here about three years, since my beautiful wife passed away. She'd have enjoyed your company very much."

"I'm sorry."

"She went to a good place, that one. I was never much of an animal lover before she came into my life. She's all the reason I take care of strays when they come by. I rescued the mother of those puppies in there." He poured some water into the coffee maker and clicked the button. "'There is only one happiness in this life, to love and be loved.' The wonderful George Sand. You take milk in your coffee, my dear?"

The last time I'd drunk coffee was before our last rehearsal. Braden took me to Quick Stop, and I'd added some sugar to sweeten mine up.

"Yes. Sugar, too, if you have any."

"Sure do." Robert pulled some down from the cabinet. "And your friends? Well, I'll just bring it all out, then everyone can help themselves."

"Don't you want to know why we're here?" I asked.

He talked while putting everything on a tray, speaking in the same way that Braden did—like they were giving a speech to a classroom full of eager learners.

"If I had to take a wild guess, I'd say you all know my grandson." He turned and flashed his teeth. "My boy, Braden. I got word that he left home. He's the reason you're here. If he's not, then I didn't cut anyone off on my way to the library this morning. If someone cut you off, you ought to get lookin' somewhere else."

I was taken aback for a moment.

"You cut people off to get to the library?"

"I'm not the most attentive on these roads. I am quite fond of books though. They are the finest remedy for a lonely soul."

He poured some of the finished brew into four cups and brought the tray into the living room.

"I've got some cookies right under the coffee table. Becca? Would you kindly pull them out?"

She reached over and placed the cookie box on the table.

"Thanks, dear. Those are some interesting drawings on your jeans. Originals?"

"Yeah." She glanced down to a dragon on her thigh. "I like to doodle."

"Very detailed for a doodle. That dragon reminds me of my time in Vietnam. Isn't the world a better place when people get along?"

"Sure is," she said.

"Bet that dragon would make a fine tattoo."

"Do you have any?" she asked.

"On this body? No. Never had one. Can't imagine what an old one would look like now."

"Thanks for the coffee, Rob." Scotty sat on the couch which swallowed his lower half. "Do you chop your own wood?" He gestured to a pile out of the window.

"Sure do. Nature is a man's best friend. I recommend you young people get out there more."

"Impressive," Scotty said.

"You can, too, when you get to be my age. There's something to Popeye eating all that spinach. Keeps you strong and sharp."

When he flexed his arm, Scotty's eyes grew.

"I'll take you as my example," he said.

"Well, kids, I don't have a decent television. Never cared for one. I only have that small one there to watch a VHS every so often. Hope that's not a problem."

Becca looked at me. Scotty glanced between us.

"I actually hoped we could talk," I said, lowering my voice.

Becca led Scotty back to the puppies.

"Absolutely, dear."

Robert began walking around the house, stopping first at the mantel above the fireplace.

"This is a little trinket Braden sent me after his first trip to Gatlinburg," he said.

It was a magnet shaped like a guitar.

"Why isn't it on your fridge?" I asked.

"We don't always have to do what the rest of the world does," he said, admiring the other things.

"Here's a guitar pick he left behind years ago. The Beatles, of course. My goodness, that boy loves The Beatles. Oh, and here's a picture of the first pike he caught just down the road at the lake. Don't know if you caught a glimpse of the lake on your way up here. He's a great fisherman."

I slid my fingers over little Braden in the picture. He must have been no older than ten.

Robert led me down the hallway. I was nervous, too nervous to ask where Braden was.

We passed a room I assumed was Robert's. There were a few brown blankets folded on the bottom of the bed. Other than that, there was nothing more than a dresser and a small desk. The next room was similar.

"This is where he would sleep when he visited. Small, but

Braden isn't the kind of boy impressed by money and all those shiny things." He looked at me. "You know that."

"He loves music . . . the meaning of things," I said.

Robert nodded strongly. "He sure does. He's a cultured one. Someone who uses his brain and takes the time to think about things. Maybe he thinks too much and too deeply sometimes, but at least his noggin works."

Robert grabbed a notebook off the side table and brought it over to me. He flipped through it, showing off dozens of pages filled with words.

"Poems?" I asked.

"Songs," Robert said, raising his wide-set eyebrows. I could see where Braden got his. "Braden wrote songs when he was here and played them to me on his guitar."

I studied the chicken scratch handwriting, grinning at the thought of Braden writing songs with passion in his eyes.

"Do you also write songs?" I asked.

"Me? No. I'm not much of an artist in that way. I do like books though. I suppose I'm just more of a hands-on kind of guy. Fixed up this bedroom. Hah. You should have seen the dump it was before I got to work on it."

A guitar sat next to the side table where he returned the notebook. I pictured Braden sitting there, strumming and singing without a care in the world. A calmness fell over me being in the same place Braden spent so much time. However, nothing was undone. The bed was made. No bags or clothes anywhere. I glanced once more in the room before following Robert back into the living room.

"Take your coffee, dear," he said, handing mine to me.

He led me out to the back porch where the sun was bright. The patio table made of wicker looked older than him.

"You know," he began, showing his age in the pained way he took his seat. "Braden's father is my son. My only child. Quiet man. Hard worker. Great provider. He and Trish have been together since they were fifteen years old, believe it or not. Three years later, he asked for her hand in marriage, and you know what she said?"

"What?"

"She said 'hell no.'"

Robert laughed, and I couldn't help but laugh with him.

"My son struggled with alcohol. He was throwing his young life right out the window for the damn bottle. Trish was a smart little gal, though. She told him that if he couldn't get himself together, he could say adios to a future with her. I admired that. Whipped my son into shape. Got him back on track. Love can do that to a person."

"Did you live close then?"

"They settled down in Tipton County. At the time, I lived much closer, about an hour away. My wife and I would come down often to visit. Braden stayed with us during weekends. I always had a strong connection with that boy. Then my Angela passed away, and I ended up moving down here. Lifelong dream. Something I promised Angela I'd do."

Angela. The letters.

He studied my face for a while. I wondered what my face looked like having barely slept.

I leaned forward.

"Robert, I—"

"I've got an idea of why you're here," he said softly.

"You do?"

"One spring, when Braden was about fifteen or so, he took a bus. Walked all the way here from the nearest bus station. Said his parents had knowledge of his leaving, but I wasn't convinced."

A bus.

I wanted to slap myself for not considering that in my list.

"He ran away to you?"

"Didn't tell his folks. Before I could even pick up the phone, Trish called me in a panic. I told her Braden was here and that he was safe and well. My son threatened to call the police if he wasn't back the next day, so I drove him. I was devastated to let him go. I'd never seen a person so down in my entire life.

"He cried and barely spoke a word the whole ride there. When I dropped him off, his mother came running out of the house. He squeezed me and didn't want to let go. I could never forget the hopeless look on his face when he finally let go of my shirt." Robert looked down. "Shortly after that, I got a call from my son saying that Braden was in critical condition at the hospital. He overdosed on some pills. That was the last I heard from anybody for a while."

I thought about freshman year . . . the longest Braden had missed school on one of his "family business trips."

"They ended all communication with me," Robert went on. "Blamed me. Said I wasn't a good influence on him on account of my lifestyle and views on life. If you ask me, blaming me was just another way of my own son getting me back for the disagreements we'd had when he was growing up. I didn't always do right by my son. I wasn't always there for him when he needed me. I had my own alcohol problems and after all those years, I suppose that cut a hole in his heart. But you see, when adults don't get along, it's the kids who suffer the most."

I watched him, agreeing with him with a slight nod as he continued.

"His mother and father wanted to control everything after Trevor was diagnosed with diabetes. That diabetes became their lives. Braden isn't the kind of youngster you can control. I've got a sneaking suspicion you aren't either."

He looked at me with a slight wink.

"Anytime his parents thought he might have stopped taking his medication, they'd send him to that quack at the clinic. He'd have good days and bad days. He'd call me mostly on the bad days until his parents caught him on the phone with me. He just needed someone to *hear* him. I told him to write down whatever he wanted to say. Just write it all down in a journal."

"Did he ever send you whatever he was writing about?"

"No, dear."

I cleared my throat, and then again because it didn't work the first time.

"I have letters here," I said. "Letters that I found under this tree at school. I thought it was just an anonymous pen pal at first, but now I'm not so sure. The name at the bottom is always Robert."

He nodded, apparently not fazed by the similarities.

"I've been writing back and forth with a man named Robert since last semester."

"I see." He leaned forward with his elbows resting against the table. "You think I wrote these letters?"

"It would make sense."

"Are they written by hand or typed out?"

"They're written by hand. Not the best punctuation, but each letter begins with a quote. You like quotes. You even greeted us with one."

"Mm-hmm." His face held the same contented smile that Braden wore.

The silence grew awkward, but I was not backing down until I had the explanation I was looking for.

Robert breathed in and leaned back in the chair. "How often did you receive these letters?"

"About every week, give or take."

"Do I seem like the kind of person who would write letters, or do I seem like the kind of person who would say what I needed to say to someone in person."

"Maybe both."

"Do you think the person writing those letters had time to drive eight hours to bury each one under some high school tree?"

"No, but they are written from a man named Robert who lost

the woman he loved. Angela. Not in the way you did, but I figured some things were changed for identity purposes."

"Well, if some things were changed for identity purposes, then don't you think there is a strong possibility some other things were, too. Like a name, perhaps?"

"You didn't write the letters?"

He chuckled to himself. I watched, wondering if I'd missed something.

"Oh, I wrote letters. About fifty years ago. I used to be a student at Tipton High. That's where I met Angela. She and I used to love leaving notes to each other under that tree. Braden thought it was the greatest story in the world when I'd talk about it."

My chest sank. I thought about all the notes under The Tree, all from a man I assumed was who he said he was. Then my chest sank even more when I thought about the possible content in the last letter.

"I saved all the letters Angela and I wrote. They're old and crinkled up now. They're in a box on my closet shelf, safe and sound. Braden loved pulling them out and reading them."

I studied Robert and how steadily he looked at me.

"Nowadays, people give up too easily. I'm not much for doctors and the sort, but from what I could gather based on his moods, the new therapist seemed to help. It gave him someone to talk to when he couldn't talk to me."

"He got a new therapist?"

"Like I said, he'd sneak in a phone call every now and then to tell me about his life and how he was doing."

"Where is he?" I asked, not caring about the begging tone of my voice. "Please tell me where he is. We're graduating on Sunday. Braden has to graduate. He has to walk with us. He deserves to be there. Becca, Scotty, Rachelle, Justin . . . we all came to bring him back. You're my last hope, Robert. I don't know what else to do."

He stared out into his backyard which resembled a forest. I could see why Braden had wanted to come here.

"Unfortunately, he's not here."

"Would you tell me if he was?"

"It always pleases me to hear young people care about something, but darling, you know what Braden would want. If you are a true friend to him, that is."

I shook my head, thinking of the promise Trevor made to Braden.

"Did Braden make you promise, too? To not tell me where he is?"

I looked into his eyes; a lightness filled them. He glanced into the yard.

"Sometimes Braden and I would come out here at night and stare at the moon." He gazed ahead. "Even through the darkness he'd fought, he'd always found a way to be optimistic. He just loved nature. It made him feel bigger than the way he felt on the inside."

We were quiet for a while. I could hear Becca and Scotty laughing from inside, and puppies barking.

"I don't have many regrets," Robert said, rising. "Granted, I've failed at many things in my life, including the relationship with my own son, but I've lived a relatively good life. If I could give you a bit of advice from my soon-to-be century of living on this earth, it would be to stop trying to find an escape and start living, Leah."

Emotions built up inside of me as he walked me back to the living room.

Becca and Scotty rose from the floor. Becca gave me a questioning look, but I shook my head.

"Drive safe out there," Robert said, opening the front door. "I hear there are crazy people cutting off other drivers for a simple library book."

I walked out. Becca and Scotty said their goodbyes and headed toward the van. I noticed Justin lift his head from the back seat.

Robert gave me a tight hug before releasing me. I adjusted the Chaplin hat on my head knowing I needed to give it back, but I couldn't find the strength. I worried that if I gave it to Robert Gregory, then that meant I would be giving up on Braden, and I wasn't ready to give up.

Everything became quiet again, which pissed me off. I expected more of a response from Robert before sending me off without the answer I came looking for.

Where is Braden?

Frustration built up in my stomach, rising to my chest. I exhaled, hoping that Robert would fill the silence with the answer I wanted: Braden was there, had been there, would be there.

But Robert didn't say a word. He just stared at me with eyes full of wisdom as if I was just supposed to accept that and move on.

The sun reflected off the axe stuck in the chopped tree trunk. I stared at it, hoping it would catch on fire. I wanted the entire woods to catch on fire.

I thought I saw Braden standing there. I knew I shouted something then. My body moved forward, but when I blinked, there was nothing but my imagination.

I glanced over the trees. I looked at one tree. It looked back at me. I looked at another, then another. They just stood there, staring back at me, taunting me with their stillness.

How was I not more important to Braden? Was I not enough for him to stay?

"Is this a Gregory thing?" I flailed my arms. "Is this some sort of game? Torture people until they lose their minds?"

Robert touched my shoulder.

He raised his head before speaking. "Ann Landers once said, 'Nobody gets to live life backward. Look ahead, that is where your future lies.'"

I gave Robert Gregory one last look, hoping to never remember his green eyes or the gentle way they wished me farewell.

On the way back to Tipton County, we stopped by Ivy Green, the home of Helen Keller. None of us had really spoken after we left Robert's. I guessed we were trying to figure out what the trip was all for.

For me, it wasn't closure. Even standing in front of Helen Keller's beautiful white house. It was smaller than I expected, probably fixed up a bit, too. I was standing on an incredible piece of history, one that I'd been wanting to see for so long, but none of it seemed real without Braden.

It sounded horrible, but I wondered if Helen Keller was better off blind. I didn't need to see my dad one last time. I wished with everything I had that I didn't have that image in my head . . . or of Braden's smile.

Sometimes I resented Helen's deafness. It was a horrible thing to resent, but at least I wouldn't have had to hear the horrible things my mom and dad said to each other. The way their voices sounded when they screamed.

They sounded like different people, terrified people. What little girl wanted to hear her parents terrified? I certainly didn't want to remember Braden's voice if I was never going to see him again.

Sometimes I wished I couldn't talk, either. I wouldn't have had to choose sides between my parents, explaining why one was right and the other was wrong. I hoped nothing I said had pushed Braden away. I wanted to say things that showed him everything he was worth, just like he'd done for me.

The senses, I began to think, were highly overrated.

I pressed my hand over my chest and breathed in a shallow breath.

An inability to feel would have been the icing on the cake. Who needed the pain of loving someone? We'd do it over and over again, and all it ever proved was that everybody had at least one case of unquestionable insanity.

I watched as the others went into the almost too-perfect house. I stared at the tree in her front yard for a while and kept turning around, hoping Braden would show up. I hoped that, somehow, he knew I would be there . . . standing . . . waiting for him.

I stroked my arm, remembering the touch of his fingers against my skin. I wished I could hear his voice and see his face, but the wind just whistled through the leaves and left.

Chapter 27

Friday, May 29, 2009
Dear Braden,

I have an envelope in my bag. I don't know what is written and I don't know if I'm ready to find out.

As I sit here in the rocky sand along the Mississippi River, I'm debating whether to throw the entire envelope into the water and watch it float away.

I've been sitting here for an hour, staring at the small waves. Jeff Buckley died on this day exactly twelve years ago. I wonder if this was the exact spot he was in before he took that fateful swim.

I keep thinking about the lyrics to "Grace" and what he must have been feeling while writing the song. He wasn't afraid to die because he was loved. So are you.

Yes, Braden. He would have been remembered for his greatness if he was still alive. So would John Lennon. So would Jimi Hendrix and all the others.

You just left me, Braden. You're gone and I don't know if I'll ever see your face or hear your voice again. I'll forget your laugh and how the touch of your hand would give me goosebumps. I wonder how it will be possible to ever move on.

I understand that it's sometimes easier to just leave, but I didn't get the chance to say goodbye. You could have let me say goodbye.

I won't though.

For now, I'll just say I love you. I always will, Braden.

Leah

When we arrived back in Tipton County, the others dropped me off at the high school. I promised them I would be fine to walk home from there.

I walked to The Tree and buried all the letters I had written to Braden on our road trip. I laid there, staring at the sky through the leaves. I didn't know how long I had been there, but I left as soon as the stars took over the sky.

When I got home, I walked through the front door. The lights were off, but the television glowed in the living room.

My eyelids grew heavier by the minute. I dropped my bag off in my room and went to the living room where Gracie was sleeping against Beau's shoulder and my mom was sitting beside him on the couch. I sat on the love seat.

My mom greeted me by raising her eyebrows, while Beau waved his hand, careful not to wake Gracie. They fixated on the movie *Marley & Me*.

I watched the next scene with them, the scene where Owen Wilson's character says goodbye to their dog, Marley. At that moment, I was glad my mom and Beau never bombarded me with questions or the need to know everywhere I went. They let me be, sitting on that seat with my arms wrapped around my legs, hugging my knees to my chest. My eyes watered when Marley's eyes slowly closed as Owen's character comforted him with sweet words. I had seen it once before, but this time was different. It was raw, as if I was witnessing it happen in real life. I wiped a tear from my cheek, leaning my head into the cushioned back of the chair, wishing Braden was there to comfort me.

When the scene passed, I left to my room, knowing it was time to face the truth.

I thought about the Braden Gregory who always seemed to

have it all. Then I thought about the one I had come to know and love.

Braden Gregory - Most Likely To Break My Heart
I pulled out the last letter, taking the heavy envelope with me. It was now or never as I sat on my closet floor and flipped it open.

  sunday, may 24, 2009
  "Never give up on something that you can't go a day without thinking about." Winston Churchill
  grandpa norris told me i needed to journal but i chose to write letters and bury them. just like he used to. doing that made me feel heard for once, even if nobody was reading them. i wanted to write down my feelings and bury them and forget about them forever. i thought if i could write while pretending to be someone else, someone as great as my grandpa then my problems wouldnt seem that real. i didnt expect anyone to find them at The Tree. when i went to bury my third letter someone named tina had replied and i didnt know it was you at first until i saw you from the backstage door a few weeks later.
  i had a plan leah. i planned to leave long before you came into my life but because of you i had a reason to stay. something to look forward to. im sorry i couldnt be stronger.
  by the time you read this i wont be there anymore. there are no strings, no age keeping me in this small town and now there is nothing keeping you here.
  i was getting counseling from hillman. i was too ashamed to tell anyone so he agreed that i could see

him after school when there were no rehearsals. because of you i realized there was no reason to be ashamed.

you looked so beautiful sitting under The Tree with my letter in your hands. when you started to respond i felt like you understood. i needed to be closer to you. i needed to be around you as much as i could.

so i auditioned for the play.

i know i hurt you when we were kids. i was a hurt person who wanted someone else to feel my pain. im so sorry leah. when i started falling in love with you i promised myself i would never hurt you again but i started to realize that it was a promise i couldnt keep.

i was looking for myself in a pool of people who dont even know who they are. you know who you are leah. you are good at things and you dont let other people stop you. that was until i realized i was standing in the way of what you wanted. you were going to stay because of me. you were going to give up college, the one thing that could give you the future you want. i made trevor and my grandpa promise not to tell you where i am because i know you would come looking for me.

im okay leah. im getting help. im getting better.

i hope you saw that the grass isnt always what you expect it to be on the other side. sometimes its ugly, brown, dead. but then sometimes it's amazing.

i put my cash savings in the envelope. i couldnt bear the thought of not being a part of your future. i know money isnt everything. use it for something good.

i love you and everything about you leah roy. espe-

cially unicorns.

The Tree is just a place, a moment in time. dont hold on to it. dont hold on to me. remember the forest.

Braden

Tears escaped down my cheeks. Wherever he ran away to . . . wherever he was, I hoped he was happy.

I nodded, looking up. I wanted to feel him next to me. I needed his comfort, but the only thing I had was the letter . . . his words in my hands.

"Okay, Braden," I said. "I'll remember."

Chapter 28

I'd walked to the high school that afternoon. Even though school was out, it was never really out for the teachers, so I knew Hillman would be there over the weekend, packing up drama club items and getting ready for summer school classes.

His classroom was an organized mess. He had been doing some deep cleaning before I knocked on his door, emptying out the cabinets filled with posters and books that he bought out of his own pocket. Teachers did things like that. Hillman went even further, spending time and money on a club that was, let's face it, close to dying every year.

I looked up from my old desk. Hillman was looking at me with those watchful eyes, tapping his pencil against his knee.

"Why didn't you say anything?" I asked him.

"Confidentiality," he answered. "And trust. I owed it to you and Scotty to keep our conversations between us. I owed that much to Braden."

"You could have told me he was seeing you after school."

"It's my job as a counselor and a teacher to honor that trust."

"Did he tell you he was leaving?"

Hillman uncrossed his legs and shifted forward. "Think of it as a fresh start, Leah. For the both of you. He will still get his diploma, even if he doesn't attend the ceremony. He can still go out there and further his education. You can do the same."

"What could I have done to make him stay?"

"His leaving doesn't mean you didn't do enough or weren't

important to him. It means he was struggling with something bigger than you could understand."

"I should have tried harder to understand."

"His depression is something that started long ago. Leah . . . it had absolutely nothing to do with you. Perhaps you made him feel better."

"You think he'll come to graduation?" I asked.

"Let's hope he does," he said. "More importantly, make sure you are there."

I pressed my lips together, looking away.

I rose and stepped to a box of props from *The Miracle Worker*. I took the Chaplin hat off my head and held it for a moment.

I thought of my dad and how I hadn't spoken to him since leaving him. Many times over the years, my mom had handed me the phone when he called, but I never took it. I had to let him go for a while, but I never gave up on the hope that one day he would be back to normal . . . the dad who would toss me the football and twirl me around when I ran into his arms.

I wasn't giving up this time either.

I wasn't letting Braden go.

I just thought that maybe one day, a hopeful student would be lucky enough to wear his hat and that maybe some of Braden's hopes and dreams would rub off on them, too. So I placed his hat on top of the box and turned away.

That evening, Becca, Scotty, and I met Justin and Rachelle at the salon.

"Quit moping about it," Becca said, forcing Scotty into one of those cool salon chairs. She pumped the chair all the way down, but he was still almost too tall for Justin to work on.

"This is pretty evil of you, Becca." Justin pulled out a bottle and a tube. He mixed the contents together into some kind of hair dye concoction.

Scotty leaned away from the mixture. The smell was strong enough to melt nose hairs.

When Rachelle came walking out from the back room in an apron, Justin wrapped a black cape around Scotty's neck. Justin had given Rachelle a summer job at the salon.

She stopped when she saw us and folded her arms. Her hair had been thinned out and cut to her shoulders.

"What's going on here?" she asked, shaking her head.

Justin gave her a hopeless look.

"Someone's mouth is a little too big," he said.

"Scotty promised that if I saw one baseball game, he'd dye his hair purple," Becca said. "So we went to a baseball game together."

"No points for keeping my word?" Scotty grimaced as Justin brought the concoction closer to him.

"I gave him choices," Becca said. "If he didn't want to dye his hair, he could have gotten a tattoo."

"May I ask what the tattoo would have been?" I said.

"Just a little strawberry." She pointed. "A tiny one right here below his shoulder. You'd never be able to see it."

"Let me tell you two things wrong with that statement," Scotty said. "One, I'd never be able to strip in front of anyone, like, ever again. And two . . . STRAWBERRY."

Rachelle ran her fingers through Scotty's hair and looked at him in the mirror.

"It's a shame," she said. "Purple isn't even your color."

Justin put on a pair of gloves and took a scoop of the color mixture.

"Here goes nothin'," Scotty said, squeezing his eyes shut as Justin plopped on a glob.

Thirty minutes later, Justin turned off the blow dryer and swung Scotty around in front of the mirror.

"You can open your eyes now," Justin sang.

Scotty slowly opened his eyes and let out a scream.

"We agreed on *dark* purple!" he hollered, standing up. "I look like a stick of cotton candy!"

Everyone laughed. Well, everyone except Scotty who couldn't unglue his hands from his neon hair.

The next morning, I put on my white cap and gown. Gracie and my mom curled my hair, going on about how my hair was so straight that curls always turned into waves. Their excitement for me was contagious and I caught myself smiling more than usual that morning.

Becca and Justin picked me up from home, gleaming in all their cap and gown attire.

I walked into the gymnasium where graduation would take place, glancing over the echoing bleachers filled with people. Students were still being seated in chairs in the middle of the gym floor.

I wanted Braden there so bad that I imagined him sitting next to me as I took my seat. I imagined the gentleness of his hand on my thigh, and when I closed my eyes, I could hear him laughing.

My mom, Beau, and Gracie shouted my name from the bleachers as the commencement began. I smiled and looked around them. I didn't see Braden's parents. I thought I saw a glimpse of Trevor, but it was just another tall boy.

When my name was called, I rose and made my walk to the small stage. My family cheerfully hollered as Principal McCoy handed me my honors diploma. Hillman gave me a fist bump as I walked off the stage. I gleamed with joy, a feeling I wished could last forever.

That evening, I finally sent in the confirmation form to Ball State. I had decided on General Studies to keep my options open. It was a start. My mom took me shopping for all the things I'd need for the dorm room life, spending the rest of the honeymoon money I hadn't used for the road trip.

A week later, I pulled Braden's envelope down from my closet shelf and carried it to my desk. I sat down and slowly opened it. I took out the money . . . so much money, and spread it over my desk.

After I'd finished counting, the total came to $9,700.00. I'd never seen that kind of money in my life and I wasn't sure I ever would again.

I kept the money hidden on the top shelf of my closet where it stayed for the next several months.

I buried one letter every week that summer, burying each in a new spot under The Tree to convince myself that someone was taking them. I did that until the final week of summer when I showed up and The Tree was gone.

I stood with my arms to my sides, unmoving, unable to breathe. Shock hijacked my nerves, so much so that I thought my mind was playing tricks on me, but I swear, it was gone. Uprooted. All of them were.

I asked the main office worker and she said that they were "reinventing" the place.

When they took The Tree, they took a piece of me with it. I would stand over the empty spot, wishing I had a picture of it since I could barely remember what the initials carved into the trunk looked like anymore. They could have at least left the stump. I could have glanced over the tree rings to see how long my name might have lived on. I even had to look at the cast programs once in a while to keep Braden's image alive since my memory of his voice grew fainter by the day.

That first year at Ball State, I wrote a lot of things for my classes, but by far the hardest thing I ever had to write was my final letter to Braden.

Saturday, December 19, 2009

Dear Braden,

I want you to know that this will be my last letter to you, and not because they took The Tree or because I'm getting tired of waiting for you. Believe me, I could wait forever. This will be my last letter because I've been holding on to you for all this time.

Like you said, The Tree was just a place, right?... a moment in time.

I thought I had moved on when, really, I was only lying to myself. It's time I stop trying to reach for those memories we shared, that nostalgia that creeps up on me every now and then.

I've realized that sometimes when you love someone, you have to meet them where they are or let them go.

I promised you I would.

Love,

Leah

Chapter 29

"Okay, everyone, I know you're all in a rush to get out of here, but can everyone gather around for just a moment, please?" I shouted from the dressing room hallway the following spring.

Cast members hurried around. I'd been volunteering in drama club at Tipton High every weekend for the spring production.

"I can't begin to tell you all how proud I am of you . . . each of you," I said. "You guys have shown what it's like to be a community and when we work together, anything is possible. When we started this play, I was worried we wouldn't be able to pull it together. I remember last year when I was in this school. We were always short on male actors. We were always short on help and finances, but between fundraising and all the dedication from each of you, you guys came together and did an amazing job."

Some students were still coming out of the dressing rooms as I went on.

I pointed in the direction of the lobby where the meet and greet was being held.

"Don't take too long back here. The audience will be leaving, so make sure you get out there and soak up your long overdue compliments. You all deserve them. And before we part ways, let's give one more shout-out to our departing seniors."

Hooting and hollering filled the small narrow hallway as each senior gave me a hug before dashing to the meet and greet.

I stood in the hallway that was quickly emptying of the cast, and sighed.

I headed their way, watching cast members rush past me to get to the lobby, which was packed with excitement and chatter.

Proud parents took pictures with the actors, and students gathered in circles, bragging about the show.

"Leah." Mr. Hillman stopped me.

Even behind the bush of his new beard, he still looked the happiest I had ever seen him. He had gotten married a month prior to a woman who apparently adored more than a goatee. It was nice to finally know more about his life and to see so much joy in his eyes.

I noticed the box of props he was holding.

"I knew you could do it," he said, standing tall.

"Learned from the best, didn't I?"

I hadn't exactly gotten used to calling him Steve yet.

In my mind, I was thanking Braden for the money he had given me. In the end, I'd decided to take out financial aid for the expenses my scholarship wouldn't cover at Ball State. I couldn't bring myself to use the money Braden had given me toward that. Instead, I pulled it down from my closet shelf that winter and donated it to the Arts for Tipton High.

If there was one thing that had saved me in high school—besides Braden—it was theatre. For others, it might have been band, choir, sports, art or anything to help them escape what they had no control over.

I was forever grateful for my escape.

"Great job again, Leah. If we don't see much of each other before school lets out, enjoy summer break."

I hugged him and thanked him once more. When I pulled away, my shirt caught onto the corner of the box he was holding to the side. As I stepped back, it tipped over and fell onto the floor.

"Sorry about that," I said, bending down to help him pick up the loose props.

Before I rose to stand, I noticed something familiar. I picked it up.

"Did we have one of these for this play?" I frowned.

Hillman rose slowly, staring at the Chaplin hat in my hand.

He gently pulled it from my grasp and placed it back into the box.

"Maybe," he said.

I watched Hillman, thinking I caught a slight smirk in his expression.

When he left into the lobby, I glanced around at the crowd of students.

I'd seen my mom in the audience that evening. She smiled and cheered along with the others. I knew she had to hurry out of there for work, but I was thrilled to see her in the audience. When the students brought me out for my bow, I heard her whistles and for a moment, I thought I saw a familiar face staring at me. When I looked again, he wasn't there.

I turned in the direction of Hillman's classroom.

Walking those hallways rarely brought up memories anymore, but that particular day was different.

When I got to Hillman's classroom, I grabbed my sweater and purse from the desk chair and pulled out the book sticking out of my open purse. My fingers grazed *Mulberry Street*, feeling the bumpy texture of the old cover. I held it to my chest.

The moments of high school graduation flashed through my mind. The excitement on my mom's face, Gracie hugging me, Beau dressed in a nice shirt and not smelling of stale beer.

Remembering auditions for *The Miracle Worker*, I looked around the classroom and smiled before turning off the light.

Still . . . I could never forget the boy who changed my life.

I spent the rest of the hour helping the office workers close up. I locked the dressing rooms and auditorium, and helped collect the box office earnings knowing we no longer needed to worry about not having the budget for another show.

As I walked out of the building, the crisp spring air nipped my cheeks, but the cloudless sky and sun quickly warmed me up.

I placed my sweater and purse inside my car. The cast would be waiting for me to come to the cast party, but at that moment, something tugged at my heart. I shut the car door and walked back to the school, taking *Mulberry Street* with me.

I had waited for him.

Every day.

Even at Ball State, I waited for his face to show up in those busy sidewalks, clinging to the hope that he was somewhere out there.

I stopped between the cafeteria and the north wing, to a now empty spot in the grass.

I'd spent the last year hoping for news to come, but it never did. One time visiting home, I saw his mom and brother at Harold's Pharmacy. I had made Braden a promise, so I didn't bother to ask.

After weeks spent waiting by my phone for a call or a text from a boy who was beginning to fade, I'd decided to get a new phone. I lost his number. I lost all the old messages.

I tried forgetting his face, too, but it would pop up every now and then when I would hear his laughter in my memories. I'd fall into thoughts of what could have been and how I wished I wouldn't have to face a life without him.

I stood on the grassy spot where The Tree used to be and sat down.

I kept being drawn back to Small Town Nowhere every time I would get lost in the pressure of college classes. The small-town life was what I had grown to miss . . . the people . . . the familiar places . . . the endless dreaming.

One thing I couldn't get rid of was the mix CD Braden had made me. Listening to it after a long day reminded me that I wasn't alone. I'd always hoped that Braden had found what he was looking for.

Sitting on The Tree's spot, I had never thought I would end up in a Small Town Nowhere, but there I was, finding myself *somewhere*.

The wind cooled my face. I placed the book beside me and leaned back onto my elbows. When I did, I heard something crunch underneath my arm.

I opened my eyes and moved again, feeling the crackle under my wrist.

I sat up and touched around the chunk of unearthed grass, digging my fingers into it until I touched the plastic.

My lips parted.

Had I missed it all this time?

I pulled out the plastic bag and took out the folded piece of paper. I shook my head for a moment, thinking I was dreaming.

I opened it and forced my eyes over the first line.

saturday, april 24, 2010

That was today.

I stopped and looked around me before reading the line again.

saturday, april 24, 2010

My heart pounded.

Was this a dream? Was I sleeping?

I remembered the way he looked as he walked into Hillman's classroom for auditions; the way my nerves melted under his stare. I could never forget the lightness of my body during our audition, after I cracked under his spell, laughing at his persistent humor.

I had given him my number.

I was so glad I'd given him my number.

The shock surging through my veins elicited a laugh from me. It was the only way I could continue reading.

saturday, april 24, 2010

I was listening to jeff buckley last night. Grace. It reminds me of you every time i hear it. Theres something in his voice, something deeper, more alive than even we are. It reminds me that we all have something to live for. Remember his voice?

I grabbed my guitar and left town. Played music down south for a while because that's what i wanted to do. It felt amazing to play again, so much that i wondered how i could have gone so long without it.

The strings, the sound, the feeling as if i was the music myself.

I stayed at Hillmans house until i was ready to talk to my parents again. Trevor knew. Grandpa Norris knew. Eventually i called my parents and worked things out. I didnt want to say anything to you because i knew youd come looking for me and the last thing i wanted to do was hold you back.

I didnt like the ending, Leah.

So i changed it.

p.s. I wrote a song about The Tree. Can i play it for you?

Braden

I couldn't stop laughing. I shook my head, laughing so hard that the tears finally came. His dramatic gestures, the way he would read *Mulberry Street* to me as we rested into each other's arms . . . it all came back to me in a flood of memories.

I was in my world; a world where the benefits were so much bigger than any fancy award or ticket sales. It was a place of hope, love, and possibility . . . endless possibility.

I lowered the letter in my lap and slowly looked up. The sun magnified everything I had come to accept; my spot at The Tree, Braden's bright grin, and the light that shined on the black of his Chaplin hat.

Acknowledgments

After moving a lot as a young girl, I finally found my home when I moved to Seymour, Indiana. For me that meant security, safety, and a sense of peace.

If not for Seymour, I would have never written this novel. I love this town and the people in it. Thank you for being the home that allowed my imagination to blossom. Thank you to Seymour High School for being a place of opportunity for me. As someone who was shy and never quite fit in, I found my courage there.

I would like to thank the Geneva Writers' Group for the endless work you do to provide writers like me with resources and opportunities to learn and grow.

Thanks to my awesome critique group, The Writaholics. I couldn't have asked for more wonderful, talented, and trustworthy women to share this story with. A special thanks to Carolina Coelho for your extended interest, critique, and belief in this story.

Thank you to Richard Scrimger. Your knowledge and guidance motivated this story to go on a diet and strengthen its muscles.

I want to thank my writing mentor, the lovely and talented DL Nelson. Your expertise, support, and generosity helped this story find its path. Thanks as well to Olivia Wildenstein for your invaluable guidance. Thanks to Anna Missa for making this manuscript shine.

Thank you to my gramma who was always eager to read my writing, provide feedback, and would have loved to hold this book in her hands.

Thanks to my incredible children for giving me the purpose and energy I needed to write this story. Your love has taught me so much, the most important lesson being to finally love myself. I am forever grateful to be your mother.

Last, but certainly not least, I want to thank my husband, Attila. Your faith in me is the reason this book came to fruition. When I'm knocked five steps back, you take my hand and lead me ten steps forward. Thanks for putting up with me even when my mind is buried under a million words. I love you with a love that goes beyond anything those words can describe. Don't stop believin'.

1. What themes can you find in this story?
2. How do you think the book's title relates to the subject matter?
3. Do you think Leah lives with mental illness? If so, explain which mental illnesses she lives with and how you have come to this conclusion?
4. What do you think happened to Leah's dad?
5. How do you think Leah's final memory with her dad affected her both socially and mentally?
6. What does being in Small Town Nowhere mean for Leah?
7. Given what we know about Leah's past, do you think Leah's mother could have done better?
8. Robert tells Leah that when adults can't get along, it's the children who suffer the most. How do you think Robert's absence affected Braden?
9. Based on the story, describe what you think is the importance of parents' roles in their children's lives.
10. What positive message can you take away from this story and what will you remember the most?

What happened to Braden Gregory? Find out in the sequel, *Letters In Mississippi*, available in 2024.

Readers get the first chapter for free!
Visit www.ginamorosey.com for your free chapter.

NERD SQUAD REVOLUTION (*noun, verb, way of life*)

definition: **a proactive approach to ending the stigma on nerdism via unapologetically being yourself.**

Join the Nerd Squad Newsletter for more details! Also, for your chance to:
- be featured as Nerd of the Month
- submit your writing
- win exciting giveaways
- receive special discounts
- access free writing material
- see sneak previews
- and much more!

Visit www.ginamorosey.com to join.
INSTAGRAM @ginamorosey
TIKTOK @ginamorosey
FACEBOOK facebook.com/ginamorosey.author
GOODREADS goodreads.com/gina-morosey

Gina Morosey lives with her family in both Indiana and Switzerland, where the green grass and blooming flowers give her the serenity to write amidst the wild and thrilling journey of motherhood. She studied Musical Theatre and Microbiology at Ball State University only to learn that writing all hours of the night causes extreme insomnia.

After making it as a finalist on Switzerland's Got Talent, she put the dream of theatre in a drawer to focus on being an author—something she has wanted to do since freaking out her teachers with handwritten horror books in elementary school.

She loves passionate discussions on all topics of creative writing.

To inquire about booking Gina Morosey for a book signing and/or speaking engagement, visit www.ginamorosey.com.

If you or anyone you know is struggling with mental illness or suicidal thoughts, please visit www.suicide.org and www.nami.org for more resources.

www.ginamorosey.com

facebook.com/ginamorosey.author

instagram.com/ginamorosey

tiktok.com/@ginamorosey

goodreads.com/gina-morosey